A GENUINE MONSTER

A GENUINE MONSTER
David
Zielinski

THE ATLANTIC MONTHLY PRESS
NEW YORK

Published simultaneously in Canada
Printed in the United States of America

Library of Congress Cataloging-in-Publication Data

Zielinski, David.
    A genuine monster / David Zielinski.
    ISBN 0-87113-294-X
    I. Title.
  PS3576.I295G4 1990   813'.54—dc20   89-35134

Design by Laura Hough

The Atlantic Monthly Press
19 Union Square West
New York, NY 10003

FIRST PRINTING

FOR PRITI,   for her
                    strength

Find me a genuine monster, whether he exists or not.
—<u>King Kong vs. Godzilla</u>, 1963

A GENUINE MONSTER

CHAPTER ONE   MONSTER ISLAND

People fucking in airplanes. The pope shot in slow motion. The difference between color and black-and-white television. Curious things like these make me wonder. I love people but they scare me.

For a long time I never talked to anyone about these curious things, not even my father. He died the day Nixon was elected president. He never got to see the New York Miracle Mets win the World Series in five games or watch civilian Neil Armstrong mash his overpadded boot onto moongrit. I saw some of that stuff on television, even though I was in Vietnam.

These days I talk to Argo. He's writing a book. I talk to him about serious matters. For instance, Godzilla is a more respectable monster than Frankenstein simply because Frankenstein looks awful in color. Argo has a computer typewriter and a gun collection and lots of unfinished business scattered across his desk—where it looks like an accident struck. In fact, he has a crooked sign on the wall: "Accidents Will Happen." I don't know if this is an excuse or a proclamation. Argo lives in a square stucco apartment building near the valley, and I visit him whenever I want.

I've lived in this town most of my life, over thirty-one years. Even though San Diego is a big town, the pope has never visited. I imagine there are thousands of people here who believe in him, too. Does it make a difference if you only see someone on television all the time then finally get to see him in person? If the pope came here, most likely more people would have to believe in him. I'll have to ask Argo what he thinks.

When I was in Vietnam no one ever fucked in the airplanes. But Sergeant Ascencion told me you could belong to a special club if you did. Argo informed me that the pope owns a special jet plane. But I don't imagine the pope cares too much about membership in any more unique clubs. I wish someday I could talk to that holy man, just for a minute. He knows dozens of languages, so we could talk fairly well together. We could have secret conversations, and I could swear never to reveal the details unless requested by the pope. Argo would want me to tell him so he could include some specifics in his books. The problem, though, is this: sometimes people don't know the difference between what's secret and what's not. The difference is tremendous.

LaWanda lives upstairs from Argo and she has an "I Brake for Unicorns" bumper sticker plastered on the rusty bumper of her Volvo, which is not secret. LaWanda believes in things that seem secret to me, though, and she says she knows the difference between black and white magic. Nonetheless, she stays inside all day and has large tits, but she's not my girlfriend.

Most of the people I meet for the first time don't understand how hard life has always been for me. I heard part of that line on television, but it still seems true, it still matches the way I feel. Never have I said this before. Too risky. Just around the corner—if there are any answers they always seem out of my reach and just around the corner, constantly moving, always eluding me, a joke, laughing in the wind.

I wish we could all have portable instant-replay cameras. If things were in slow motion I could understand them better.

Most of the time things seem secret to me. Argo says it's the same for everyone, but I think he said that because I was boring him with questions. I never try to tell personal stuff like this to LaWanda. It's more fun to pretend I know a wealth of secrets, like the pope. She does the same to me, I can tell.

Argo lectured me the other day and said it wasn't good to keep too many things secret. So, when he asked me what I was up to lately, I admitted I was jacking off at night a lot. He laughed, but it was his good laugh, and he said, "That's like letting air out of a balloon." But I told him, "I saw this lady doctor on TV last week and she said it was good for you. She even wrote a book, just like you." That's when he lit his white meerschaum pipe—whenever he gets serious, Argo lights that pipe and lowers his voice. Sometimes I have to strain to hear him. I don't always understand everything, but I nod my head anyway and try to make my face look as dangerous as his. "That little bitch doesn't know what she's talking about," Argo said behind a cloud of smoke. "You should do yourself a favor and get laid. Rejuvenation, Nick. That's what we're talking about. God, if only Celia were in town."

I learned not to ask Argo any more questions once he starts talking about Celia. I only saw her once, and she is the most beautiful woman I ever met in person. She used to be married to Argo. He said she got tired of him because he always wrote the same old thing. One time last week when Argo was drunk, he showed me their wedding pictures. Argo and Celia looked silly, like little kids. He laughed when he told me the knife they held to cut the cake was upside-down. "The story of my life," Argo said. Then he sent me out to buy him another bottle. When I got back he was passed out on the living room floor, snoring. When that happens, I sneak to read the book he's working on. The latest one is called *Elvesizer's Cold War.* I wish I could be like that character, Eddie

Elvesizer, the main hero. He's always doing it with different women.

I once told Argo it looks downright funny when people fuck. I saw LaWanda doing it before. I walked into her apartment for a visit, and when I heard these weird noises from her bedroom, I looked in and saw her yelping on her hands and knees tangled up in the sheets with a skinny sailor bumping her from behind. They both held their eyes closed tight, and I didn't know if they were experiencing rejuvenation or not.

After Argo relit his pipe—because it went out when he tried to remember where Celia was—he talked to himself and flipped through his address book. I felt strange, like I wasn't even in the room with him. When Argo puffed out fresh smoke again, he said, "You know, Nick. She had the most delicious little tantric twitch to her hips. It just drove me wild. Turned me into a damn animal. Nothing held us back. I remember this time we were out in the snow fucking, it was splintering cold and I could have cared less."

Sometimes when Argo talks, it's easy to slip away and think my own thoughts. Sometimes I would rather remember than listen.

When I got back early from Vietnam, I played baseball in the minor leagues. I had been drafted twice—by the U.S. Army and the San Diego Padres—but before I could play ball I had to play soldier. Sometimes it snowed and the playing field was erased. We never played a game in the snow. We just sat in our motel rooms and played cards and watched TV. That was in Walla Walla, Washington, Northwest League. They had a good TV station there that showed the best monster movies of all time. One week they had a Godzilla festival, and I got to see my favorite movie again, Monster Island. That's the one where Godzilla's son and a Japanese boy are friends. I once told Argo that he was like Godzilla's son and I was like that boy. He

4

didn't understand. I pretended to be just kidding so I could keep that thought secret.

Sometimes on guard duty I pretended I was on Monster Island. I'd drop a Willie Peter into my grenade launcher and let it fly—floop!—and sit there in the foxhole surrounded by sweating sandbags with my eyes wide open trying to pick the exact moment when the phosphorus would explode. All that light would hurt my eyes, but I loved to watch the dark night get split open down the middle. The barbed wire looked so sharp, and the dirt and pebbles looked clean and perfect like a huge expensive rug made out of plastic beads. With the explosion still trapped in my ears, I'd lay my cheek on a sandbag and close my eyes and pretend big monsters were growing out of blobs of black night—monsters I remembered from movies and monsters I made up. The ones I made up were the scariest. The worst one looked like a giant wolf with two mouths and pointy fur and red orange eyes big as burning trash cans. The grenade explosion was his growl. Whenever I saw his ugly face I had to open my eyes. He scared me more than the VC I couldn't see. I named that wolfmonster Brak and I see him still.

A few weeks ago I was waiting for a bus downtown and almost fell asleep on the bench before Brak's face filled up my head. I snapped open my eyes and right then an old woman crossing the street too slowly fastened to a silver walker got smashed by a freshly waxed black Corvette. Paramedics hauled her away and I waited for the next bus so I could watch. Argo says only guys with limp dicks drive Corvettes. Sergeant Ascencion had a picture of a blue Corvette in his wallet, and he used to show it to me with pride when he got drunk—before he took me off guard duty.

Argo tossed his lit pipe onto the floor and grabbed the wedding photos out of my hand. "It's no use," he said. "She was, is, and always will be a fucking untamed ungrateful

5

unrepentant monster." I want Argo to put some monsters in his spy books, but he always says his editor would never play along. I think Eddie Elvesizer could handle a few monsters with ease. When the late great Nick Adams starred in *Monster Zero*, he handled three at the same time: Godzilla, Rodan, and the frightening Monster Zero with three dragon heads who spit special-effects lightning. That movie was great particularly because Godzilla was cast as a good monster for a change.

Argo says he's getting sick waiting for someone to make a movie from one of his books. He wrote eleven different Eddie Elvesizer books and sometimes he writes westerns and romance books, too. Where he gets all his ideas and experience living in a filthy apartment I'll never know.

I read the Eddie Elvesizer books because those are the only ones I can get at Esmeralda's liquor store. I won't ask Argo to lend me any others because he already does me too many favors. I can tell he doesn't want me around when I come over and he's working, but he always talks to me anyway.

He said a writer friend of his wrote a script for a low-budget karate movie and was never paid, even though the movie was filmed and distributed and later sold as a video. Each time Argo tells me that story he laughs hard. Then he says, "America's the only country in the world where people get out of bed in the morning only because they think they're going to get lucky. No one works hard anymore. They're all waiting for a bag of money to fall on their fucking heads." I've been listening to Argo talk mean like this for a long time, and I still can't figure out why he's so different from Eddie Elvesizer.

When I saw the pope on TV, he was riding in a funny glass car waving to a zillion people. I think one important reason people believe in him is because they want more luck. Sergeant Ascencion had a big silver cross around his neck, hooked to his dog tags. He said it was his lucky cross. LaWanda has a drawer full of black candles. One time she let me help her light them and cast out some spells—for bad luck. In Soviet Slugfest, Eddie Elvesizer told a KGB mole, "Tough luck, comrade. You'll need it where you're going," right before he shot the Russian in the face and left him for dead in a dumpster outside Falls Church, Virginia. I don't know if I'm lucky or not. If I were writing Argo's books, I would make Eddie Elvesizer say instead, "Good-bye, comrade. Now you don't have to worry about a bag of money falling on your head." Then maybe Brak would claw out the Russian's heart and bite it into four chunks with his two mouths.

If I were lucky I wouldn't be the way I am. The doctor said I suffered slight brain damage at birth, choked by the umbilical cord. If I were lucky I would have a girlfriend. In Vietnam I had one girlfriend, but she was quickly killed. In Walla Walla I never had a girlfriend. Ernie Lazaro brought a girl on the team bus to Spokane once, but she wouldn't do it with the white guys. Coach Mulhauser tossed her off in the dark before we got to Pine City, anyway.

I hit two home runs in one game once. But I know that wasn't luck because I tried to hit them. It was the day after I came back from Seattle. I'd had lunch in the Space Needle by myself and stayed up there for three hours looking out everywhere. The waitress said it was all right if I stayed because they weren't very busy. She told me I looked peaceful and I waited for her to come back out of the kitchen, but she never did. The next day Coach Mulhauser said he thought I looked like I was on drugs, so I hit the home runs on purpose to prove I wasn't. He benched me after the second one. He said he wanted to let this new guy get some playing time, since we were suddenly so far ahead.

In my closet at home I still have the bat I used that night, which I never used again. I know there are two more home runs *in that bat left over from the night I should have been up to hit two more times.*

I couldn't understand how Argo could call such a beautiful woman as his ex-wife Celia a monster. He said there were some things I was never meant to understand. As he groaned, bending over to retrieve his smoldering meerschaum, I told him the Space Needle was a monstrous construction but that it was the most beautiful thing I had ever seen. Tapping ashes into the trash basket, Argo said I was just lucky to catch it on a nice day. The time he visited Seattle he was with Celia. It was raining, and she couldn't wait to get back to the hotel so they could fuck before he was supposed to give a workshop for a writers' conference. "The most horrible day of my life," he said. "I showed up drunk with jism stains on my slacks and almost got tossed out of the auditorium. But I guess it did do something for my image." I watched smoke rise from the pile of crumpled balls of paper in the trash basket, wondering if that waitress in the Space Needle would have let me fuck her. We could have done it near the windows and not have stopped until the restaurant spun around in a complete 360-degree circle.

We were called the Walla Walla Bears. I always thought that was a ridiculous name for a baseball team. Baseball is too beautiful a game. The teams should have more appropriate names. The Japanese have a team called the Swallows. I saw them play the Tokyo Giants once, during the war, when I was blessed with some sudden R & R. When Sergeant Ascencion clicked his M16 to automatic he called it rock & roll. From Tokyo, I brought him back a poster of Godzilla with yellow Japanese writing crisscrossed all over the bottom. Godzilla was green and dripping with wet seaweed. He was crushing some skyscrapers that looked like toys. Sergeant Ascencion tacked up the poster in his hootch next to his postcards of jackalopes from

Texas. Later, somebody taped a Polaroid photo of Sergeant Ascencion's face over Godzilla's reptile head. The sergeant didn't care. After he was killed by friendly fire I took down the poster and burned it, watching his photo-face shrivel and turn shiny black then dusty gray. Months later, when I was with the Bears, I bought Ernie Lazaro a plastic model of the Space Needle in Seattle, but when I got back with the team I found out he had been sold to the Houston Astros and sent down to Tucson. After that, I called Coach Mulhauser "Mulehead," and I never gave him anything. The Space Needles would have been a better name than the Bears but still not exactly right. I always had a feeling for an even better name, and sitting in the dugout during games I would try and capture that name in my mind—but the right word never did come. Never.

I wish I could make up words like Argo does. Someday I'm going to ask him to teach me how to write a book. That is, if he doesn't get killed or sold first.

In the meantime, I must become rejuvenated. Argo gave me that word, and it fits—it stands for something I have needed all my life, something I have never been able to discover in my America—something right around the corner.

As Eddie Elvesizer would say, "Her initials are: LaWanda Hernandez."

No one knows where I live except Argo and the VA, since most of my best friends were killed or sold. Mrs. Raylak is my landlady and sometimes she forgets to collect the rent. She belongs to the Nebulae Society, a space alien association that owns forty-seven acres on the way to the desert past Jamul. Mrs. Raylak drives out there regularly with Mr. Rainey and his wife, Neeta, and with hands held in a circle at midnight they all wait for the aliens to land. The last time I paid Mrs. Raylak the rent, she returned the receipt slipped in between the pages of a green paperback with red letters: *They Are Coming: How Shall We Greet Them?* The binding broke and the pages slid out before I could finish. Sri Annabelle Afton wrote the book; I wondered if she was a friend of Argo's. The color photo on the back showed her in a satiny purple dress with her hair coiled and fluffed into a beehive style. She didn't look half as exciting as Eddie Elvesizer, but some of her ideas were much more amazing. Not only did she believe in space aliens, but she had visited twenty-three invisible realms in various dimensions beyond our solar system.

I get up with the sun every day. In the winter I sleep longer. I yearn for a change, but most of the time I feel controlled by cosmic forces beyond my personal vision (a phrase I borrowed from Sri Annabelle, page 18). Last night's weather report on TV announced sunup at 6:01 a.m. When I first opened my eyes in the morning, the red stick letters on my clock radio glowed 6:02:43. For the following fifteen minutes I strained through my cat exercises. Miki called them cat exercises when she taught me in Saigon. We did them together. Sometimes I would cheat and smooth my hand through her shiny black hair when I was supposed to be stretching. Not long afterwards she died when a bomb exploded in a restaurant, and she never got to see California like we planned.

Every time I squeezed her hand and told her about the beauty in San Diego, she smiled and peeked at me through her tiny fingers. It was a custom for the Vietnamese women to hide things from men. Even so, when I told her we should get married, she shook her head fast and stung me with Vietnamese words that sounded like she was talking backward.

Argo says women know things men can never know, and for this reason we despise them secretly, even if we don't admit it to ourselves.

It would be a good thing to be able to wake up closer to the exact moment of sunup, right on the perfect second. That way I could return to the world just at the instant of first light and leave my dreams entirely in the dark. Miki's hair was black. I could never make her understand how full of light it was when we walked through the hectic markets. Her hair seemed to glow from underneath.

When I pushed myself through the morning exercises, I imagined myself reborn into an unimagined dimension, clean and sparkling and rich. But that thought was eliminated by the cold fact that I still possessed one minute's worth of live dreams, dreams that would have been erased if I had woken up on time, precisely at sunup. Ever since I once saw myself die in a nightmare—sleeping on guard duty with my M16 tight and cold against my cheek—I try to do anything I can to kill my dreams. When I mentioned this to Argo he laughed, and I

11

tried not to let him see the hurt on my face. He said all I had to do was get some pussy, the magic cure-all, the all-important release, the biological imperative impalement—on and on, he showered me with words.

I have two feelings about his advice: I think he's right and I think he's wrong. Making decisions has always been terrible. And I have two feelings about that, also: either I find someone to make the decision for me, or I wish I were another person. Sometimes it's impossible being me, Nicholas Ames. Anyone else. Most of the time I wish I could be anyone else. On that horizon line. I exist there in the middle, hiding, in a foxhole, in the dugout, talking now into thin air, where it's difficult to breathe, where my skin turns blue and I strain, wishing, hammering my fists into the wall begging for some freedom, 365 days a year, panhandling for a new identity.

Yet when I think this way I rebel—when the central part of me is overshadowed by borrowed voices, when I begin sounding like Argo. Or like a voice from the television.

I like to watch TV when I eat breakfast. It helps me forget who I am. After finishing my exercises, I checked the *TV Guide* listings and couldn't believe Channel 5 from Los Angeles was going to broadcast three monster movies in a row. To find one on that early in the morning was too good to be true. LaWanda would call it a sign. Yet I was cautious about watching just part of the first movie. Keeping those three movies from entering my mind would balance out the dreams that were still alive. The way I figured it, the process worked along these lines: I woke up late all week—the dreams overflowing in my mind, working on me, would have no effect as long as I kept those three monster films trapped inside a dead television. Those unseen movies would even the score so I could concentrate on LaWanda. First breakfast, and then rejuvenation, revitalization, restoration, renewal—sex.

I dug out an old black tablecloth from the closet and draped it over the top of the TV surrounding the screen, just like I saw a magician do once at a USO show before he made a vase of flowers turn into a flock of pigeons.

This early, it was dead quiet in my house. I ate my cereal slowly, chewing each bite into liquid before swallowing. After I cleaned up the kitchen spotlessly, I tried to send my thoughts to LaWanda.

She said she could read minds from miles away. I tried to disguise my thoughts just a little, though, so she wouldn't be completely sure it was me in case she was receiving—Argo would be proud of me for including that touch of mystery.

I didn't want LaWanda to know exactly what I had in mind. Whenever I fucked before—each of the three times—it just happened and I never performed any planning. Now I was.

To fuck on purpose still seemed funny. Silly. Argo always talks about fucking Celia, about how great it was, but he sounds like he wanted to hurt her instead. And when Ernie Lazaro brought that girl on the baseball bus, they did it in the cramped bathroom in the back—they sounded like they were hitting one another, banging into the tin walls and howling like overfed dogs. In Vietnam, Miki kept her eyes closed and she was silent.

There is a lot of sex in this world. Everyone has to like it, even if they say it's bad. Argo should write a movie script for the pornos, but it should have monsters fucking. Godzilla could fuck the Bride of Frankenstein, for health reasons. What was it that transformed Godzilla into a good character in *Monster Zero*? Did he get laid in between movies?

LaWanda thinks Argo is wasting his time writing those Eddie Elvesizer books because they don't possess any imagination. I should give him more of my ideas, to pay him back, because he has done me many favors—especially when he tells me all about sex and provides his life as evidence.

Sometimes I have to fight to turn off these thoughts. My mind is always working, like a separate creature taking up space in my head—sometimes that creature is friendly and sometimes I have to fight it for control.

I settled into my couch and got comfortable and tried to imagine LaWanda's face so I could send her my thoughts. At the same time, I tried to imagine I was a slightly different person, to confuse her somewhat. But the more I concentrated, the more uneasy I became, shifting and twisting—fighting the temptation to explore the flurry of memories that suddenly poured into my mind.

I pushed myself off the couch; the cushions seemed like angry marshmallows trying to swallow me whole. On my knees, I walked across the room quickly toward the television; I could see myself in the gray screen growing bigger as I approached. Gripping the antenna with both hands, I aimed it toward LaWanda's apartment across the park. Between here and there was the wall to pass through, park buildings, the fountain, the Space Theater. I didn't know if my thoughts were powerful enough. Were they as strong as television waves?

There is a huge radio tower not far from my house, down toward the shipyards. You can see it through my back window. I had the abrupt urge to climb that tower, to struggle with the rusted metal, dragging myself to the top. One night on the news I watched a Mexican man clinging to that very tower. He was going to jump because he didn't have a job. A priest showed up riding inside a yellow fire truck. He prayed for the man gripping the tower. Eventually, the man climbed down, but only to be put in jail.

Would LaWanda love me if I had a job? Would she? Does

she think less of me because I live on checks from the government? Those checks will stop in a month, anyway. She doesn't know that, Argo doesn't know that, Mrs. Raylak doesn't know either.

Argo said I should be a philosopher, but what does he know? I just need something. If nothing else, if I got a job people might think I was a different person. That would be worth it alone. Argo is Argo, but he's really a writer. And I used to be a soldier—even though Sergeant Ascencion yelled at me, "Ames! Do you call yourself a soldier?"

All that time, I felt like I was something else inside. But at least I was a soldier.

Even though I still clung to the antenna, I couldn't focus on LaWanda. This was all Argo's fault.

Argo isn't really a writer, even though he says he is. LaWanda isn't really a waitress, because she wasn't born a waitress. I am Nicholas, but I want to be like Eddie Elvesizer—even though I could never really become him. Though occasionally it seems like I have, when I close my eyes. Nicholas is nothing more than a name my father chose. Brak is a name I chose, a name more powerful than any other. If during a job interview I announced myself as Brak—a personal monster just as terrifying as any other, as good or bad as Godzilla ever could be—I would be asked, "Brak who?" To that I would just have to laugh.

A company that would hire me as Brak would be the best place for me to work.

My fingers surrounding the antenna were as red as the flesh of a plum. LaWanda's face blossomed in my mind—I wanted her, yet at the same time she seemed to be interfering with my reaching beyond her, behind her. A trick. My mind was playing a trick. Sergeant Ascencion said it was time to pack it in when you couldn't trust your own mind.

I wanted new energy. I wanted to be stronger, powerful. The commercials on TV promised these things—promises transmitted to me through television waves, not unlike thoughtwaves.

There are so many waves surging through the atmosphere that thoughts need to be extra powerful to travel to designated areas—to fight through all the interference and competition. There are waves from television and radios—countless radios like CBs and shortwaves and stereos and police broadcasters. There are more waves beamed from the sun and other planets, not to mention gravity waves and thoughtwaves from hordes of people all over the globe. Waves that force us to dream. Telephone waves and electricity waves and pure energy waves. All kinds of sound waves. If we had more potent eyes, we could see waves everywhere crossing and bouncing around in different colors—X rays shooting through us or light waves curving over us like neon tubes in the shape of our bodies. So many waves out there, in there. One reason why there is so much cancer today—I've heard—is because these waves crash into the atoms of our flesh and knock them off course.

The only way to cure cancer is to shut down most of those waves, which would be impossible even for someone strong as Godzilla or terrible as Brak.

I hoped the aliens would be strong enough. When they landed on private land near the desert, they might be confused by all the earthly waves—what could they think, studying Mr. Rainey and Neeta and Mrs. Raylak and Sri Annabelle Afton trembling in front of light-bleached mesquite plants, all those waves trapping the humans in an enormous plaid forcefield?

Would the aliens try to help them or put them out of their misery? How could they tell the difference between thought-waves and television waves? The aliens might casually absorb a television wave and witness a monster movie from Channel 5, thinking quite honestly that the movie was a thought transmission from Sri Annabelle Afton. At the same time, the aliens might think they were being attacked by the Nebulae Society, with the help of today's television satellites and forceful beams from the SuperStation.

If I were an alien, I wouldn't know where to start.

My face ballooned, reflected in the shiny glass screen.

For now, Lawanda had to be enough.

She sleeps late because she works until three in the morning. I was afraid she couldn't receive my thoughts because she was asleep—the most I could ask for was my thoughts mingling with her dreams, unnoticed, unfelt.

Even so, I tried to aim the antenna at the perfect spot for the choicest delivery. It could be good enough for her just to dream of me. It could. She sleeps in the daytime, and most of her dreams aren't killed by the dark like mine. If she had good dreams about me, when I showed up later she might want to fuck, she might want to restore me.

In Vietnam, I thought about Miki all the time when I was out in the field. Before falling asleep I forced myself to dream about her. Dreams can be just as real as people. Not real like you could eat the food in dreams and stay alive, but real like the way they turn inside out but keep on going.

There is a canyon down the hill from my house. When the birds begin singing back and forth, I sit by the window and look down past the eucalyptus trees and wonder what the birds are saying. It's like a forcefield down there in the canyon, too, except the waves are different. When cats walk through hunting, the birds tell one another to be careful. When the birds sing and chirp, that's one type of wave. A tree storing up sunlight in order to grow is another kind of wave, which has much slower vibrations. At the bottom of the canyon is a two-lane road busy with traffic most of the time. All those people driving so close together without crashing is another kind of wave, more likely a combination of many fine and erratic waves. It's like a perfect picture when I look through my window, because all those different waves lancing through the canyon weave together in a pattern. One kind of wave influences another kind. The bird-waves change the catwaves, and after years and years the treewaves change things also, but very slowly. When the road was built down there, different waves were created—waves emitted by humans and different from all other types of waves. Humanwaves are not just crackly and dangerous like electricity, or smooth and golden like trees growing, but both at the same time.

Still gripping the thin silver antenna, I made one last concentrated effort—I thought about doing it to LaWanda and I felt suddenly warm. That warmth comes out in waves, too, which others can feel—and which in turn is more than just a warm feeling.

When it grows too loud and the sun comes up and there are more cars streaming down the road, I have to get away from the window and do something else—because the world becomes too mixed together for me. I need to be able to determine differences; when it becomes too noisy, I can't tell if a bird chirped or a car horn honked or what.

The television felt dead. Frustrated, I ran into the kitchen and dug through the tool drawer for a screwdriver. Then I unhooked the antenna wires from the back of the TV and sat down in the middle of the living room the way Miki taught me to sit. With my legs crossed in my lap, I peeled open my jeans. My prick was soft, and I had to dig it out from between the slot in the front of my underwear. When my prick grew hard, I touched the antenna wires to the bulging red head. It felt strange; a tiny charge made me quiver the same way I did

18

when touching my tongue across the connectors of a nine-volt radio battery.

Sending my thoughts to LaWanda wasn't going to work. Sending pure sexwaves might.

I thought about the time I caught her fucking that skinny sailor. Her face was scrunched tight. She held her mouth open and her tongue flopped in and out. She shook her head up and down like a horse would. Her hair bounced all around, and she laughed and uttered slow deep sounds, and she laughed again.

I touched the wires harder and pictured Mr. Rainey doing it to Neeta, and Ernie doing it to that girl on the bus, and Eddie Elvesizer fucking two United Nations nurses at once when he was a soldier of fortune in Zaire.

Argo says fucking is the only thing people live for, if you want the bottom line. There is so much fucking going on in the world each moment; no one can keep track of it all, not even with computers. There is always somebody fucking somebody else somewhere, keeping the sexwaves alive. Was there ever a moment anywhere at any time when no one was doing it? When most of the people in the world are fucking, do more good things happen or more bad things? When Neil Armstrong stepped onto the moon, were most of the people in the world fucking? When B-52s unloaded arc-light explosives on the people of North Vietnam, were not as many people fucking?

My sexwaves grew stronger in a twisting surge, and I wanted to jack off. I pressed the wires down harder until they hurt, which made the waves feel darker.

I wished LaWanda were awake. I wished I could see my sexwaves beaming out through the end of the antenna. LaWanda claimed she could see auras that surround people like a rainbow along the curves of their bodies. From the colors of the auras she can tell if a person is good or bad or sick or healthy.

Sexwaves must appear gloriously beautiful and scary at the same time.

Michael from Oregon was in my platoon. He wore beads all the time and painted colorful designs on his helmet—peace signs and protest slogans and flowers. He told me if enough people prayed together at the same time, the war would end just like that. But it never did.

Sex must be more powerful than prayer, because everyone has to fuck. I suppose even the pope must fight against his sexwaves.

I jabbed in the wires too hard. They split the soft skin on my prickhead enough to raise fresh blood. I heaved the antenna wires against the wall. My prick felt so big in my hand, I was afraid the blood pumping through the veins would spurt out the end—like I was coming but shooting red instead of white.

Blood trickled hot across my fingers and dripped down onto the rug.

I wanted LaWanda to feel how strong I could be with sex.

My prick was harder than ever.

If LaWanda were with me, she would be astonished by the bouquet of sexwaves flowing out from my prick all across the room—sexwaves ricocheting back at us and encircling us and forcing the colors in our auras to convert to bright, bright colors.

ALPHA
BODIES

When we went out on patrol around Chu Lai I pretended
we were in the TV show Combat, that I was the character
Littlejohn, that my M16 was really a BAR. As we slid through
the jungle, I hummed the theme song. Sergeant Ascencion told
me I was a fool to sing, but I couldn't stop myself from
pretending. The jungle swallowed us whole—that had never
happened to me before. But I had seen plenty of episodes of
Combat. When we stopped to eat, Sergeant Ascencion always
wanted to trade C rations if he ended up with spaghetti; I just
told him to pretend it was something else, his favorite Mexican
food. It was impossible to get him to play along. And he didn't
look anything like Vic Morrow, the actor who portrayed Sergeant Saunders on Combat. Even so, Vic Morrow was killed in
real life on the set of a movie about Vietnam. The more I
thought, the more confused I became—the tighter the jungle
enclosed me. I pretended. I lived.

When I fuck LaWanda I don't want to pretend.

I had to put medicine and a Band-Aid on my prickhead
to avoid infection. I doctored myself in the bathroom, carefully, trying to ignore the burning pain. The drill sergeants in
boot camp taught me all about first aid.

During basic training at Fort Polk, Louisiana, we trainees
were finally allowed to leave the post after three weeks of
marching through the swamps and swimming with snakes.
Dennis Clinksdale, a local kid, took a cab into Leesville, the

little town right outside the fort. We didn't see him until the following Monday morning. I was shaving, staring at my unfamiliar short-haired head in the mirror, when I noticed Dennis stumbling toward the urinals. Pissing, he rested his head against the wall and screamed. He never left the company area after that, warning us not to waste our money in Diseaseville.

I'm cursed with thoughts. I'm afraid it's a disease. All the time I'm thinking, remembering, never forgetting anything except what I'm supposed to do, what I'm responsible for. The Band-Aids. Standing in my bathroom staring at a white metal box of Band-Aids, fighting back the exhibitions in my head.

I tossed the box under the sink and sat down on the furry toilet-seat cover, wondering about LaWanda. How could I fuck her with a bloody prick? She'd think I was carrying something toxic. She'd think this, I'd think that. The curse. The thoughts. The games. Around and around, retreating, pretending—I heaved the glass medicine bottle into the bathtub; it shattered with a stinging crash and red splashed all over, which made everything worse. LaWanda seemed so far away, sitting on top of Mount Fuji, and I crumpled in a ball in the valley below, my legs severed from one quick slice of a samurai sword, bleeding—but I had to squirm up there and get her, at all costs, for my sake.

LaWanda. She works at the Beaumont Station restaurant down in Mission Valley. I visited only once, with Argo, when he decided to celebrate selling yet another Eddie Elvesizer novel. The restaurant is built around old red boxcars; the inside is stuffed with railroad souvenirs, which look awfully fake—and I felt funny trying to eat normal food and pretend we were sitting in a train station. Argo ordered some freezing champagne, and we drank that in a hurry, teasing LaWanda when she told us to leave for our own good, before the manager threw us out. But I wanted her that night. I wanted to stand up and take her and tear the old-time photographs off the walls and strip that place clean until it was just LaWanda and Nicholas, lean and alone.

What a dream. Another dream tangled and arrested and silenced by fear. I know, I know.

Many times I've been on the brink of revealing my fears to Argo, but it's so hard when he's always chattering about being a man. I've never told him my fears of being unlike anyone else. In Nam the company all called me Dudley. Our supply sergeant was a huge purple black man named Lee Otis Jefferson who always laughed at me when I requested new boots. He said, "Here's your banana boats," and slapped the boots down on the supply counter. They were a sick color of green with black rubber soles; the laced edges flopped over and sagged down. I hated to ask for something from that sergeant. He had puffy yellow eyes that filled up most of his face; his head looked like he borrowed it from The Mole People, *a movie that starred Hugh Beaumont before he became Beaver Cleaver's father.*

In the perfect movie, I arrive at LaWanda's apartment just as she wakes up. She answers the door in her robe and doesn't mind when she catches me admiring her tits—in fact, she wriggles pleasantly causing the robe to slide open even further, to tease me, to play with me. Taking my hand, she leads me into the bedroom; I don't have to ask, I don't have to imagine, I don't have to stare into hideous yellow eyes or endure bellowing laughter just to receive what I deserve.

I didn't bother to clean the mess in the bathroom. LaWanda was waiting. I left all the broken glass and the red puddle in the tub, following the part of Nicholas that wanted out, that suddenly decided to walk over to LaWanda's apartment instead, taking the shortcut through the park.

My house, surrounded by two overgrown pepper trees,

sits in the backyard behind Mrs. Raylak's bigger house. As I put my clothes on quickly, I realized how calm it was outside—the trees accepted the early-morning sunlight, the air was still, the telephone wires arced gently across the yard. Then my mind was invaded by the thought of robbers breaking in after I was gone. The family next door had been robbed two weeks ago. Investigating policemen swarmed through their house, and cop cars packed the street. None of the policemen would give me a ride or let me listen to the radio, even though I'm a veteran. No suspects were ever placed into custody.

It took me years to realize there is always fear droning beneath calmness. This neighborhood is calm, at first glance, most of the time. But only on the surface. Overseas, indoctrination teams taught us to look beneath the surface of Vietnamese life. I learned never to point my feet at the Vietnamese when I sat down—to do otherwise was disrespectful. Some of the calmness in our neighborhood comes from television. In the evenings, gray light streams and flashes from most of the living room windows—inside everyone is watching their favorite show, or at least waiting for those favorites to come on. Now that so many Vietnamese are coming over here, they need to learn our customs, to respect the calmness—when visiting they must join in and watch TV in silence, for example. In this way, we can all forget the fear.

West of my house, toward downtown, there are hundreds of Vietnamese families moving in, filling up old apartment buildings and shabby clapboard houses. When I walk through that neighborhood I have to dodge all the children romping in the streets and on the grassless yards. Old women sit cross-legged on the porches, wearing long colored skirts and rubber flip-flops—and I picture I'm strolling through Saigon again. As the sun glimmers in the shiny black hair of the children, and as I hear those women call out in high shrill voices, I'm

24

transported—I can easily remember again all the sounds of that crowded city: the persistent blare of shopkeepers crying out and small cars and motorcycles racing past and the music from bars and boom-boxes pounding and shrieking. When I hear those women on the porches call to their children in high shrill voices, I'm transported.

But once I went too far; once I lost myself. In that same Vietnamese neighborhood I almost jumped out of my skin when I heard a garbage truck clamped onto a dumpster bang that dumpster against a concrete driveway. For a quick moment I thought that booming sound was an exploding mortar round. I was transported to the evening I saved Sergeant Ascencion's life. We were shelled mercilessly outside Chu Lai. As loud as I could I screamed, "Incoming!" The sergeant was terribly drunk and couldn't figure out right away what was happening, so I ran to him and yanked the back of his sweaty fatigue shirt with one hand. It took me just a few seconds to drag him down into our bunker. When we crawled back out later, when the calmness returned, in the spot where he had been lying drunk was a good-sized crater—his can of Budweiser floated at the bottom ripped inside out and shining silver.

There is plenty of violence in our neighborhood. I can't always see it, but I can feel it sitting there, pointing its toes at me.

Making certain my front door was locked behind me, I stepped across the yard over the shadow of the pepper trees. Through a side window of the front house, I could see Mrs. Raylak on her couch reading one of Sri Annabelle Afton's books—this book, like all the others published by the Nebulae Society, had the same colorful photograph of an alien spaceship on the cover. The title read *Planet X: Land of Eternal Peace*. There was a Planet X in the Japanese movie *Monster*

Zero—an interesting coincidence, I would say, even though Argo would no doubt cough, "B-F-D."

Spread all across the wall behind Mrs. Raylak's head was an enormous map of the Milky Way galaxy. The outside wire for the cable TV poked right through Polaris. The only reason Mrs. Raylak got cable, she told me, was to watch the local public-access channel—the Nebulae Society broadcasts a show all morning long re-creating adventurous visits to other planets at video studios in their east county headquarters (an old warehouse painted green next to the Salvation Army store).

Mrs. Raylak told me some time ago that when Mr. Raylak finally died after years of suffering from cancer, he was absorbed into another dimension more spectacular than imagination itself and that he was waiting there for her, beyond the stars. When I shared this fact with Argo, he laughed like Lee Otis Jefferson used to laugh before blurting out, "If that dimension is so damn beautiful, what's keeping her here on earth?" I didn't think Argo was being fair, so I never told him any more stories about Mrs. Raylak, even though he sometimes asked, "How's the Space Queen these days?"

Mrs. Raylak has plenty of faith, and she attends regularly all the Nebulae Society functions—but I still find it hard to believe the aliens are going to land near here anytime soon. We're not ready for them yet, for one thing. Still, I *do* think that whatever we can imagine can come true—even if only in a movie. And no one can say that movies aren't true, because everybody watches them all the time—in theaters and on video at home. There might be as many people all over the world watching movies right now as there are people fucking, if not more.

Mrs. Raylak looked very happy reading her book, and I wondered if I looked that happy when I watched TV. I couldn't imagine a life without television. When *Star Trek* was first broadcast, I used to watch intently, jacking off each time Lieutenant Uhura appeared. She never did much except follow Captain Kirk's orders, but she had beautiful dark legs and lips that could soothe me to death. Once in a while I grew afraid that she could see what I was doing—then I would go soft and wait quietly for the next episode.

Pushing away from Mrs. Raylak's side window, I slipped and almost crashed into the wooden fence. Straining to grab on to the hollow knobby branches of her poinsettias for support, I made too much racket. Long knife-shaped red petals stuck into my hair. When I glanced up to check if Mrs. Raylak had noticed the commotion, there she sat waving pleasantly. I couldn't hear her, but her lips were moving with these words—"Come in." As she slipped a tasseled marker into her book, I tried to untangle myself from the poinsettia. I watched her slip the book into a neat row on the bookcase next to the television. The top row of the bookcase held a shrine, something like the shrine Miki built at her mother's apartment in Saigon—but Mrs. Raylak's was brighter and cluttered with colors. Miki's was created around a laughing plaster-of-Paris fat man who gripped lighted cigarettes and smiled behind clouds of sweet incense; Mrs. Raylak's was shinier, adorned with chains of metal beads and photographs—one of Mr. Raylak staring into a night sky, and another of Sri Annabelle Afton hidden underneath a white robe. A third photo depicted the alien landing site—a cleared-out dirt circle surrounded by low scraggly underbrush. My father used to take me out near there when I was a kid, before they had condos, to try our luck fishing at Otay Lakes.

There was a red stop sign sticking up out of the lake by the boat dock, and some trees submerged up to their top branches. Next to the window of the rental office were hundreds of snapshots of the biggest fish caught, the most fish, the largest bigmouth bass with jaws wide open like a Japanese lantern. My dad rented a wooden boat and we slid quietly out onto the glassy lake, holding ourselves warm as we slipped through pockets of early-morning fog.

We fished for a while without much luck. Even that early my dad was drinking lots of beer, and soon he had to row in to shore to piss. He left me alone in the boat; I waited for him, lulled by little waves slapping against the hull.

Dad disappeared into the bushes and I searched for something to eat in the ice chest. It was still cold and full of golden beer cans.

The front of the boat was jammed into the sand, and the shoreline smelled like garbage. Hunks of green moss were packed up around the tules or crisping on the beach. Flies soon discovered the boat, and I fought with them while I dug a sandwich out of the bottom of the cooler. The sandwich was squished sopping, and I could barely unwrap it from the waxed paper.

Then I heard the bushes move. But it wasn't my father. It was a skinny Mexican man, and he just stood there staring at me. He pointed at the sandwich and quickly looked back to where my father was peeing. Then he pointed at the sandwich intensely, poking his finger back and forth like a spear. With his other hand, he grabbed his belly, talking mean to me in Spanish.

I was scared, but I didn't want to stand up. My father told me never to stand up in the boat. Instead, I leaned over as far as I could and held out the sandwich until my arm hurt. I didn't want to throw the food at him. The Mexican man ran over and slopped in the shallow green water, soaking his black dress shoes. The sandwich seemed to float out of my hand as he received it softly.

When my father returned, the Mexican man ran as fast as he could down the beach before crashing through the bushes out *of sight. We could hear him breaking branches and swishing through the high grass. My dad just laughed and lifted the boat free from the sand.*

Again without talking we glided out to where we had been fishing before, near the concrete dam. After dunking in the anchor, my dad ordered me to fetch him another beer. He wiped off his mouth with the back of his hand and spat into the clean water. His white spit floated away from the boat like a tiny galaxy of stars, and he grumbled something about the governor and all the illegal aliens as he stabbed the opener into another cold can.

Brushing poinsettia leaves and yellow pollen from my shoulders, I waited patiently on Mrs. Raylak's porch, listening to her struggle to turn the locks. After the recent robbery next door, she had had a man come over and install two new dead bolts. When he was drilling the holes, I stopped by to watch, and he told me, "These locks won't stop anybody who really wants to get in, but the old lady'll sleep better at night." He blew sawdust into my eyes before the drill screamed again; then he said, "A hundred bucks for peace of mind is a bargain." I laughed to myself then, because Argo maintained there was no such thing as peace of mind, just piece of ass. I tried to tell that to the locksmith, pretending I had made it up, but his drill drowned me out.

The door finally inched open, creaking slightly like doors in scary movies.

"Nicholas! Please come in. I was just about to call you, but you probably felt my thoughts and saved me the trouble. How are you, young man?"

I nodded, hoping I had brushed off all the leaves and flower petals.

"It's getting so hard to dial the phone anymore with this arthritis."

Mrs. Raylak grinned up at me; her eyes sparkled, but the

corners of her mouth were tight with pain. She reached up to close the door behind me and I stared at her hands; her knuckles were swollen knobs and her skin was as thin as tissue paper.

"In or out, Nicholas? In or out?"

I stepped inside and the door slammed shut. It was nice in her living room—spicy with air freshener and thick with antiques. It always seemed curious to me how such an old woman could have strong feelings about space travel and other modern ideas. Mrs. Raylak believes in the power of thoughts, too, but in a more old-fashioned way than LaWanda. Mrs. Raylak accepts aliens from other galaxies, and LaWanda has seen demons and spirits from lower worlds. I had most of my troubles with earthbound situations, so I suppose I wasn't ready for these other levels. Yet.

"Here, sit down next to me on the couch. My, you're looking fine."

Her couch was so perfect I hated to sit there, because I always left a large dent in the cushion and messed up the lace doilies covering the headrest.

"Would you like something to drink? I've got mineral water. It was on sale."

"No, thank you. I ate a big breakfast."

She sat down on the ottoman and crossed her legs, resting her twisted hands on her knee.

"That's good, that's good. No wonder you're looking so well. Now. Nicholas? I need to ask you a favor."

Mrs. Raylak talks very slowly to me, which is nice, even though her words are colored with polite suffering. Even if I lose track of the meaning in her words, I can understand how strong she still is—as she battles to smile through the aches. Argo could learn a lesson from her. He talks fast, and he talks too much—always trying to catch up with himself. Mrs.

Raylak, though, has to strain to stay right where she is—because death is always pointing his feet right at the ottoman.

The more I sit with her, listening to her voice stretch and quiver with random strength, the more I see that death is an earthbound situation. The tension in her voice tears into me worse than the sight of any bloody corpse I saw in wartime.

"I can't mow the lawn today, Mrs. Raylak. I've got to . . . I've got a date."

"You have? Well, that's wonderful. Yes. I'm proud of you, Nicholas. The lawn can wait, of course. But there is something much more important I need to ask you."

There was a tightness in her voice, pulled to the limit like the secure bun of hair on the back of her head. I looked straight into her eyes, and for a moment it seemed she was gone and I was gazing into two blue disks as thin and clear as the skin of a blown-up balloon that squeaks when rubbed against your pants, where it sticks violating the power of gravity.

"Perhaps you and your date would like to accompany us this evening, Nicholas. What do you think? Mr. and Mrs. Rainey and I are driving out to the X-site together, and Sri Afton would like us to bring along as many alpha bodies as we can. It's dreadfully important, because the alignment is unique tonight. We won't have this pattern in the heavens for another three hundred years. Oh, Nicholas, do come. It would mean so much to the society!"

"I don't know. She works at night. But maybe Argo."

"No, no . . . I think it would be best if you came without Mr. Argo. Besides, I'm not certain if he's an alpha body or not. I have a hunch not."

"How can you tell?"

"Hmmm? How? Well, it's all in the books. It's explained in the approved literature. But we won't worry about that now.

Mr. Rainey is arriving at eight. Can we count on you also, Nicholas? With your girlfriend, perhaps? Please say yes."

I was assigned to Alpha Company in basic training. Third Platoon, Alpha Company. I felt invisible after my head was shaved. Channel 5 was showing Invisible Invaders *with John Agar on the late show, but I had already seen it twice. Alpha. Alpha beta. Alpha-Bits. Oldsmobile Omega.*

"Nicholas?"

"Yes? Yes, I might be able to."

"Wonderful, wonderful. I won't forget this, young man. And neither will Mr. Raylak."

She closed her eyes and gripped the string of purple metal beads around her neck. The skin under her chin was papery and splotched with blue veins, as delicate as her eyelids. When Mrs. Raylak spoke again, she sounded like a different person.

"You be here at eight sharp, Nicholas. And wear as many white things as you can. Do you have a white shirt or some white slacks? Mr. Rainey has some extras, but I daresay they'd be too small."

"I've got a new blue shirt."

"No, that won't do. Blue is a gamma color."

"I didn't know."

"Oh, I'm sorry, Nicholas. I didn't mean to snap like that. It's just that today is a perfect alpha day. I've been on guard against gamma influences all morning. By the way, does the head of your bed face south?"

"No, but if you want me to I can—"

"It's fascinating when you think that the Van Allen belt, well, perhaps another time. You see, I'm going to help with Sri Afton's next book on radiation, and I've been so busy studying and taking thought readings. Yes. But I'm so glad you're going to come with us this evening. You don't know how much this means. We were going to try and send you a thought command, but Neeta said it would be best to come right out and ask. Sometimes we just have to use words, even if they *are* so primitive."

I opened my mouth prepared to say something, but Mrs. Raylak froze my tongue staring at me with her head tilted and her eyebrows twitching. So I just nodded. She nodded back and then stared at me for the longest time, in silence. Held in her eyes, I ground my hands together and scraped my feet through the shag carpet. When I took a chance and looked away, she grunted and wouldn't stop grunting until I stared into her face again, into her fragile wet eyes. She seemed ready to cry, which made me feel sad. I had to look down at her pointed nose for relief, startled by the number of gray hairs coiling from her nostrils.

"Well, Nicholas? Well?"

I checked back to see if I had tracked in any dirt or leaves, but the carpet was clean. The couch was spotless, and there weren't any flower petals hanging off my shirt. Still, she seemed to be warning me.

"Aaaa-hummmghh."

Then again, like she was trying to start a motor.

"Ni-cho-las . . . ?"

There was too much force in her eyes, making me nervous. The thought of fucking LaWanda sometimes made me nervous, but not this badly. As Mrs. Raylak juggled her eyebrows and leaned closer, I squirmed on the couch—which was strange since there was no suspicion of sex in this room, and nothing to be afraid of.

"I . . . there might be lots of people in the park today."

"Oh! That's wonderful. Then you *did* receive my message."

Possibly I did. But I wasn't sure. The couch felt as

insignificant as a cloud beneath me all of a sudden; I thought I would fall in, absorbed by swirling vapors; my heart narrowed its beating. Mrs. Raylak's face curved back at the edges in a fish-eyed flash.

"Sri Afton is so right. Thoughts are truly powerful, Nicholas."

Yes, this I already suspected. Squeezing the armrest, I steadied myself. Sex. Thoughts. The recovery of my power. The power to revive. Someone else was doing my thinking for me, an intruder within the walls of my skull. Mrs. Raylak smiled. Come. Make me come. She was too close.

"You certainly must be an alpha body. That makes me quite pleased, young man. Quite pleased."

Embarrassment flooded through me when Mrs. Raylak patted my knee. As a defense, LaWanda's big tits ballooned in my mind. Thoughts could make me come, they were that powerful. Argo's voice. Interrupting. He said he got bored fucking Celia and had to imagine other women to get off. If sex is as powerful as Argo claims, thoughts had to be just as strong if they could force a climax. Those days were gone for Mrs. Raylak—so her thoughts had to be stronger, with no sex-forces to interfere.

The couch hardened beneath me. My mother. I never saw my mother alive.

"Yes, and you seem pleased about something. What's this about a date, Nicholas?"

Pictures of LaWanda slid rapidly through my mind, out of control. My prick stiffened, playing a trick on me. I tried to cross my legs to hide it, but there was too much. My foot plopped back onto the rug with a clomping sound. I tried to force the thoughts to stop. Thoughts against thoughts, until explosions in my head transformed into butterflies then into naked LaWandas—in the park she slowly rose up out of the square goldfish pond; on the moon she tore off her silver space suit and danced around easily, bouncing in the vague atmosphere; on television, she ripped through the screen and lured me closer, taunting me with her slippery lips.

"Are you sure you wouldn't like a drink, Nicholas? You look like you need . . . something."

"Okay. Sure."

Mrs. Raylak skipped out of the room, grinning just before she disappeared into the kitchen. I pressed down on my hard prick with both hands trying to squash it. The softness didn't begin until I heard ice cubes clank into a glass.

Godzilla and Rodan were quick-frozen inside huge glass balls so Nick Adams could tow them through the soundlessness of space on the way to Planet X.

"You know, Nicholas, the X-site is so spectacularly beautiful in the evening. The stars seem so close, like you could stretch out and touch them. Grab them right out of the heavens. Oh, it's so delightful to watch the skies. To wait. Knowing. I believe we're being watched, too, and the aliens are closer than most people think, waiting for the right time, waiting for the faithful to develop their awareness. Oh, all I had left was a diet Coke. Here, Nicholas."

Mrs. Raylak wasn't aware of the lump in my pants, I knew that much. Even Mr. Raylak in the photograph couldn't see; his face aimed up and out of the gold frame—a light glowed in his smooth skin, and his eyes were brighter and more colorful than they were in real life. There was still pain, and the Band-Aid was too tight—but my secret was still a secret. All my secrets were held deep and tight within me. For protection.

"You're correct, Nicholas. I agree completely. But it's fun to talk out loud, anyway."

"What?"

"In case we're being watched. This way, we can share with the aliens. Sri Afton doesn't know if our thoughts can be read by other beings or not. So it's best we communicate, with words instead of thoughts, for their sake. Here, now drink this."

The glass was freezing, stinging my fingers. Brown soda

bubbled around the chain of ice cubes. Inside I heard fizzing and saw thousands of bubbles—more than there were stars illustrated on the living room wall—bubbles electric in my hand, exploding, churning, dying, changed back into raw space.

"We don't need that many tonight, but we do need at least thirty-six. Lately it's been so hard to get enough together—enough alpha bodies, particularly. Our group is changing all the time, and if it weren't for the Raineys . . . well, you can always count on them. Since my husband withdrew from this dimension, membership has lagged. He helped attract others. There was a Hernandez couple and some of their friends who used to come, but ever since the withdrawal . . ."

"LaWanda's last name is Hernandez, too."

"I bet she's a sweet thing, Nicholas."

"I hope so. But I should get over there now, before she has to go to work."

"Yes, of course. Oh, my, you *were* thirsty. One gulp, Nicholas. I hope that girl knows what she's getting into. There. Now . . . Nicholas, look out!"

When I stood up, a spiked cramp tore into my crotch. I crashed back hard onto the sofa, shaking the end table and knocking over the lamp. When the lamp smacked the wall, the metal cones surrounding the light bulbs tore into the paper Milky Way, shredding half the galaxy.

"Oh . . . my God . . . Nicholas. There. You just run along now. I suppose I can tape this and salvage Polaris. What would Mr. Raylak say? He's probably watching us now."

She grabbed the sides of her tiny gray head and held her eyes closed tight. My prick was throbbing. Hoping Mrs. Raylak wouldn't notice the bulge, I inched backward toward the front door.

"Columbus found a world, and had no chart," she said in a deep voice.

I moved closer to the door.

Snapping open her eyes, Mrs. Raylak grinned freely.

"What happened?" she said. "I think I blacked out for a moment."

"I should be going. Now."

"Yes, I think I might have been channeling. Just for a moment. That felt like Mr. Raylak. Didn't it?"

"It's time for me to change the channel, too. I'll talk to you later."

"Yes. Of course."

As I turned to leave, Mrs. Raylak jiggled her head like she was trying to make it empty. When I grabbed the doorknob, she scraped the torn galaxy map.

I slipped out of Mrs. Raylak's house without speaking, unaware of her thoughts, leaving her with a handful of ripped stars and a broken light fixture. It was a relief to find myself outside again. Out on the street, I walked swiftly. A group of Mexican kids playing hopscotch on the corner stopped skipping when I passed by, staring at me as if they knew what I had just done, their eyes holding the apology I forgot to offer.

The fastest route to LaWanda's cut through the canyon past the end of the municipal golf course. My shortcut sliced across one of the greens, but my progress was halted by a pair of golfers. I had to wait on the edge, in the woods, while two men finished playing the hole. The fat one in a blue hat sighted down the length of his putter at the flagstick as if aiming a rifle. His opponent sighed, fanning himself with his white hat. After rehearsing a few strokes, the fat man tapped his yellow ball. At the last moment, the other man yanked up the flagstick to allow the ball to clomp into the plastic hole. "Nice bogey," he said. The fat man did not reply.

It felt strange to stand so close to these men without being noticed. They seemed more real than I did, too, out in the sun with their clean colorful clothes. Their bright blue and green and yellow shirts and pants reminded me of the time my father took me to a used-car lot on my sixteenth birthday. As I hugged the rough bark of the tree, holding myself in the shadows, scenes from that day fell into my memory.

Colored plastic pennants snapped in the wind, strung up all around the block of shining cars. After school that day, my father had rushed me into his Dodge for the drive to La Mesa, where he promised to find me something dependable for five hundred dollars. But first and foremost, he said, he wanted to teach me how to buy a good car, to show me the ropes. As we walked onto the lot, preparing for the advancing salesmen, he whispered, "Son, you have to learn to stand your ground." His words were punctured by the steady clicking of the plastic flags.

A man in red slacks eased between two cars and smiled, his teeth gleaming in the lights. My dad hissed hard in my ear: "Watch me now, you might learn something." His breath was thick and warm with beer.

The salesman grabbed my dad's arm with two hands and shook it hard before pulling us from car to car. That salesman gave way to two others after we took a few test drives. My father told me the '57 Chevy was the best all-round deal, but he wanted to wear out the salesmen before he got down to business. I wanted the shiny gold Buick Skylark instead, but my father scoffed. The Chevy was to be mine, "no matter what," because it was a much cleaner car. But I liked the way the Buick burned in the lights when I squinted my eyes.

On our last test drive, the two of us squeezed into a green Fiat two-seater. My father drove it madly, too fast for too long, fighting it up and down hills. Then he stopped at a neighborhood bar across the railroad tracks, jamming the front tires hard into the curb.

I waited outside, counting the moths flitting around the streetlamp; then I counted the boxcars on a train that rattled past—the game I invented had this rule: more boxcars than moths, and the Buick was mine.

We drove frighteningly fast on the way back to the car lot. Hopping out of the Fiat without opening the door, my father asked me, "Did you learn something today, boy?" I said yes because his eyes wanted me to say yes.

As we surrounded the front of the Chevy, my father argued loudly with the latest salesman, slapping his hand flat against the hood and knocking the black-and-yellow price sign loose from the windshield. The salesman seized the sign and jammed it back into place behind the wiper blade, holding his other hand down on top of my father's.

In the office, after clearing his throat, my father counted off twenty-five twenty-dollar bills one by one, and after each hundred dollars he looked back at me and winked.

I was afraid to drive the Chevy home, but my father insisted. The car seemed so huge inside, the front seat as large as our old couch. I had trouble shifting gears with the column shifter, and I fought to keep up with my father racing ahead of me in our old Dodge. Worrying that he would lose me, I stole glances at myself in the round glass over the speedometer and didn't recognize my own face; black-and-white numerals spun in my eyes and the red needle pierced my forehead.

That big Chevy never ran easily after that, and I never had enough money to get it fixed. Whenever I tried to talk to my father about helping me out with repairs, he tightened his throat, his eyes bulged, and his lips thrust together thin and taut. This expression always stood for "The End."

I made that car explode a thousand times in my dreams.

As the fat golfer reached down to snatch his ball out of the cup, the other man—wearing red-and-white spiked shoes—stomped on his plump hand. They yelled and shouted, and as their voices raged I took cover behind some low-hanging branches, peeking through the leaves. Taking out his wallet, the fat man pinched out a flurry of paper money, throwing the bills at the other man, who watched them flutter down onto the green. Instead of bending to pick up the cash, he hoisted his putter over his head. His arms shook. His face blossomed pink. The fat man with the empty wallet laughed, but only until he was axed with the putter hard and straight across the back. He flopped flat across the scattered money and groaned like an animal. The other man continued to beat him; then he pounded on the short grass of the green and dug up holes of fresh brown dirt, screaming, "Here's some more holes for you! Maybe—this—will—make—it—easy! You hog!" Wrapping his overflowing arms around his head, the fat man mumbled, "Stop, please, I love you, I love you. . . ."

I forced myself to keep still, to breathe slowly and deeply, surrounded by shadows and leaves—in hiding, in conceal-ment, in ambush, in disguise. While I watched, afraid of being seen, the two men struggled in the bright sun; their crisp brand-new golf outfits were luminous against the shining grass.

The fallen golfer curled his knees up against his chest as the other man circled him and putted dirt clods—when a clod splattered against the fat man's forehead, he sobbed. Snicker-ing, the other golfer shouted, "Take that, big man. Let's see Mr. America cry like a baby for a change."

Three golf carts raced down the fairway. One swerved out of control and overturned, flipping the passenger and his bag of clubs. He jumped free and ran after the other two speeding carts, eventually leaping into the back of one and wrapping his arms around the driver in a bear hug.

"Here comes the cavalry, motherfucker," said the golfer in the white hat. The sneer on his face and the roar of the approaching golf carts brought to mind the monster battle at the close of *Godzilla vs. Megalon*. That was a spectacular movie because it left out Godzilla's silly son Minyah and the Monster of Too-Strict Mothers, Momagon.

The men in the carts barreled up onto the green. Two of them leaped out and grabbed the attacker in the white hat. He tried to fight them, stabbing his putter like a sword, but he was quickly wrestled to the ground, his face jammed hard into one of the holes he had slashed. The third man knelt down next to the fat golfer, who moaned whenever he was touched.

"That's all right, let the woman cry," the angry man said, his face smudged with dirt. He didn't stop cursing until someone slugged him hard in the belly.

With help, the fat man rose slowly to his knees. He lifted his head and blinked, looking straight at me. Without smiling or yelling, he simply stared, his eyes dull and wet, his lips a small straight line.

When he smiled all of a sudden, I couldn't smile back. Blood oozed from one corner of his mouth and speckles of dirt dotted his chubby face.

Holding a wounded arm close to his side, the fat man leaned down to scoop up the paper money. With a cluster of green in his fist, he waved at me. His friends glanced my way, over his shoulder, but I ducked from their sight at the last second. I peered back out cautiously; the fat golfer tried to speak to me. Just as his mouth opened and the sun glistened against his wet teeth, his eyes shut tight; he collapsed in half, squeezing himself with both arms. His friends eased him down. His hand loosened, and all the money—pinched into a crumpled green knot—came rolling out like a golf ball. The End.

"Hey, there's somebody watching in the bushes!"

I ran straight ahead, crashing through branches across the spongy green, the golfing clothes a kaleidoscopic blur of seething color. I ran up the hill and over the jangling chain-link fence, down the bluff to the road up Florida Canyon almost to the back entrance of the Naval Hospital.

As I leaned against a Caution sign catching my breath, car after car passed by, hissing down the asphalt, and I stared at each driver—but no one answered.

I hiked out of the canyon and entered Balboa Park from the back, near the fountain and the Space Theater. Climbing out of the canyon was sweaty work, so I stopped to rest on a concrete bench in front of the fountain. Clusters of tourists with bare white legs took photographs of one another. I discovered this park on my own, since my father never brought me here. He rarely took me anywhere special, except for an occasional hockey game. He loved the fights on the ice, but they scared me because I thought all the spectators inside the Sports Arena were going to join in the battle. Each time we attended a hockey game, I saw the same fan screaming from the front row—an overweight young man in a blue suit and black tie; he continuously waved a rubber chicken on a stick at the meanest player on the opposing team, who, in that league, was usually Mad Dog Madigan. I wondered what that fan did when he wasn't at hockey games harassing Mad Dog with the pink rubber chicken. And for that matter, what did Mad Dog do when he wasn't high-sticking and body-checking and sitting in the penalty box? Why did he make a career out of violating the rules? Why did these fans pay ten dollars for the privilege of behaving strangely?

That fat fan reminded me of my dentist. When he calmly poked into my mouth I would wince, unable to speak, the suction dish gurgling by my elbow—and I would imagine that even though the dentist was neat and composed in his clean white smock he was actually dying to dash for a rubber chicken stashed behind the door, which he needed to taunt all the patients in the waiting room.

Our old mailman was another one who never said much, whose clothes were always clean and pressed—but I figured he had another rubber chicken stuffed into the bottom of his huge leather mail pouch and that he ached for someone to make a wrong move so he could break it out and dance around the violator shaking this rubber bird close to their unbelieving eyes while he cackled and tossed letters into the air like confetti.

But I could never picture my father doing anything like that, even though he was generally calm and quiet—even after he had a few drinks. Often I wished more than anything he would do something silly for me, but he never did. Not playfully, anyway.

The spray from the fountain was cool, and through the wisps of water vapor I could see the outlines of the Natural History Museum. Years ago, on a school field trip to that museum, our class huddled around a monstrous gold pendulum, waiting for it to knock over helpless wooden pegs. I enjoyed looking at my face in the swinging gold ball. The reflection would be frustratingly tiny at first, then all of a sudden my face would balloon and the pendulum would miss the peg by a cunthair (Argo's favorite expression) before arcing back. That action was supposed to prove how the earth rotated in space, according to the explanatory plaque mounted on the safety railing, but I could never understand the details. I was too afraid to ask for help, anyway. Even so, the sad fact of the matter is this: too few people these days make the effort to really explain things to anyone's satisfaction. Or so Argo has told me. And I believe him.

It was refreshing to sit by the fountain, with the water jets spraying up high then crashing down on the people playing in the pool with their children. The spray created a barely visible sphere of mist, and all around the top edge were rainbows dazzling against a sky the color of light blue stationery.

When I shifted my head too far to one side, the rainbows disappeared—due to the rotation of the earth. But I couldn't be certain. An entire day could be wasted trying to figure out such things, but it was more fun to simply watch them all take place and unfold and proceed.

There are always plenty of beautiful girls in the park, and of course I enjoy watching them, too. I never get much further than the watching part, however; so studying how guys try to pick up girls is also a fascination—especially when those guys fail.

I've seen all sorts of dramas in these courtship situations. It's especially sad, though, when one of the best-looking girls gives in too soon. The ones I respect the most are those who pretend the guys aren't even there.

I've seen guys get violently angry when certain girls wouldn't talk to them even though they stalked those girls halfway across the park. Those guys enjoy cursing, "Fuck you, bitch!" as an insult, which is a ridiculous thing to say since that's what those guys desire in the first place.

Watching girls, watching movies, watching men crush one another's ribs with golf clubs—I'm always looking in from outside. I never tried to follow a girl around the park, because

I tell myself there is enough to enjoy just through watching. With water spouting and gurgling and rippling all around me, I watched—and pain scissored through my crotch as my cock swelled up. The Band-Aid was slipping loose. A swollen rubber chicken. Smashing my dead father's face with a rubber chicken tied to the smooth varnished head of a golf club. He never taught me how to pursue women. He showed me how to drive, but that was about it. And now the state of California wouldn't even let me have a driver's license.

On the other side of the fountain two girls kicked off their shoes and rolled up their jeans preparing to wade in the cool water. They looked perfect through the spray, like a page from a magazine. One had long brown hair that spilled straight down over her shoulders and grazed the white concrete bench. She continued folding up her pant legs then sat back down to brush the hair from her eyes. Her friend was already in the fountain pretending she was going to splash water. I could have begun broadcasting thoughtwaves but decided against it, not wanting to interfere with their fun.

The girl with the long hair finally fixed her pants, and she entered the water timidly. I could feel her fear, especially when the other girl threatened her, kicking up longer and longer arcs, keeping her close to the retaining wall.

Suddenly, three sailors took over the bench next to mine. They all had short bristly hair, and their skulls shone through around the ears. One of them slung an oversized radio over his shoulder on a multicolored guitar strap. Music erupted, thumping in a contrasting pattern to the fountain sprays. It was wrong. The design was ruined. Closing my eyes I saw a cartoon of the fountain pump squirting out of control, overburdened by a surplus of foreign rumblings and vibrations.

Then I observed another cartoon—the projector in the Space Theater sizzled a hole in the domed ceiling with the

46

intense power of a laser. The building split in two, emitting a cascade of visitors and science exhibits and charred souvenirs. Across the street, the Natural History Museum shook and thundered before the walls crumbled into dust—the golden pendulum swooped out of control, spinning ferociously, knocking tourists unconscious without mercy.

The music changed direction. The three sailors strolled over to the bench in front of the girls' socks and shoes. Aiming the radio at the girls, the smallest sailor balanced it across his knees, adjusting the strap around his neck. I could hardly see him hidden behind the immense silver speaker grilles. If I scrutinized him from the wrong angle, the sun glanced off the shiny knobs and hurt my eyes.

A city bus out on the road behind the fountain scraped its gears. A family behind me chattered fast in Spanish. I sucked in a deep breath and yawned; when my jaw opened full it cracked at the joints under my ears—and for a second I couldn't hear *anything*.

Then my ears popped, like they did at high altitudes. In that moment I was lost. When I could hear again, everything was painfully loud. The Mexicans shoved swollen babies into creaking strollers; the babies' eyes were painted on; why weren't they crying? The music thumped; the fountain water sizzled. The babies had to be in pain. I pressed the heels of my hands against my ears with terrific force, craving silence, until I floated, freed from the net of noise, released.

When we got shelled in Chu Lai I used to count the seconds between explosions. Sergeant Ascencion jabbed me in the shoulder as we lay in the bunker. "What are you always counting for?" he said. "We could get blown inside out all the way into next week, and you'd still be counting."

CHAPTER FIVE

THE ONLY THING A MAN COULD DO

I wanted LaWanda. She could save me from myself, from the park, from the hideous sound of beatbox interruptions, from the panic of lust at a distance. But the more I craved her, the heavier I felt—a lump of human clay deposited upon a park bench, reshaped by the sun, splattered by fountain spray, perforated by strange looks from tired tourists. There I sat behind my eyes, taking refuge in memory, too afraid of the present moment. LaWanda could change the channel.

The fountain hissed, the music throbbed. The past. With the power of thought I could replace this entire scene; I could leave and reenter. Alone.

Decades earlier, and I would have been sitting in the center of the world's fair. That's why the park was created, as a center of commercial celebration—the Panama-California International Exposition. I've seen pictures, faded black-and-white photographs. All the ladies wore dark frilly dresses that must have weighed tons. When I think about those ancient people, I imagine that they saw things in black and white, that they lived in a completely black-and-white world, thinking drab ashen thoughts. I know that isn't true, but it still seems like the world was more painful back then, and not as comfortable and vibrant as it is today, with all the colors we enjoy on TV and on billboards and in magazines. Colors make things entertaining, but black-and-white things seem more real.

Monster movies in black and white are the best—believable as documentaries. Authentic. When I watched Billy Reid die, his legs blown off by a VC mortar round, my hands crusted over with blood that dried hard and black. We fought the war at night. Only our nightmares were in color. The VC wore black pajamas—the same fierce black as umpires' uniforms.

West of the fountain, across from the Natural History Museum, stands a row of old Spanish-style buildings; one of them used to be the Aerospace Museum. Inside was the original *Spirit of St. Louis*, the little silver plane Charles Lindbergh flew to Paris. Alone. Somebody set that museum on fire, somebody kidnapped and killed Lindbergh's son. Sometimes flames can burn pure white.

The city suffered the loss but soon raised enough money to build a new museum; this one stands at the southwest end of the park, near the municipal gym, on a bluff overlooking the freeway and the skyscrapers downtown. One of those skyscrapers is the El Cortez Center, purchased recently by a religious man who transformed an old hotel into a headquarters for his movement. Bible students study the word of God in redecorated suites and penthouses, preparing for ministries of their own, in the shadow of glass bank towers. The religious man had caused the city to suffer once again, destroying another landmark. The night before he took over, television news reporters visited the El Cortez Sky Room for the last time, mingling with teary revelers who sloppily retold stories of honeymoons and proms and anniversaries; an organ bellowed in the background; the reporter, a veteran of thirty years' broadcast experience in San Diego, dribbled tears onto his microphone. Behind him, the night was black as felt through the Sky Room windows.

I used to play basketball at the municipal gym in the park, and occasionally Bible students from the center would drop by—bony white kids, the type who grow up worshiping guys like Bobby Knight and Pete Rose. The local blacks loved to play against them, upstaging their Midwest tenacity with graceful Southern California foolishness. I lucked out once and ended up on a team with four local players; they made me the center because I was the biggest and the slowest. Our opponents, all thin and pale, shouted, "Praise the Lord!" each time they scored a basket. At first, I thought they were just kidding around, maybe a little stoned even, like we used to get playing football in Chu Lai with a dented helmet for a ball. But the further the future ministers fell behind, the more desperate their shouts became—their eyes and the cords in their necks bulged out with trouble.

The game grew taut, and my teammates fell into stride magically, passing the ball with dizzying flourishes. They drew me into their rhythm, until I found myself running faster, with little effort.

Then I went up strong for a rebound, leaping higher than I thought possible, snatching the ball free from a network of slashing hands. Coming down, I crashed into one of the Bible kids. He slapped down onto the shiny wooden floor, screaming. With his face a knot of pain, he struggled to reach down and grab onto his leg. The ball of his calf muscle had slipped up close to his knee. I clutched my own leg, feeling a jolt of sympathy.

One of the fallen player's friends shoved us out of the way and knelt down on the court. I stepped back up to watch, though—because as the friend pressed both his hands against the injured kid's forehead, he began speaking backwards. He sounded even stranger than LaWanda when she casts spells.

While the poor guy lying flat on the floor tried to keep his leg from twitching—as he scrunched up his face with his eyes

50

closed tightly—his friend yelped louder and louder in a curious language. It didn't sound like Spanish, which I heard all the time all around me, even on television; and it didn't sound like French, which I heard everywhere in Vietnam; and it wasn't German because it lacked the throat-clearing sound I knew from war movies. It was an alien tongue. I was drawn to the sound, feeling I should know its meanings, yet frustrated because these otherworldly murmurings were so peculiar. I wanted to understand, but the sounds slipped away, teasing me.

My teammates backed farther away, staring at one another with their eyes wide open. As the impassioned squeals and yips grew louder, they broke free, running to an adjacent court to shoot random baskets. Laughing, one of them fell down and mimicked the injured Bible student, spinning in a frantic breakdance circle on his back.

I wanted to dash over and join them, but I couldn't find the strength to move. I felt I was being forced to stand there and watch.

All of a sudden, the kid emitting the strange language shoved his hands up toward the ceiling and shouted, "Geee-zusssss, O, sweet Lord Geee-zussss! Heal this man! Please, plu-eeeze, make him whole again!" He scooted closer to his wounded friend, slapped his hand on the straying muscle, and continued shouting. The fellow on the floor still sobbed, but he tried his best to fight off the agony. He knew his leg was warped and ugly, but he somehow trusted the grating shrieks of his friend to blot out the truth.

When I realized I was the only one standing close by, I backed off slowly and forced myself to stop staring. Finally, the lame player rose to his feet; his friend walked him off the court, bouncing him on the good leg.

51

I still don't understand what happened.

LaWanda could help. She could do an awful lot for me, if I were man enough to ask for help.

Things would be so much easier—my life would be smooth and pleasant and error-free—if she would appear, if she would come for me now, if she would tear me loose from this fountain, from the fountain of my thoughts and memories and dreams. She was the one; she was the one I needed; she was the being who could cast free the monsters that gnaw at the edges of my mind, those invisible creatures fueled by anger and fear—so playfully evil, so deliciously invisible, so hard to kill.

A few buildings down from the Space Theater, next to the burned-out husk of the old Aerospace Museum, stands the fortresslike House of Hospitality. Outside it's decorated with stucco towers and rows of monstrous imps and naked women. It reminds me of the Vietnamese temple Miki showed me— the temple towers were taller but adorned with similar complicated details carved and twisting above the doors. In Vietnam, the temple appeared to have been there forever; the House of Hospitality looks fake, as if it were built for an old movie about rich Spanish families fighting peasants and foreigners. Miki brought fruit or flowers to her temple every day; others brought cigarettes and stuffed them smoking into the mouths of laughing little Buddha statues painted shiny red and gold. Inside, protected by gleaming panels, sat a larger Buddha atop a black lacquered table. The temple held nothing else but people. To me it seemed almost too simple. I enjoyed myself there, surrounded by the comfort of muffled voices and subtle fragrances. Together, we remained silent, bowing. After Miki died, I returned to the temple, making sure I honored whatever remained of that original sweet tranquility we shared.

The fountain spray crashed, and the music and voices

gathered into a tight net of trouble. My head hurt. My crotch vibrated with slicing soreness. I had never seen that many people in the park before—that many grinning and shuffling and coughing people, with the sun blasting off their foreheads, too intense for any movie, too touchable and sweaty and close. When threading my way through a crowd like this, I had to remain anonymous—even if I brushed someone's shoulder by accident. It was time to make the effort. I needed a new scene.

Breaking free of the bench, I infiltrated the crowd, pointing myself west toward Sixth Avenue a mile away. I was reasonably certain no one in the area had ever seen me before, and I could count on never seeing any one of them again also. Blocking my path, a Mexican boy slurped white ice cream from a broken cone; a few sticky drops splattered onto my shoe. I ignored it, still invisible. The aliens in the movie *Invisible Invaders* had to slip inside dead human bodies in order to attack earth properly. But those aliens were violent, and I didn't feel that way. Violence was an external force; my life was shaped by how well I reacted to that force. But never did that force initiate from within. At the conclusion of the movie, all the countries in the world were forced to work together in order to eradicate the alien threat; the final credits rolled over a still shot of the United Nations building framed by a fake tree branch.

I broke free of the crowd and slipped through the arched entry to the House of Hospitality. Inside, cactuses and palm trees and thick bushes offering potent red flowers all encircled the sunny patio. LaWanda would have to wait for a while, I decided. I wanted to go in and stand by the wishing well.

In the center of the patio was another fountain, quiet and pleasant—the statue of an Indian woman pouring water from a pot. The statue was carved delicately from gray rock; the woman's face was wide and smooth, but she didn't smile like a gold Buddha. Instead, she held the pot loosely, tilted downward, to suggest pouring—even though a small pipe poked up over the lip of the pot streaming water. Why an Indian would not be taking water from the well instead of putting it back was a question.

The patio was tiled and ringed with black wrought-iron benches. Above the plants was a second level of offices and party rooms; on the first floor there were more offices, a restaurant, and a ballroom behind mammoth black wooden doors. I looked up from the statue to study the people—many of them searching for the nearby public rest rooms—and wondered how many were alpha bodies, hoping one of them would instantly transform into LaWanda.

I fished some pennies out of my pocket to feed into the wishing well. Before I released each coin, I envisioned LaWanda naked, her hair swirling around her breasts, her lips holding my name.

A family stepped past me, juggling cameras and guidebooks. The mother said, "I've wanted to see this place for years, Henry."

Each coin I tossed cut through the water, drifted down to the dirty green bottom of the well, and landed head up, scattered in among dozens of other pennies and fat worthless pesos.

The family stopped, and I observed them by leaning forward and peeking around the statue's head. The sun struck them full force; their shadows were small black lumps tangled in their feet. The mother pointed upstairs, where no visitors were allowed. The little boy struggled to take a Polaroid photograph; when he peered into the viewfinder, the rest of his family spread out. He danced up closer, tried to focus, and his family shifted out of view once again. His father wore a brand-new baseball cap, too small for his head. His mother had scruffy blond hair, on fire around the edges from the burning sun.

The Polaroid camera was too big for the boy to hold properly. It quivered in his little hands as he leaned down to focus, one eye squinted shut. His mother turned white for a quick moment. "Go around to the other side, Ricky," she said. "You don't want to take a picture of the back of a statue."

The woman pushed her boy forward, and he stumbled. I slipped in closer, to make sure he would be all right. Opening her mouth to speak, the boy's mother stared straight at me, so close I could see her real eyes through her sunglasses. "Ricky. Ricky. Just take the picture. Get it over with, now. Now."

The camera whirred and spat; the square photo inched out of its slot. The boy reached for the picture, but it slipped from his tiny hand.

I stepped away from the wishing well and bent down to retrieve the photo. The mother walked past me, too close; I could smell her perfume—like roses inside a cold department store. She grabbed her boy tightly, pinching his shoulder, and yanked him away.

As soon as I touched the picture, the black square in the middle changed color. First the blue sky appeared, and then the green shrubs in the background. The statue and I were dark like solid shadows. I waited for us to grow lighter. I could almost see the spots where our eyes and mouths were supposed to be.

Since it wasn't my picture to keep, I wanted to give it back to the tourists, but they had walked away quickly, over to the ballroom doors. The mother dragged her son; his red tennis shoes scraped on the concrete as he tried to slow himself down. They all turned a corner together, and the boy caught his foot underneath the bottom edge of a clay pot. The pot held a palm tree with leaves pointed like knives. The mother tugged viciously on her son's arm. He cried so loudly, more people stopped to watch. When the boy finally pulled free, the entire family ran off as if the mother were chasing them all.

I crashed into an old man accidentally. After I apologized, handing him back his hat, the family was lost.

To fill in their absence, chimes sounded from the tower at the Museum of Man down the street. It was the pattern that signified half past the hour; but I didn't know what hour. In the army they used a different time system with lots of zeros that I never got hold of. When I finally had ninety days remaining on my tour of duty, Billy Reid called me a short-timer. To honor that occasion, he presented me with a calendar showing ninety days in tiny boxes all outlined by a naked woman. The ninetieth and final box was right on her pussy. Each day I colored in a new box, then stuffed the calendar safely into a bandage pack on my helmet. After a few weeks the calendar became torn and ragged—from being folded and unfolded, from the rain and humidity and sweat. But I filled in those boxes religiously, even though by the last day the woman's pussy had faded out completely.

LaWanda was no doubt still asleep. It was early for her, even though the sun was high in the sky. So I decided to return to the patio. After examining my Polaroid, waiting for the shadows to come to life, I noticed a man leaning over the second-story railing above the restaurant. He wore gray pants and a matching shirt, the thick variety that plumbers and television repairmen wear. I wanted to spy on him, but the benches in all four corners of the patio were occupied. Since I had thrown away all my pennies, I couldn't stand by the wishing well any longer. Instead, I leaned next to a pillar pretending to empty my pockets into a sand-filled urn dotted with cigarette butts. The gray man upstairs held a clump of keys on a rope, and he dangled them over the railing as if he were fishing, moving them in a slow, careful arc. The shadow from the keys flitted in between the feet of meandering tourists.

LaWanda told me that dreams were keys to the soul. She once described a dream that portrayed her out walking with a boyfriend from high-school days. The heat grew unbearable. Then this guy mutated into the devil, and just like that he was giving her a vivid guided tour of hell. LaWanda interpreted that dream for me, but I've forgotten the details. She has dictionaries that explain precisely each element of a dream. The devil stands for something important. And if the devil were riding in a Cadillac, then he would stand for something different. I told LaWanda that it would be fascinating to watch other persons' dreams as clearly as watching a movie. But I don't think she heard me. The shadows in my photograph were still shadows—as unfocused as my understanding for the thoughts in the man's head above me, the man strangely twirling his keys. If I could see his thoughts as clearly as a movie, I would qualify as a more fantastic spy than even Eddie Elvesizer—and I wouldn't need any secret guns that looked like toothbrushes, or painful torture gimmicks that used European electric current.

The cigarettes in the urn were the same type Argo smokes. He has a frame around the license plate of his car, "So Many Women . . . So Little Time." LaWanda just has a simple red bumper sticker, "Caution: I Brake for Unicorns." I know why Argo has his, but I'm not sure why LaWanda has hers. I never asked her, because I didn't want her to think I was stupid—because why would a woman want to fuck a stupid man? Argo said he would like to suck LaWanda's pussy until her head caved in, but he said that when he was perilously drunk and was having trouble finishing a book—he even slammed a half-full beer can into his file cabinet from across the room and said *I* might as well finish the book for him. But I didn't offer; not that night. Instead, I volunteered to fetch him another six-pack before the stores closed. Argo only made it through two cans. He fell across his desk, passed out cold, and I carried him into his bedroom. Then I returned to his study to read the last line he wrote: "In that situation, the only thing a man could do was." There were more words, but he had crossed them out sloppily with felt pen. I couldn't read them, even though I held the page up to the light.

Upstairs, the gray man reeled in his keys and stuffed them into his shirt pocket. I leaned back against the wall next to the men's rest room as he strolled past a row of doors, then down a passageway along the side of the ballroom, where he disappeared. I had never noticed that passageway before, even though I had once slipped into a wedding party in that ballroom to try the cake.

LaWanda was married once, to the man of her dreams, she said. But he was smashed to death by an Amtrak train in Del Mar one night trying to prove his manhood—she called it *Rebel Without a Cause, Part II.* The last thing he heard on this earth, she told me, was the warning whistle screeching atop the locomotive.

When the Museum of Man chimes rang again, I forced myself to leave the House of Hospitality. It was filling up fast with hungry, curious tourists. I was beginning to feel weak, crowded in. Outside in the parking lot, facing the art gallery, is a massive statue of the hero El Cid atop a black horse. He clenches a long iron spear with a metal flag attached to the back end. *El Cid* was made into a movie once, starring Charlton Heston, but it wasn't much good; human heroes don't make very entertaining monsters.

But he was a hero for a good reason.

As I stared at that black iron statue, shivering, I gathered together all the thought-energy I could muster and aimed it at El Cid's hollow metal head. Just the size of that creation, blotting out half the sky, seemed to calm me, cleaning the grit off my mind's eye.

If that statue came alive—if El Cid strained and creaked into motion—his brute horse would first of all trample cheap little cars and people; and El Cid himself could jam that spear through windshields and brains and splash a trail of blood and sparkling safety-glass chunks; he could gallop over the tops of cars and buses and crush them flat all the way from the Sculpture Garden, past the Old Globe Theater and the Museum of Man, across Suicide Bridge and along Laurel Street, until he trampled his way down the hill to the international airport where he could bust right through the restraining fence on Pacific Highway, clomping right out onto the landing strip puncturing the fuselages of jumbo jets and ripping loose sheets of thin metal riveted in patches on the wings, jabbing his spear into tires and pilots and unsuspecting visitors; he could then bust up the entire airport and keep on going, stomping through the navy base tearing up all the ships and crushing the heads of trainees marching through the Naval Training Center, trashing the sailboats at the marina in Point Loma, demolishing all the wooden docks and revealing weed-fringed barnacles and rotten rubber tires, allowing his horse to crunch his hooves right through the slats; then he could charge up the hill gutting the homes of rich people until he reached the ridgeline, shattered Jacuzzis and security systems in shambles at his feet; up there he could tear back the reins and force that beast to rear up on his dull black metal legs so El Cid could survey the entire city, from the broad harbor entrance into the bay, past the glittering glass skyline, out toward the low, fat mountains in the east; kicking his horse back into motion, El Cid could continue galloping until he achieved land's end,

59

knocking over the old lighthouse, rolling it down the cliffs like a toilet-paper tube to collapse against the rocks below; swirling his spear, El Cid could rush the national cemetery uprooting thousands of white crosses like so many limp daisies, gouging ugly holes, tearing up manicured greenery; and by this time he would be harassed by police helicopters and the SWAT team and marines; bullets would zing off the metal horse and ricochet from El Cid's helmet; rounds from bazookas and LAWs and wire-guided Dragon missiles would explode into dust; El Cid would laugh so loud everyone would stop and look at one another in bladder-emptying fear; then he would shout out something in Spanish that would sound like heavenly music echoing from his empty iron soul; he would swing his spear around and around and the metal flag would flap as he delivered a speech; but no one would understand, and El Cid would laugh again—a ripe hollow cackle that would ring true with bronze firmness—and he would trot his horse past all his attackers, back to the park as if nothing had happened; thousands of fans would follow behind; the minicams would fight for close-ups; and El Cid would lead everyone and glide his horse up onto the pedestal in front of the House of Hospitality; just like that his life would disappear and everything would return to normal—despite the fact that there would be mutilation and destruction in a line for miles showing his furious path.

CHAPTER SIX   EATING BACKWARDS

El Cid's eyes guided me to the pay phone on the corner. The suggestion was strong: call LaWanda. Yet hero or not, El Cid couldn't possibly understand the central problem—if I asked LaWanda for permission to visit, she might not consent. Then all my plans would be shot down, destroyed more completely than a slab of concrete stomped into pulverized dust by an oversized bronze horse.

The heat drove me out of the park. The crowd of tourists and the intensity of El Cid's unapproving glare compounded the weight of the sun on my back. I needed movement, to keep my mind off the itch and burn in my crotch.

I seemed to be the only one leaving; swimming upstream, jostling families and sailors and a pair of newlyweds in matching blue T-shirts—"I'm with Stupid" and "I'm Stupid"— eventually I arrived at Sixth Avenue, the thoroughfare separating the grassy fringes of the park from the restaurant-church-and-apartment beginnings of downtown. A cold six-pack would be more appropriate than a phone call, so I headed for my favorite liquor store in Hillcrest. LaWanda enjoyed liquor more than she did faraway words amplified through hard plastic.

The first—and last—time I called her my wishes were refused. Argo had introduced me the day before, going up in the elevator at their apartment complex. He told me later she would do anything for anybody, so I decided to ring her up.

No, I couldn't come over, LaWanda said, because she was right in the middle of a new art project; the house was a mess, and she needed to be alone. A few weeks later, Argo dragged me down to see her, telling me I made a lousy drinking partner. He and LaWanda shared the rest of his beer while we all watched *Monster Zero*. Snickering like depraved children, we made up our own conversation for the characters, screaming when the Japanese actors continued moving their lips after completing their dialogue. Argo says it's healthy to laugh at imperfection. But today was one day I hoped would be laughter-free.

LaWanda's favorite drink is a tall gold can of Olde English 800 malt liquor. Usually—or so she claims—she prefers a beer right after waking up. I know she likes pills, too. She has plenty, in every cabinet, prescribed by her psychiatrists. At last count she had three doctors, a man and two women, and that seemed crazy to me.

I don't mind giving her beer in the morning—morning for her, even though it might be well past noon—but when she chokes down her pills I have to turn my head. LaWanda emphasizes her need, for extra energy and added relaxation. But I think she forgot *how* to relax; somehow, the pills remember for her.

Toward the conclusion of *Monster Zero*, Argo dashed into the bathroom to throw up. While he retched, the monster from Planet X screeched so loudly I had to turn down the sound. LaWanda fell asleep on the couch beside me. Her body was luscious and warm, heaving with each deep boozy breath; I scooted closer to her warmth, staring inside her sweater at the curves of her breasts. She began grumbling and slurring weird noises, talking to a stranger in the language of dreams. The gray light from the TV covered our bodies with a film of dancing particles. LaWanda's contortions and grunting increased—until the warm feeling between us stopped flowing. I slipped off the couch and walked on my knees to the TV. Every time the monster from Planet X began to shriek, I cranked up the volume extra loud, hoping to inject that violent cry into her dreams. Those pills had stolen her away from me.

By the time I reached the liquor store, I was frying from the heat. The coolness inside welcomed me. The store was run by a Vietnamese family, and all of them helped out, each one performing a separate but necessary function. Two young girls sat by the window and braided a baby's hair. Sweeping the floor, an old woman in a long flower-patterned dress shifted smoothly away from me as I walked toward the cooler. In the back corner, a thin man straightened the mosaic of magazines on the wooden rack.

I felt as if they all knew me, and that I knew them—but we never exchanged more words than "Thank you" and "Good-bye." Even so, I had a feeling they understood I had been in their country once; I tried to act respectfully each time I visited, pausing before the cooler pretending to make my decision—though I knew right where the malt liquor was kept.

The family's quiet voices, the rustling of the broom, the aroma of perfumy incense and foreign vegetables—it was too much like Saigon. I closed my eyes, briefly, and imagined the cars swooshing past outside were actually hundreds of bicycles and mopeds and three-wheeled taxis. I magnified the family's voices times a thousand and saw myself surrounded by a boiling crowd of black-haired heads. I understood their language the same way I understood music—never did I know what they were literally saying; instead, I listened for the colors and the tensions and the volume and tried to figure it out from there, accepting and smiling and not expecting to be hurt or deceived. That's how I had communicated with Miki, listening and smiling. She was dead, but at certain times I felt she was close by, singing to me from the silence of another dimension.

The refrigerator motor stopped and snapped back on, erasing my reflections. Digging out a six-pack, I took it quickly up front. The lady behind the cash register wore her hair pulled back in a long slippery ponytail. Handing her some money, I noticed where her real eyebrows ended and her eyebrow paint took over. She dropped the change into my outstretched hand, careful not to touch the skin, and said "Thank you" as quietly as a kitten, and I said in Vietnamese the only words Miki had taught me that I could remember: "I wish you a happy New Year." The lady smiled. Her skin was smooth and clean, but she had too many missing teeth. Bowing slightly and hiding her smile, she said "Thank you" again without looking up. The ponytail slid around off her shoulder, and she flipped it back with a flash of her tiny hand. When I scrunched the top of the brown sack together, it crinkled loudly; the two little girls stopped braiding the infant's hair and shielded the child as I walked past. As I ducked through the doorway, an electric bell signaled someone was coming in—even though I was leaving.

From the liquor store, I walked straight to LaWanda's apartment: past the used-book shop with the same old hardbacks fading in a wooden bin for twenty-five cents each; past the theater next door that screened the curious foreign films Argo enjoyed; across University Boulevard; past the bank on the corner that changed its name every few months; down through the medical center where my father used to make me wait in the car while he saw a doctor I wasn't supposed to know about; and then over the freeway bridge decorated by a foot-high Roman numeral date carved into concrete—built in 1950, the same year I was. Finally, I arrived at the apartment complex, which was tucked up against a bare, raw cliff, like a fort with a parking grotto underneath. I searched for LaWanda's car to make sure she was home; there it was in parking spot number 37—her green-and-white Gremlin with a smashed-in door on the driver's side.

It was cool in the shadows, the chill exaggerated by shiny automobiles and cinder-block walls. The sack of beer frosted my ribs; I held the six-pack high, away from my crotch, afraid to interfere with the sexual energies, or with any heat I had accumulated from walking and dreaming of LaWanda's body. The sexwaves needed to broadcast freely, absolutely, and with a purpose. Those were the words Eddie Elvesizer used to describe his philosophy of life; I forgot who he was speaking to, or in which book, but I could always remember those three words.

Since the parking garage extended so far underneath the apartment building, I wondered if living there was safe. A medium-sized earthquake could easily rattle the thin gray pillars that held up everything.

The complex above the garage was three stories tall with outside hallways, almost a perfect cube except for the midsection—a hollowed-out cement patio cluttered with swollen urns full of rubbery green plants enclosing a Ping-Pong table in need of a net. Argo said the landlord purchased those urns on sale in Tijuana, in the aftermath of a pottery factory fire; some of them were still smeared with greasy black charcoal and ashes. During my last visit to Argo's place, I dashed out late to retrieve him another bottle; when I returned, he was hugging the edge of an urn next to the laundry room—"eating backwards" was the phrase Miki used to describe throwing up. Argo made so much awful noise I thought he was coughing out his guts. I expected to see him choking on a slimy knot of intestines. Instead, in between attacks he rubbed his throat and moaned and reminded me how much of a bitch Celia was.

Many of the tenants were home, since it was Saturday; I could see them watching TV and drinking and washing dishes. The dryer in the laundry room howled; a girl folded sheets in there by herself, unaffected by the broken appliance, concentrating on the task of keeping the sheets from brushing the ground—a neat trick, since the cement floor was heaped with clumps of lint scraped off the dryer screen. I hoped LaWanda folded her laundry with as much care, since I didn't want to be fucking her with wads of multicolored lint stuck all over the bed.

In the patio, a slender guy and his girlfriend sunbathed on a soft red towel. They both lay on their bellies; their backs gleamed with suntan oil. It must have felt tremendous to smear oil on that girl's shoulders. Though her friend had probably done it so often it was now a routine—like Argo says writing his books has become a deadly routine, even though I can't wait to read the next one. Rubbing on that oil would be wonderful, as far as I was concerned. I'd spread oil across both hands, then I'd kneel above her—barely touching her sides where they slope inward then flow back out around her soft hips. When you barely touch someone, the sensation is more intense, because there is room for the current to jump. When the waves from two bodies mix in that space of air, something magical occurs. With my hands slick with oil, I'd gently press on her shoulder blades and rub tenderly to smooth the oil all over before pressing down a little harder—then harder, with my fingers stretched out all the way so I could feel as much of her warm skin as possible. Each time I circled my hands around her back to where her spine flowed into her ass, I'd contemplate fucking her, the two of us immersed in gallons of oil fucking so slowly.

66

I wondered if that sleeping man ever thought about pleasing his girlfriend the same way I did. He just dozed, looking dead, baking in the sun like a bear-claw pastry, his arms wrapped around his head and stuck together. Argo says he got tired of fucking Celia six months after their marriage—but I think it was something else that split them apart, something he will never tell me about. The clues are not even in his books.

As I walked into the stairwell, my prick was on hard. It felt good and it hurt at the same time, and I didn't care. A prick is a prick, and the sad thing is this: too many men pretend they don't have one. Ernie Lazaro wasn't that kind of man. After we lost three games in a row to Spokane, he ran around the locker room in his jockstrap, using a Louisville Slugger baseball bat for a pretend prick. He slipped the handle of the bat inside the top of the strap, sneaked up behind Sandy Hageman—the pitcher who lost the game in the ninth inning giving up four straight doubles—and Ernie said, "I shalt fuck thee who fucks me!" before he slammed the round end of the bat into Sandy's butt when he bent over to dry off his feet.

LaWanda lived on the third floor; it felt peculiar to walk up the stairs with my prick solid and sore. The Band-Aid had worked loose; it chafed my thigh, yet I was too embarrassed to reach into my pants and fix it. The thought of touching myself in public was repulsive. Miki was the only other person in this world who ever touched me. She used to hold my prick with both hands, wrapping her thin fingers tightly around the shaft. The head stuck out the top of her brown hands as red as a tomato, and I laughed in front of her, reminded of the way kids back home chose first-ups for baseball games: one guy threw a wooden bat into the air and the captain of the other team caught it with one hand; then the first guy wrapped his fingers around the bat above his opponent's hand; they continued until they ran out of space; the guy with at least two

67

fingers beneath the handle won. I tried to explain that process to Miki, because she demanded to know why I laughed so hard. But I couldn't explain. I lost myself wondering how children invent such games to begin with—then my prick went soft in her hands. She frowned and attempted to resurrect me. I failed that night, and the following morning I was back in Chu Lai so fast my time with Miki seemed as brief as a hazily recognized dream.

All the lights in LaWanda's hallway were burned out; it was difficult to read the numbers on the doors. As much as LaWanda protested—or so she said—the apartment manager rarely had time for minor maintenance. According to her, the only time he'd come around in recent memory was in the wake of a squadron of brown-shirted cops descending on the apartment next door to break up yet another fight between LaWanda's violent neighbors, Cindy and Ed Hogan.

For entertainment, LaWanda and I sometimes enjoyed sitting on the back of her couch, pressing our ears to the wall, listening to the Hogans yell at one another. During a particularly ugly fight, Ed heaved a remote-control channel changer at the TV when it was on full blast; LaWanda and I heard the set emit a comical *poot* after the screen shattered. Cindy howled, "You killed Jerry Lewis!" because the crippled kids' charity spectacular was broadcasting that weekend. We had that show on, also. LaWanda had pledged ten dollars, but as far as I know she never paid. When Jerry loosened his tie and wiped sweat off his face before requesting the final cash count, LaWanda cried, wiping her eyes as the numbers rolled and spun inside the huge tally board encrusted with cheap blinking lights.

But LaWanda would never be able to cry as wildly as Cindy Hogan. That woman yelped like a diseased hound; and when Ed smashed anything and everything in his path, the two of them created a weird song of urgency.

I never did understand why those two fight. LaWanda said it's the only way they can express their love. Jerry Lewis chattered about love nonstop on his telethon, which only made the issue more confusing. His love was money and Ed's love was cruelty. I knew we needed love, and the songs all celebrate love, but I was sad for not knowing what it was—even though everyone else in this world, from Jerry Lewis to the Beatles, seemed to know.

In front of door 37 I stood still and listened for LaWanda. I didn't know if I wanted her to be asleep or awake; I just listened. Between the two black numerals on her door was a glass peephole; I squinted and looked through it; her couch was tiny as a fly's head; her curtains were closed. That's all I could see before my eyes hurt too much and my neck ached terribly from leaning over so low.

The door opened. My heart cranked free another notch. LaWanda grabbed shut the top of her blouse, sucking in air loudly in a reverse scream.

"Nicholas!"

"Hi. I was—"

"Speak of the fucking devil."

LaWanda's hair looped and snarled around her head—curly, wispy, spiked, and dull. It held her face captive. Her eyes shimmered like wet black beach rocks; jagged red veins split her creamy eyemeat, encircling my reflection. She was ready for sex.

"What are you doing here?"

"I'm not in the mood for games."

"Oh, Nicholas, for Christ's sake. Can't you see—"

"Don't you feel it?"

Tingles seared my hands as I took hold of her shoulders. She was cold and bony underneath the frilly white blouse, and she smelled of yesterday's cigarettes—but a ripple of thick sensation snapped through the blue veins in her neck, throwing her against my chest, initiating warmth, eliminating all thoughts save one: the vision of my lips descending toward the veiled brown halo on her breast.

"My God! Get *off* of me."

LaWanda shoved away from my chest and slammed into the hollow door, vibrating the cheap wood on its hinges.

"Sometimes, Nicholas, you can scare the shit out of me."

The six-pack under my arm felt extremely cold all of a sudden.

"But maybe that's why I like you, who knows?"

When she smiled, I felt twisted up inside. The mixture of the space between us and the skin-level memory of her body against mine shaped a thickness in my throat, trapping words between swallows.

"I had a feeling you'd stop by today. In fact, we were just talking about you."

"Look out!" I hugged LaWanda for protection; the sack of beer plopped to the carpet. "Hold it right there, pal." A man wearing boxer shorts sneaked through LaWanda's living room, advancing on the doorway.

"Put her down, you big goon."

Happily, I remembered some crucial lines from an appropriate Eddie Elvesizer story. "I don't know how you got in here, but you best find your slimy way out. Now. Or you'll have to answer to this."

"Nicholas, let go of me. You're squashing my back."

"Oh, is this the clown you were telling me about, sugar?"

"Yes, it's Nicholas. Just Nicholas."

"What do you mean, just Nicholas?"

"Hey, buddy. Enough with the King Kong impersonation. Let her go before she gets hurt."

"King Kong? Who the hell do you think you're talking to?"

"Harold, would you apologize. He's killing me."

"No, I'm *not!*"

"Ouch!"

"Let . . . let her go, dumbshit. Now."

"Out of the question."

LaWanda's breasts felt fine pressing warm against my belly. A cold spot on my arm left over from the six-pack quickly melted from the touch of LaWanda's body.

"Put her down, jerk. See this? I'm dialing. I'm dialing the police. Damnit, Wanda, what's the number? What is it?"

"Nine one one, stupid."

The tighter I squeezed LaWanda the more seriously she slumped in my arms.

"Nicholas, sweetheart, just let me go. Okay?" She said this softly, so the man couldn't hear.

"Why do you got so much damn extension cord?"

Harold danced crazily. The curled phone wire spun around him as he tried to whip it loose. His undershorts puffed out between the tightly wrapped cord; he looked like a man underwater for the first time at the beach with air bubbles swelling up inside his swimming trunks.

"You smell good, LaWanda."

"Nicholas, just put me down. Of all people. You. Hurting someone."

"I'm sorry."

When I set her down, I peeked one last time into her blouse and caught the dotted brown rim of one nipple. Quickly, while she fluffed her hair back into place, I snicked up the bag of beer and wrestled one can free from the plastic holder.

"Your favorite."

"Give it to Harold. I'm going to fetch my clothes out of the dryer."

After LaWanda ran down to the stairway, all that remained in front of me for one precious moment was a rush of sweet air. I didn't turn my head. I just stood and stared, wishing somehow she'd reappear in the same spot, like Lieutenant Uhura on *Star Trek* beaming back to life inside the *Enterprise*, her body re-created from swirling sparkling molecules.

"There, there's the nine. And the one. Now, wise— Hey! What'd you do with Wanda?"

"La—Wanda."

"Who the hell are you? John fucking Wayne?"

"In case you forgot, he was a terrible actor. He only made one decent movie, *The Barbarian and the Geisha*."

"What boat did you come in on?"

"I walked. All the way."

"I believe it."

"Here, this beer's for you."

When I stepped inside the apartment, Harold hopped back out of my way and practically tripped over the phone cord. I popped open a can of beer; it spuzzled like cotton lava.

"No, thanks."

"What are you afraid of?"

"Just who the hell are you, anyway?"

"Just who the hell are *you*, anyway?"

"Wanda never told me about any Frankenstein-looking friends. What are you, kin?"

"Why not? And I can tell you the name of every Frankenstein movie ever made, including *Frankenstein Conquers the World*, *Frankenstein Created Woman*, and *Hollow My Weenie, Dr. Frankenstein*, which is the actual name of one of my favorite films from 1969."

"What, are we on a game show already? You're too precious, pal."

"I'm worth my weight in gold. Gold is a precious metal. These cans are getting warm."

"So toss them in the fridge. Do I look like the maid or something?"

"When LaWanda's not here, you're obligated to be the host."

"Hey, funny man, I got your host right *here*."

Harold grabbed himself. His hand was hairy black, and his arms were tanned brown as wall paneling up to the middle of his biceps. The rest of his skin was as white as his shorts. His arms looked as if they belonged to someone else. His feet were the ugly type that appeared to have been run over by a car, and his toes were yellow, crinkled in opposing directions. To avoid him, I stepped right into the kitchen; it wasn't that far away from Harold, but at least I could shield myself behind the refrigerator door.

As usual, the same bottles of ketchup, mustard, and salad dressing sat on the shelves—leaving plenty of room for the tall cans of Olde English 800. I busted each can free from the plastic rings—three cans went on the first shelf and two on the second. I poured the last can into a glass decorated with pictures of Marvel Comics superheroes. I never read Marvels much anymore, because the stories are all too sensible; all the characters have fancy origins—not like the rest of us regular people, or monsters who appear accidentally. For instance, I know more about where Spiderman came from than about why *I* was born. Fancy origins seem entirely ridiculous. There are too many other circumstances to wonder about.

I slammed shut the refrigerator. Behind me, in the other room, Harold kicked closed the front door; an echo filled the apartment, vibrating through the cold eggs and a little Tabasco bottle. Harold leaned against the door, staring at me. If anyone squinted through the peephole, he could see the shaggy hairs coiling along the side of his neck; it would seem as if a stupendous hairball had swallowed the living room.

"Do you always barge into people's apartments to drink cheap beer?"

"Do you always wear your underpants in the middle of the day?"

"Look, bulkhead-face. You owe me an explanation."

"The moon has a dark side because it does not rotate on an axis as do the planets."

The hairball disappeared. The room opened up for anyone peering inside through the door. Harold moved toward me, hitching up the elastic of his shorts. Whenever I see anyone walking on such damaged feet—at the park or the beach—I imagine them to be in great pain. Painful feet. It was so moist and steamy in Chu Lai, when I removed my boots I peeled hunks of dead flesh off the bottoms of my feet like rinds of bacon fat. Sometimes I poured beer on the wounds. Cheap antiseptic.

"Get your snout out of that glass and look at me!"

Sergeant Ascencion used to yell at me in the same harsh

74

tone of voice, but he was supposed to—he was required to be cruel for our own good. Billy Reid reminded me it was only the sergeant part of his personality doing the yelling. But whether or not Harold possessed different personality parts was still a mystery. For the moment, all I knew for certain were two things: his feet were a mess, and the whitemeat of his eyes was grilled by jagged red blood vessels.

"That's better. Finish your drink and get out of here."

"No."

"Apparently you didn't hear me."

"What?"

"I said, apparent— Hey! No room for wiseasses. Heave-ho, chucklehead. Now."

"It's not now anymore."

"Now!"

I raised up my superhero glass between us; when I shut one eye and refocused, Harold's head fit perfectly on top of Invisible Girl's shoulders; and her tits were full of beer.

"If you're not out of here by the time I count three, I'm going to have to kick your loony ass sideways into next week."

"I'll miss the landing tonight."

"One . . ."

"Wait until LaWanda gets back."

"Two . . ."

Invisible Girl's tits crashed flat into my face; beer splattered into the air and rained onto my head. I waited for Harold to say, "Three." He slapped the glass out of my hand; it tore loose and smashed against the kitchen counter. He gasped; chest heaved. The bone over my right eye throbbed.

"When I say get out I mean *out!*"

"I . . . don't want to."

"Just what the hell is the matter with you?"

"I just want to . . . visit."

"Can't you see the fucking writing on the wall?"

I closed my eyes, trying to escape. Memories. Once, when LaWanda had saved up ten books of Green Stamps, she took me to the redemption center to trade for a clock. She had always wanted a nice big clock to adorn her wall. The choices were limited, and LaWanda reluctantly chose one depicting the Mexican-American border crossing and the mural that announced, "Tijuana, the Most Visited City in the World." I hung the clock over her television and plugged it in as soon as we got home.

The clock is still there on the wall. Across the room, deep blue curtains hid the sliding glass doors. Through those doors was a balcony where I liked to sit and watch life down in the patio; LaWanda never sat with me; she didn't like the sun, even though that meant she missed the sight of many luxury sunsets burning the roof edges of her apartment building.

The wall opposite LaWanda's kitchen was decorated with nothing more than a small brass-and-glass mirror LaWanda bought in Tecate; two candle holders coiled down from the mirror, fitted with stubby black candles that dripped onto the tattered couch. Too many things in LaWanda's apartment were black—her furniture, her waitress skirts, her T-shirts, her books, the circles under her eyes, the shadows behind the television.

"What the hell are you looking at, Baby Huey? Huh? Didn't you hear what I said? Didn't you? Maybe you'll understand *this!*"

Harold pounded his fists into my belly; he grunted and pumped his arms in a blur. I clenched my muscles awfully tight. Bent over, his chin stabbing into his chest, Harold rocked his punches and his hair danced. As he grew weary, I hopped toward the counter—just as he pulled one arm back—

before he could slug me again. When Harold missed with his jab, he twisted sideways, and we almost collided. Dodging him, I winced from a jolt of pain blasting through my sore prick. To avoid his body, I leaned in beneath the kitchen cabinets, breathing hard. For support, I stiffened my arms against the countertop, holding up most of my body weight— and in the process I slammed my right hand straight down onto a slice of broken glass. The shard of glass gouged in deep and protruded like a clear horn. There was no pain at first, and time seemed to have stopped as we stared at the puncture. Then my hand bled swiftly, and blood flowed over the glass, coloring it cranberry red.

"You dumb fuck. Now look what you did."

Fat drops of blood plopped down onto the counter between the saltshaker and the sugar bowl. I squeezed my wrist with my good hand; I could feel fresh blood swelling up within my arm—as if all the blood in my body were flowing straight down into my slashed hand to rush out the fresh hole. As I held my hand up high, the blood still spilled over my constricting fingers.

"Nicholas!"

Immediately after stepping inside the living room, LaWanda tossed her clean clothes onto the floor like they were burning garbage.

"Hey, it's nothing," Harold said. "The goon just sprung a little leak. Here, give me those."

"What?"

"The underpants."

"My panties? Are you crazy?"

"Easy, babe. They're clean, aren't they?"

"My kitchen. You've ruined my kitchen."

"It didn't take much. Now be a good nurse and give me

77

those, please? There, that's a girl. Now, Tiny, why don't you just lower that dinosaur arm of yours. What are you trying to do, anyway? Paint the ceiling?"

Blood trickled off the pointed end of the glass spike; fire mixed with the blood still pumping into my hand. LaWanda's eyes glistened with electric fear; I caught myself reflected in her large black pupils. Transforming my face with a smile, I sent her a pleasant thought.

"Over the sink. That's it."

Harold shoved my hand under the faucet, and cold water erased all the blood. Once again there was nothing but clean glass poking out from my pink skin.

"This might hurt, so get ready."

Harold gripped my hand tightly. His skin didn't feel real under the stream of water that swept back all the hairs on his arm in one smooth direction. I couldn't understand why he pressed the glass *in* gently; my hand erupted with pain; Harold was splitting me open. But when I opened my eyes, the glass had been removed. Harold showed it to LaWanda, turning it like a jewel in the light. That was the first time she smiled at him all morning.

"I didn't know you were a medicine man, too."

"And you thought I was good for only one thing."

"It looks like your one thing wants to tell me something."

I saw it, too, but only by accident. LaWanda laughed and Harold moved up close to the sink, trying to hide it. He took hold of my hand and spoke softly for a change.

"Just let me wrap this up. That ought to do until you get to the hospital. You're going to need some stitches in your claw."

"You're not going to drive him over there . . ."

"No . . . ah . . . I've got to take you to work. Remember?"

"LaWanda's shift doesn't start until five. Look at the clock. It's not even one yet."

"Yeah, sure. But today she's got to go in early. Right, honey?"

"And you've got to go in right now," LaWanda said.

"Oh, Jesus. We've got a problem here, big guy. You couldn't just hoof it, could you? It's only three blocks. You've probably got twice as much blood as the rest of us, anyway. What's a few pints between friends? Hey, easy. I was just kidding."

My hand beat violently beneath the bandage Harold had made from the silky underpants. I struggled to send more thoughts to LaWanda; she stared too intently at Harold, and I was afraid she was sending *him* thoughts. The aching intensified, which certainly interfered with the strength of my thought-broadcast.

I wanted to be so much stronger, so that even stabbing pain couldn't wear me down. I wanted to touch LaWanda, to run my hand through her shiny hair—but I was afraid to drip blood on her neck.

"Hey, don't look so sad, Spartacus. We'll get you over there somehow. Right away. Call a cab for him, would you, sweetheart."

"Then what'll you do for me?" LaWanda said.

"Just get on the phone," Harold said.

"Don't yell at her."

"Argo's home, isn't he, Nicholas?"

"He should be. Eddie Elvesizer has to escape from Monte Carlo before Friday."

"Right, right," LaWanda said. "He'll be glad to take a break and get you over there in his Jeep. You sit down, Nicholas. I'll call Argo for you. It'll be Vietnam all over again, with *him* driving."

All over again. Again and again. Billy Reid listened to Jimi Hendrix tapes constantly; each time I visited his hootch, he was smoking dope and singing along—pretending he was playing a guitar, with his eyes closed, fluttering his long black fingers, sucking in his cheeks before shouting out, "Baby, are you . . . experienced?" Guitar solos would coil and scream in that little room. Billy cranked up the volume for the solos. When the tape was over, Billy switched it around and played it again. After a few months, the tape sounded old-fashioned and scratchy, sometimes fading in and out like the radio. Billy explained that was special effects, alternative percussion. The tape was only a year old, but it played like something from another century. Whenever it broke, Billy spliced it together with Scotch tape. After a while, there were so many jumps and gaps that when I listened to Hendrix I thought there was something wrong with me, too.

" . . . Yeah, Argo, we had a little accident over here. . . . No, Ed didn't murder Cindy . . . Nicholas just hurt his hand. . . . To take him to the hospital or something, that's why. . . . He's sitting right here, I can't tell him. . . . Okay. . . . Bye."

"Is Argo coming?"

"No, baby. You just go on down there yourself. Are you still bleeding? Let me see."

"No. It's all right."

"Just let me take a look."

"No."

"Nicholas. What's wrong? You're not mad at me, are you?"

"Jesus, Wanda. He's not a kid. He's a fucking veteran and all."

"Shut up."

"I'll be all right," I said.

"You sure?"

"I just feel a little weak. That's all."

"Criminy, you didn't bleed that much. Come on, Wanda. We've got to get . . . going."

"Is that all you ever think about?"

"Look who's talking."

"It won't be long now."

"See you, Nicholas. Sorry about . . ."

"Bye."

When door number 37 closed behind me, LaWanda laughed like someone eating cotton candy throwing softballs at metal milk cans for prizes at the fair. I couldn't make out Harold's exact words, but his voice joined hers in a harsh pitch. La-Wanda laughed again; then she whooped loudly as if Harold had suddenly thrown cold water on her back.

The disembodied aliens in *Invisible Invaders* murdered people before sneaking in through the pores of corpses. After taking on a new body, they shuffled around the countryside so that earth people could see they were actually who they said they were—the same person they had just murdered who only moved and spoke a bit more slowly than before. When these aliens were invisible and looking for someone to kill, for a body to inhabit, they would creep along dirt roads and trails— the movie would depict close-ups of an empty road, followed by a swooshing noise; then a small mound of dirt shifted forward. These mounds of dirt would slide ahead leaving a trough behind. This was evidence of an alien walking on an unfamiliar earth landscape. Even after taking over a fresh body, these aliens traveled sluggishly—arms straight out and legs stiff as lumber. Ultimately, John Agar found a way to slaughter these invaders with sound waves, and in the process he saved the entire world from destruction.

I reached the stairwell without lifting my feet, scraping along like an alien. John Agar was Shirley Temple's first husband. I could never imagine anyone fucking Shirley Temple—

not Harold, not Argo, and especially not John Agar, who had to keep himself strong enough to combat concealed invaders from the shadowy side of the moon.

Reluctantly, I lifted my feet to navigate the concrete steps. My heart strained and hammered flames into my hand—like I had been bitten savagely by Brak. Rising up the steps, I walked blindly; in my mind Brak snapped his two jaws shut on Harold's neck—blood squirted in thick red jets that dissolved high into the air and reconstructed the sunset—and the horizon became as red orange as Brak's sparking, flaming eyes. He twisted Harold's head, gouging through tendons and veins, teasing the spaces in between Harold's spine bones with the tips of his spiked eyeteeth; Brak's mouths were messy with blood and foamy spit and chunks of flesh crimson on the shredded edges.

"Nick! Holy shit, are you okay?"

". . . My hand."

"Yeah, careful. Watch that last step. Boy, what'd she do, bite it with her snatch?"

Brak's long vicious teeth converted to slippery layers of rubbery pussy-lips that could be peeled back again and again as if tearing toward an artichoke heart.

"Go ahead and lean on me . . . whoa, not so hard, son. You look like I feel. Worst hangover I've had in . . . days. Yow, you're a heavy one. Easy now. Let's get down to my place and check that ugly thing. Lookee there, the old used-undies tourniquet. Hope you don't get infected."

"They were still warm. LaWanda just washed clothes."

"That's a first. Hey, don't pass out on me yet."

First and last. First things first. I held on to Argo's shoulders and let him carry me along. On my first mission with Third Platoon of Alpha Company, one of us got killed and I never learned his name.

Lieutenant Wheeler had us sneaking through high grass;

the grass brushed delicately against my arms and tickled, so I carried my M16 up under my chin. I had slopped too much oil onto my rifle, cleaning it just before we moved out, and bits of grass stuck to the gunmetal. Lieutenant Wheeler signaled for us to get down flat, staring straight ahead and waving his arm low behind. The grass hissed around me as I fell—that was the last sound I heard until that guy screamed.

"Just a little farther. Talk to me, Nick. You all right?"

"It hurts."

"Yeah, you and me both. Come on inside."

Argo pushed me through his living room, forcing me to dodge piles of junk: empty record album covers, crinkled beer cans, a shiny bag of Cheetos, the tipped-over coffee table. Even the bathroom was a mess; Argo kicked a box of papers out of the way so we could stand together over the sink.

"Let's peel off these little pretties and see what we got here. Jeez, they don't even smell good. But what did you expect, eh, Romeo?"

"She said I had to go to the hospital."

"Well, I don't know about that. Especially at today's prices. It looks like you're going to live, anyway."

"Who's Harold?"

"What?"

"Harold who was in his shorts in LaWanda's apartment."

"Sounds like she found a tame one for a change."

"The guy's an asshole. He slugged me for no reason."

"Nobody does anything for no reason, son. You didn't go over there today for no reason, did you, Nick?"

"But that's different."

"Is it? Think about it. Hey, did that hurt? Sorry. Try to hold still. I've got to wash that thing off."

"He called me King Kong, the jerk."

"Oh, he did, did he? He must have quite an imagination.

84

Of course, anybody who would run around LaWanda's apartment in his shorts must be full of imagination. She really knows how to pick 'em."

"What's that stuff?"

"Just a little hydrogen peroxide. Either you let me pour on this magic healing elixir or we take you to the hospital."

"It's going to hurt."

"All by yourself you figured that out? There's hope for you yet, Nick."

"I hope so."

"Can I write that one down? I've been searching all day for words of wisdom to jam into Eddie's mouth. If you'll pardon my insensitivity, I'm glad you received this little injury. I've been stuck all day on the same page. The story of my life, don't you know. Of course, this hangover didn't help much. They got some new Spanish champagne at Esmeralda's and I had to celebrate, so I bought two bottles. One white. One black."

"What did you celebrate?"

"What? The fact that they got in this new champagne, that's what."

I forced myself not to flinch when Argo poured on the medicine. The cut in my hand burned and sizzled; white foam fizzed along the open raw slice. Hissing.

We waited in the grass for choppers, and our ammo was almost gone. I thought Charlie would rush us for sure. All my clips were empty, taped together like Billy taught me. I pressed down on the spring-loaded top parts that were shaped like bullets, wishing those fake bullets would turn into real ones so I could reload.

When the choppers chugged in above us, their swirling blades blew down all the tall grass. I could suddenly see where we were all hiding, holding down our helmets and looking upset, as if we had been sleeping deeply and now someone had torn loose our bedsheets.

Those resupply choppers missed us and dropped the fresh ammo on top of Charlie, but it didn't matter; we got lifted out an hour later. Sergeant Ascencion sat next to the dead guy, patting him on the shoulders, sometimes smiling and nodding his head. I couldn't hear the sergeant's voice over the helicopter noise, but he talked to the dead guy all the way back to the LZ.

"There. All done. Welcome back to the land of the living."

"Thanks, Dr. Argo."

"Got your sense of humor back, too, I see. Must be my bedside manner. Maybe it's not too late yet to put in that application to medical school."

"It's only about one-thirty."

"Yes, yes. I can always depend on Nick. I've got to hand it to you. Many times you've rescued me from the shattering depths of despair, from the most doleful doldrums, with your apt pronouncements."

Argo yanked gauze tightly around my hand; my fingers tingled from cut-off circulation. He continued tugging and wrapping and using more words I couldn't understand, words I'd never heard before.

"There, that should put an end to today's LaWanda caper. Unless you've got plans for those panties."

"I'd like to tie them around Harold's neck, that's what."

"Now, now, Nick. Let's not be antagonistic. I'm sure it was all just a simple misapprehension."

"No, it wasn't. You don't understand!"

"Nick, please. My head."

"But what about my prick?"

"What about it? Did she slash that, too?"

"I need to fuck, Argo. Just like you said."

"Yes, one of Dr. Argo's recurring themes. But can't we talk about this over a couple of cool drinks? Repair work always stirs up a powerful thirst."

"I left a whole six-pack over at LaWanda's."

"That's all right. She'll make a nice lunch out of it. I've got something much better for us. Hopscotch your way out to the couch and I'll be right there."

When I stepped on the Cheetos bag, it crinkled and crunched. I fired hundreds of rounds in Vietnam, but I don't know if I ever killed anyone or not. Friendlies killed Sergeant Ascencion, but we never were told who it was, exactly. Billy Reid said he knew which artillery unit was responsible, but he couldn't prove it. Another mystery.

Argo converted one of the bedrooms in his apartment into his workroom; he calls it his laboratory, and it's overflowing with books and manuscripts. The centerpiece is his fancy computer, the one he bought after selling *Eddie Elvesizer: Assassin*. Argo presented me with a free copy; in that one, Eddie Elvesizer uses a computer of his own to destroy and torment enemies. I think Argo bought his computer so he could become more like his character. More lifelike.

Lieutenant Wheeler said if it hadn't been for modern technology, Sergeant Ascencion would be alive today.

The lieutenant stumbled into my hootch when a bunch of us were sitting around drinking beer and smoking dope; but he didn't care, because it was the day after the sergeant got blown away. The lieutenant said we had R & R coming; he turned to leave, then turned back around at the last minute and tried to say something else. We all stopped and waited, holding our cans and pipes halfway down from our open mouths. Lieutenant Wheeler's head was bent over, and hidden behind the swirling smoke inside the hootch I saw his bald spot staring at us like a pink flesh eye; he scraped his boot across the dirt floor and his lips smacked open. But he still couldn't say anything.

After the lieutenant left in silence, Billy Reid said, "Was the LT really in here, or was I just trippin'?" We didn't get R & R until the next month. When we picked up our passes, Johnny Aspen, the company clerk, told us that Graves Registry in Hawaii had misplaced Sergeant Ascencion's body.

All the way to Saigon, Billy Reid said every five minutes, "A fucking conspiracy, that's what it is," and he hocked huge oysters out the chopper door, leaning over to watch them disappear.

The paddies beneath us looked like glass checkerboards, and I wondered if Billy's spit changed the rice where it landed— if it made the stalk it covered grow shorter or change color.

I met Miki that time in Saigon, and I acted in an appropriate manner, just as the Nine-Rule Card said—the same card I had been studying since I received it at indoctrination my first day in-country: "Treat the women with respect, we are guests in this country and we are here to help these people"—even though Miki helped me more than I helped her.

"So, you seen any good movies lately?"

Argo handed me a cold tall glass without pictures on the sides. He sat in the reclining chair facing me; when he pushed back, the footrest snapped out too fast and he almost tipped over backwards, spilling some of his sloshing drink.

"Don't mind me, I just live here."

"I was going to watch Channel 5 today, but I didn't because I had to erase some of my dreams."

The drink was cold, but it was hot, too, when I swallowed.

"Wait. Run that past me again."

"They show three movies in a row, which is a lucky sign."

"Who told you that? They always have three movies in a row."

"Not three monster movies."

"So what's the difference?"

"Monster movies tell more about real people than regular movies."

"Is that so? But what's this about dreams? If you're having trouble sleeping, well, you know how to cure that, don't you?"

"Godzilla is really inside us, like the movies are all really inside the television."

"I tell you, Nick. You need it bad. I thought LaWanda would come across for you, but maybe I was wrong. Your timing might have been off, though. I mean, if she won't give it up, then . . . boy, this is a good drink, if I do say so myself. You know what this is? Go on, take a guess. If you do, I'll run out and *buy* you a piece of ass, for Chrissakes."

"It's good."

"Damn straight."

"It's got a great bite to it," which is what my dad used to say.

"Yeah, a man's kind of drink, if I might be so bold. I call it an Argonaut. A Wild Turkey spritzer is what it is. The fuel of great literature. If it weren't for this stuff, Eddie Elvesizer— that incisive spokesman for our troubled age—would be still-born back on page one of book one. And a fine book that was, too. Did I ever give you a copy? *Las Vegas Firefight*? The critics were falling all over themselves back then. Couldn't say enough good things. Now they just take high quality for granted, the sorry slobs. Oh, to think how my books have graced this wondrous land of ours, stuffed into the racks at bus station gift shops and all your finer supermarkets. How many uneasy souls have found solace in following the rambunctious escapades of that postexistential devil, Edward Farragut

89

Elvesizer? Consider the lonely gas station attendant on the bitter arid wastes outside Barstow, moving his lips carefully as he savors each word, choking on the dust stirred by passing tractor-trailer rigs, but paying no mind to the momentary inconvenience as he strains to follow Mr. Elvesizer's ardent decimation of bothersome Oriental martial-arts experts. Or the kid in your high school no one ever talked to, who went out and shot the president or somebody like that—I'm sure he has the latest copies delivered to his cell, and I bet he doesn't share them with anybody. Even yourself, Mr. Nick. Perhaps you, too, have been sublimely touched by one of my tomes. Tell me true, Nick. Is this not so?"

"There're no monsters in your books. I told you that before."

"Yes, indeed you have. And a point I've considered time and time again. Perhaps some day we might collaborate, you and me."

The more I drank, the better it tasted. But I slowed down when I noticed that Argo had more in his glass than I did. I made a personal rule long ago never to drink more than he.

A few years back, right after I was released from the team in Walla Walla, Argo brought me to a local theme bar called the Grand Slam. The place was filled with sports paraphernalia—posters, pennants, insignias, team photographs, trophies. A group of guys near our table were the type of fans who knew all the statistics; they even knew who I was in addition to my batting average from the year before. They bought me a few drinks, and Argo kept butting in telling them he was a famous writer—which eventually chased the fans away. That's when Argo and I challenged one another to a drinking contest, because Argo needed to prove to me that *he* wasn't a minor leaguer, that *I* was the only one who could make that claim. After fourteen shots I got sick and wobbled to the men's room;

I never made it all the way. Instead, I barfed across a wall poster of Hank Aaron smacking home run number 715—I'll never forget the image of those big red numbers surrounded by glops of glistening orange puke: "7-1-5!" The year of my release I hit seven home runs in fifteen games, even though I rode the bench most of the season.

"This is a good drink. You know how I can tell?"

"No, my son. How?"

"Because my hand doesn't hurt so much anymore."

"Ah, yes, the curative powers of distilled spirits. Sorcery, Nick. Nothing short of voodoo extremism. And that's too bad about your hand. If it's any consolation, you should have a nice scar there eventually. A badge of honor from the pussy wars. Something to be proud of and not concealed, no sir. You're a valiant soldier, Nick. You just need a different strategy. Or better tactics. Oh, hell! You just need to get laid, that's all."

"I know. You told me already."

"If I told you once, I told you a thousand million times. But that's not getting the job done, is it, Nick? You're still sitting before me in desperate need. Oh, just to look at you, one quivers with pity. You need it so bad, Nick. It's stenciled into your face. It's scrawled across your crotch."

"Can you see the waves? Is that what you mean?"

"Waves? Like, wave bye-bye, maybe."

"But, why?"

"Why? Why do you have to eat? Or shit? Because it is written, Brother Nick. Saint Nick. Nickelodeon. Nickknack."

CHAPTER NINE

But sometimes I don't know what to say; my tongue lies flat in my mouth like a dead thing. Argo waits for me to speak, to say something, anything, staring at me with eyes big as tunnels. But it is so much easier to remember, to let my memories run free like an undirected movie, uncut and uncensored, flashing and coiling and writhing beyond my eyes. Words are unable to contain what I remember and what I feel, but those little words are all I can use, and I fight with them, each one of them, trying to wrap them around my memories, trying to force them to harness my thoughts, straining to find the right one, the one that has some power to it, some fire, some precision. But the result too often is thin and the words create nothing more than a hollow echo of what really happened or what I really experienced, the same way a Polaroid snapshot is either more colorful than the scene it imitates or overexposed and brown as pond slime.

"I ought to get a patent on these Argonauts. Are you sure you don't want another one, Nicolito?"

I shook my head no. Once again Argo slipped back easily into his recliner, even though I wished he would tumble over worse now than he did the first time. He grinned at me, his teeth greasy white. My eyes closed.

In basic training, the drill sergeants promised to march us out to the rifle range at night; we were scheduled to attach black starlight scopes to our M16 rifles, enabling us to see in the dark. After chow, on the afternoon before we were to hike out to the rifle range, Drill Sergeant Chubasco pounced into our barracks and announced we were on alert; he stomped in front of our bunks along the shiny center aisle, a wide green linoleum strip we were forbidden to cross, which we kept waxed for inspections as lustrous as a new car. The sergeant's ghostly footprints violated the gloss.

Drill Sergeant Chubasco ordered us to remain in the company area until further notice. I stared down at his shoes riding the linoleum strip; he seemed to be floating on clear sky, and I wished he could have fallen right through to the bottom.

Frustrated, Sam Gulli from Brooklyn hopped up onto his bunk and complained. He said his brother Joe, who was already fighting over in Hue, had written to him about the starlight scopes. Sam wanted to use one desperately. It was on the training schedule, he argued. So we had to use them.

Sam Gulli told me once he was going to steal one of those scopes and mail it home. He said he was going to stock up on military gear, to protect his family from the inner-city riots. But he was National Guard and not regular army like the rest of us, so he was going to end up fighting in an entirely different war.

As Sam Gulli shouted and complained, some guys surrounded his bunk and shook it from all four corners. Sam grabbed on tight to the gray railing by his pillow. Those guys rocked his bunk so hard that Sam's dog tags twirled around his forehead and slapped against his nose.

When it became obvious Sam was about to cry, the fun vanished. It was replaced by silence. We wandered around the barracks in our T-shirts like we were lost.

Someone mumbled that since we were on alert, Fort Polk

might be under communist attack; another guy answered back loudly, saying maybe there had been a riot down in Lake Charles or New Orleans. A loud laugh answered in the corner; and someone said he hoped there had been a riot in Leesville instead and that the worthless town had been torched to the ground. Most of us laughed at that vision, and some of the fun returned to the atmosphere inside the barracks—the quiet returned again after someone else said that Nixon had probably declared war on China.

The waxed floor looked even deeper, bottomless, and the sergeant's footprints floated, pointing in all different directions.

My eyes opened in rhythm to the pounding in my hand. Argo returned to focus, still grinning. "But when was the last time *you* got to have some pussy?"

"My, Nicholas. Such rage unleashed. Perhaps a little story will soothe you, child. Let me see, it wasn't last night, that's for sure. I think. And if it wasn't last night I really don't remember when. But wait one moment, kind sir. You're not suggesting I follow my own advice, are you? Certainly you don't believe I need to get my wick wet just to carry on, do you, Dr. Nick?"

"I do."

"But don't you see? We're talking apples and oranges here. I just cannot get laid too often; otherwise, I'd be destroying my precious drive. That creative center. The heart of it all. Because it's really a question of balance. And energy. All the same force, Nick, pounding through our inner depths, and you have to allow it to seep out somehow. I don't know how many wrinkled, whining babies have been spared the ignominy of birth because I've devoted myself to my craft, to writing my novels, to nurturing Edward Elvesizer, my son, my suckling son. How do you think I afford this sanctum sanctorum? Eddie pays my rent, buys my booze, and I can't

94

simply respond to every quiver of my cock and forsake the man to whom I owe my *life*. Such as it is."

"Then maybe *I* should write a book, instead. Then I'll be better."

"Better? What means *better*, Nicalliope? Toot me a carnival tune from out that Mardi Gras mind of yours."

"Will I be a better man if I fuck LaWanda?"

"Ho! Step right up, ladies and gents. Listen to me, Professor Nick-Einstein, the master of relative curatives. I've got a little elixir here that can change your lives, literally change your hat-in-hand, what-do-I-do next? lives. For the better, to boot. Yes, for the better. For just one-tenth of your last paycheck you, too, can indulge in the vitality-restoring powers of Fuck-a-Bunch tonic. Distilled from the finest Colombian vegetation with extracts of you-name-its and what-have-yous, imported from all over the world, from the moon, from Mars, from the stars themselves . . ."

"*Will* I, or *won't* I?"

"Hey. Nick. You want the truth? You want the God's-honest-no-bull-straight-poop truth?"

"Of course."

"Well. The . . . truth . . . is: I don't really know."

"But you said—"

"I know what I said. Ah, shit. I know only too well what I said."

"But I have to do *something*."

"Is it too dark in here? Go turn on that lamp. The one unto your left."

Our platoon leader at Fort Polk went down the line, checking the other barracks to see if anyone knew why we were on alert. When a plane buzzed low overhead, we tried to guess what kind it was and where it was coming from and going to. An argument began, revolving around three different types of

95

aircraft: B-52 or 747 or C-130 transport. Each person saw what he wanted to see, and some were willing to fight for what they saw.

When chow time came again, word went around that we were supposed to get back to the barracks and pack up our web gear. Sam Gulli's hands shook so badly he couldn't hook his buttpack to his belt. "We're all gonna go," he said. "We're all gonna go early. Tonight. We're gonna get on that plane and go straight to Vietnam."

We waited until it grew dark, checking and rechecking packs, straightening wall lockers, shining boots with spit and fresh cotton balls. When the cattle trucks roared up outside, we didn't say anything. We continued working in the quiet. Drill Sergeant Chubasco stepped inside easily, but he still messed up the freshly buffed center aisle.

The sergeant ordered us outside. We drew out weapons from the supply shed and lined up in platoons beside the mess hall. Specialist Dempsey the cook stood in the doorway leering at us, picking his teeth with a fork. He always wore white pants instead of olive drab, and his pants were starched and clean because he ordered others to do all the kitchen work. He stood in the only light, pretending he was the only one who knew the secret. When he noticed how frightened Sam Gulli was, he spit on the ground; each time Sam whimpered, Specialist Dempsey spit again. Soon, there was a puddle of clear ooze pooled in front of the toes of the cook's black jump boots.

We loaded onto the cattle trucks one platoon at a time, clomping our boots and clattering our plastic gun butts on the pavement. The entire company crammed into two trucks; I was crushed against bare metal by a wall of bodies and had to hang my arm out an air hole to keep the blood circulating.

The truck whisked by telephone poles and pine trees as it turned sharp corners, and as hard as I could I pressed my arm *flat against the outside of the truck to ensure my arm would not be torn off at the socket. Too many guys were smashed against me, and I couldn't pull my arm inside.*

A few cigarettes were lit, and they glowed brightly when the smokers puffed. No one said anything. The only sounds were the truck shifting gears and the shushing sound of lungs releasing smoke.

Then, in the back, from the darkest part of the trailer, a chant began quietly: "I wanna be an Airborne Ranger . . . living on blood and guts and danger." But no one answered or joined in.

"Nick, do I really look like I have all the answers?"

"But if you don't, then who does?"

"Eddie's maiden aunt Edith."

"Argo!"

"Do people still worry about things like this? Tell me true, Nick. Do people still walk around seriously, their heads bursting with multicolored existential question marks? Is that why they look so glum in the supermarket? Because of all those unanswered questions? Maybe that's our fate, Nick. And maybe I've been left out in the cold here. I just didn't receive my ration of questions. But the rest of you plod right along, full to the brim with interrogative necessity. I suppose the average person receives, let's say, twenty Big Questions at birth, right? And he totes these questions around day in and day out, searching for answers, just like playing rotation pool with his brain stem. Right? First you go after Question Number One. You look everywhere for the answer. And it gets frustrating because you can't tackle Question Number Two until you knock off the first one. Yes, this explains quite a bit. The Big Wheels in this life, like Donald Trump and mysterious Middle Eastern arms dealers . . . well, they're the ones who've managed to work their way through, maybe, ten or twelve questions. Hell, Hugh Hefner probably has the answer to Number Fourteen, even. And you, Nick. There you sit, Argonaut in paunch, wrestling with setting the questions in order, not to mention answering them. Yes, first comes One. Then comes Two. Switch those others around. There. Now comes Three. I've often wondered what you're doing in there, when you slip away from me. I used to think you were dreaming, or savoring my last transmission, or lusting, or otherwise enjoying yourself. But, no. You're shuffling your questions. And you still don't have them squared away, do you, son?"

"I just had one question."

"Aye, but there's the rub, BooBoo."

"What do you mean?"

"There! Did you hear that? Yet another question. You're full of them, my boy. Simply chock-full to the brim and overflowing. Unlike my drink. May I have another? Ho! Of course I may. What kind of a question was that? And what kind of a question was *that*? You see, Nick. You've got to be careful. Seek and ye shall find, but keep asking and all ye shall receive is someone else's BS. Or your own BS. What does it matter? BS is BS. Yet in and through it all, one fact remains: I need another drink."

The cattle truck turned hard; the trailer tilted so far I was forced to grip tightly onto the air hole to keep from tumbling across someone's helmet and a pair of M16 muzzles prodding my thigh. When we recovered and rumbled down a dirt road cutting through a pine forest, guys jumped up and fought for a look outside.

"Where the hell are we?" Sam Gulli said, and someone shouted, "At your mama's house!" After the laughter died, there were more questions and even more answers: "To the airport to ship out"; "Naw, we can't ship out till they give us orders"; "That's bullshit! This is the army, not a travel bureau. They can

ship you out faster than a motherfucker!"; "We be diggin' in 'round the fort"; "You're crazy. We ain't even graduated basic training yet"; "Motherfucker, we graduated the day we got here!"; "Hey, I'm gonna graduate your face if you don't git offa me!"

The truck rolled slowly. There was no moon, so all the pine trees together looked solid black—except at the tops where the needles stuck out like thousands of tiny bayonets poking into the purple night sky, allowing in the light from the other side that created thousands of starpoints. I wished for more light to leak in. I pictured all of us firing our rifles at once, cracking off rounds on automatic with full banana clips curling out longer than our arms, jagged flame cones flickering on the ends of our muzzles as sharp-toothed bullets tore into the night sky until a king-sized sheet of darkness busted loose and slipped down in a curve to the horizon like an avalanche of pure black, revealing immaculate daylight.

"Nick, did I show you my new gun? And don't get me wrong. I know that sometimes a gun is only a gun, despite what you amateur psychologists might say to the contrary. Come on back to the lab and I'll show you. You sure you don't want another drink? The third time's the charm. Looks like I'll have to let Eddie slumber until tomorrow."

"Is he still in Monte Carlo?"

"Yeah, the little sleazebag. He happens to be winning bigger'n shit at baccarat, whatever the hell that is. My editor thinks Herr Elvesizer is too—how do you say?—blasé to play something simple yet endearing like poker. But who the hell does he think reads my books, anyway? When was the last time you played baccarat, Nick? Maybe you can teach me someday."

"In the army we had a saying: 'This is my weapon and *this* is my gun. This is for fighting and *this* is for fun.' We had to do push-ups if we used the wrong word. So I don't know if I want to see your gun or not."

"Sergeant Nick! Did I hear you correctly? Are you questioning my sexual orientation? Are you suggesting, in your none-too-implicit manner, that I may be overly fond of my own kind? Let me point out, Señor J'Accuse, that you remain standing there in an illustrative pose squeezing your manhood with your—gasp—brawny lunchhook."

Even with Argo shouting at me, I still couldn't stop remembering that night in boot camp.

Inside the cattle truck, I wanted to be able to sight our destination down the dirt road and be the first one to figure out where we were headed. Until it hurt in new places, I strained my neck out the air hole. But I could only see up to where the truck's headlamps burned through the trees.

The trailer dipped into a rut and scraped the overhanging pines; I yanked back my head right before a wave of branches scratched across the air hole. The trailer leaned deeply sideways; some guys lost their balance, took headers, stumbled—they were tossed back rudely the other way when the trailer jumped loose onto the road again.

The truck driver ground the gears, and the scrunching noise stabbed into my ears. Just when we all shifted back into our places, the air brakes hissed strongly, and the truck ceased rolling. The engine rumbled, vibrating the trailer in rhythms.

The back doors tore open, and Drill Sergeant Chubasco stood framed in the glare from the headlights of the other truck behind us still chugging down the road; it appeared as if the sergeant was wearing a cloak of bristling yellow fur, almost as prickly as the outlines of the pine needles. "Let's move it, let's move it! Over there in front of the bleachers!" Drill Sergeant Chubasco stuck out his arm straight, pointing steadily through the trees; we scrambled swiftly, turning to run down the line his finger suggested through the darkness.

I couldn't see the bleachers; I just hustled behind everyone else, butting into someone's backpack when he stopped abruptly. Lights clicked on and saturated the forest with a stinging blaze. "Let's go! I wanna see nothing but asses and elbows!"

Argo's voice blacked out the memory. "You won't believe the deal I got on this thing, Nick. I tell you, that Ed Hogan might be a complete fool when it comes to handling women, but he sure knows how to score . . . weapons. You ever see anything as fine and dandy as this little baby? Huh?"

"It's an M16."

"Close, but no panatela. What you're feasting your eyes on is a sleek and mean Colt AR-15. Customized. Ed filed down the firing pin so I can go au-to-ma-tic. Dig?"

"Rock and roll."

"Whatever you say. You're the veteran in the family. Just let some dizzy squidlips try and break into this place. I'll sho-nuff play him some rock 'n' roll. You can't be too safe these days, Nick, no matter what your taste in music might be. Yes, sir. You seen any crime statistics lately? It's just as well. They're enough to make a grown man—or even you—cry and cry and cry. And when he gets done crying, if he still has any wits about him, he takes the next logical step—stylized self-defense. Oh, this is a sweet thang, Nick. Makes a man feel proud to be an American. Just hefting this dangerstick makes me feel red, white, and blue all over. Excuse me, Nick, but I feel like putting the Constitution to music. A drumroll, please. And yes, I know it's against the law to have one of these customized killers. But trash that censuring scowl and revel with me in the delights of wicked protection. Such high-powered sin, it makes me giddy."

"Too many Argonauts."

"No, my friend. This is a rush of a different caliber we're talking about here. Danger, Nick. The prospect of pure, unadulterated danger. Don't you know, there's always going to be fuckers who want to kill and sorrier fuckers who want to be killed. I'm just ensuring myself a place in the middle, out of reach of the madness at both ends."

I closed my eyes; Argo was not making any sense to me. None at all, and I was mad at myself for not following his words.

In the bleachers, we crammed together shoulder to shoulder. Drill sergeants yelled, and guys dragged their rifles across the backs and heads of others when they charged in to fill the empty seats. Out in front there stood a battered wooden podium and a blackboard; in the distance was the firing range. I could barely make out the silhouettes of the green targets at the end of the firing lanes—the same plastic targets we had been blasting all week, zipping off round after round, and reloading hundreds of clips, punching down that spring and hooking our thumbs inside, bleeding on the bullets and still firing—from the prone position, from the kneeling position, from the standing position—continually jabbed by Drill Sergeant Chubasco's pointer if our arms sagged or our rifles pointed at other trainees in other lanes.

All week long, those targets kept popping back up, no matter how many holes we shot into them. From the bleachers, I could begin to see them all out there like shadows—no faces, just the curve of a head and shoulders; but they stared back nonetheless—green torso monsters that would never die.

When a fat sergeant appeared below us, he hooked his thumbs into his belt and rested his belly on the edge of the podium. He was so fat his gut swelled out farther than the ends of his boots. His head was tiny and looked like it belonged with a different body; I thought someone was standing behind a headless soldier, trying to make it seem like the sergeant was a whole person.

"Attention!" the fat sergeant squealed, and as we stood

most of us laughed. "Good evening, Sergeant!" we had to yell. As more of us laughed, Drill Sergeant Chubasco reached in from the side and dragged guys out onto the ground, even some who didn't laugh, and forced them to do push-ups underneath the bleachers. One guy dropped his rifle and was forced to pump out an extra fifty. More of us were collared and ripped out, right and left; I couldn't see how the sergeants could reach in that far, but they did. "All right, men," the fat sergeant continued, "tonight we're going to learn about night vision."

I could barely hear him speak above the grunting below, but I pretended to comprehend each and every word. He showed us a series of charts and lectured half the evening—but all I heard clearly was this: Don't stare into the night directly, searching for targets, but sweep your eyes around in overlapping circles. Plus, he said it took thirty minutes for the eyes to adjust to darkness. That seemed like too long a time to me. As you waited, the things around you changed unnoticed, and you could never tell exactly how, or even if, they were changing.

The fat sergeant slapped a chart with his pointer; the chart depicted a GI's head sticking up from a foxhole; leaves poked out from around his helmet; in front of the GI was a straight-on drawing of a tank; and next to the tank was a squad of infantry with big shoulders and helmets that looked like ladies' hats; and next to the soldiers was a bunker and the Swiss-cheese barrel of a machine gun showing through. Out from the GI's face was drawn a dotted-line spiral that curled around and around the tank and the soldiers and the bunker, to show that the GI's vision never resulted in a direct engagement, as the fat sergeant said. Never.

"Yes, Nick, things are circling in, getting too close. A man's got to survive the pinch somehow. You just can't wait around for The Big Crush. No way. Which is how it should be, if you ask me. *Carpe diem* and pass the ammunition."

"What things?"

"What does it matter? As long as I've got this baby here and enough ammo to keep her well fed, who cares? Let 'em come and get me. Let 'em drop out of the skies, even, and I'll get 'em every one. I got the Jeep packed up and ready to go on a moment's notice, if worse comes to worst. You cover all the bases, you survive. *Comprendes?* No use in messing with this kid, no way."

"What if they came tonight?"

"Tonight? *Esta noche?* Luck be a lady tonight. A hot time in the old town tonight. Who knows but the world may end tonight."

"The *Tonight* show, starring Johnny Carson."

Behind his computer, Argo resembled a machine gunner
trapped inside a gun emplacement; stacks of books and papers
teetered within his arm's reach, and a shaky wall of books
loomed in the background. From the depths of his writer's
bunker, Argo asked me to fetch his bottle from the kitchen;
when I returned, he shakily aimed his rifle at the closet door
where he had pasted color and black-and-white photos of
people and places, headlines from the papers, advertising
slogans, postcards—including Polaroids of Celia with cutout
spots where Argo had razored free his image. There were
larger photos of Celia, so crisp and bright they seemed to have
been shot by a professional: Celia spread her hands across a
carpeted hump; she wore a red dress with a black bow tight
around her neck; her eyes searched out beyond the white
borders of the picture, somewhere over Argo's shoulder. He
pointed the rifle at her, using the Wild Turkey bottle for a gun
rest.

"I don't know how many times I've blown her brains
out."

The trigger clicked. Then Argo whacked the black plastic
gun butt with the fat edge of his hand, spinning the rifle in a
sloppy circle. He lost his grip, and the rifle clattered against his
computer before tumbling to the floor.

"Now you have to give me fifty push-ups."

"Yeah, whatever you say, Sergeant Nick-Rock. Fifty

fuckups, maybe. Fuck-ins, fuck-outs, the whole nine yards. The whole ninety-nine yards, for that matter. Now do you have a clue, trainee? Are you beginning to get the picture, receive the transmission, grasp the message? It's energy release, bucko. That's your problem. You've got some kind of awful psychic dam blocking your energy flow. Look at you, Nick. A big strapping guy like yourself. You should be strapping it on with a vengeance. If only women knew, they'd be begging for it. You'd have to fight them off. Maybe you'd even have to avail yourself of Ed's firearm clearinghouse for protection."

"If they knew what?"

"Nick, do you just go through life moving from one quizmaster to the next? Am I some sort of Monty Hall guru in your big old eyes? Where are the needful women, Nick? Behind Door Number One? Two? Three?"

"You said they knew."

"Said they knew what?"

"Argo, you're too drunk already."

"Ho! You say I'm drunk? *Borracho?* Swacked, plastered, and boiled? Am I stinko, Nick? Three sheets to the wind? 'Tis but an illusion, *mon frère*. What you see is raw energy flow. This divine Wild Turkey is blasting through vasculature and viscus, tearing me wholly asunder right before your very eyes. What you see is a man nearer to God than thee, though to gloat would render the satori unsatisfactory. This is what we all strive for, Nickisattva. Release. I'm releasing all over the place. Immersion in Godhead, here I come! Watch me now, Nick, watch me. Deliverance here, Nick. Redemption. Even Swami Eddie Elvesizerji wants *this* stuff, whether he knows it or not. Freedom, Nickolaiovich. Burning through the Siberia of my soul. I'm not drunk, I'm a rotten saint corrupting the monastery with my stench. Drunk? Heavens, no. I'm . . . not . . .

drunk. This is simply rest and recreation. Re-creation. A reeking creation if there ever was one."

Argo's breath was deadly, and his words were too much for me all at once. Unending. Diarrhea of the mouth, to use one of his favorite expressions. He could wrap himself up so tightly in his own words, I could disappear without him noticing.

Billy Reid and Sergeant Ascencion took me with them into Saigon. We drank beer all afternoon in a crowded bar, exchanging places back and forth going to and from the men's room. Later, as we stumbled out of the bar—while I was making certain my wallet was stuffed into my front pocket—I lost them. Crossing a busy street, I scooted to avoid a crazy moped driver and hopped up to safety on the other side. I turned, expecting to see Billy and the sergeant right behind—but there were only Vietnamese boiling in all directions. Cheap neon lights blared all around me; even so, I searched using night-vision tactics, spiraling my eyes from one end of the street to the other, as far as I could see without losing focus. I stood next to a kiosk decorated with newspapers; the words were incomprehensible; the writing seemed to be backwards as if reflected in a mirror. Trying to make sense of the headlines, I held the sides of my skull as an ache throbbed behind my eyes—then and there, I pictured a gigantic mirror that reflected the entire street scene. I had the feeling that the headache would dissolve only when I reopened my eyes, the throbbing erased by the sight of the real street.

That was when I first saw Miki, the woman Argo never met.

"Shit. Not too wise tossing guns all around the room. Sonovabitch could go off and it would be Hemingway's Ketchum, Idaho, right here in the laboratory. Why hasten the inevitable, I always say. Cheers, Nick Adams. Damn, that's good stuff. Sure you don't want some? Come on. It's good for you. What's the matter? Didn't they teach you how to drink in the service? What *did* they teach you, anyway, besides termination with extreme prejudice? I had Eddie say that once, right before he slaughtered a beautiful raven-haired Nicaraguan literacy-campaign supervisor. She died with his seed still warm in her tubes."

"It makes you crazy, Argo."

"So what means crazy? I make a good salary. I work out of my home and get all the tax breaks I deserve. This is crazy? I should be *more* crazy, that's what I should be. You ever see a crazy man with a fine computer like this, with a mammoth hard disk, plenty of fast memory, and a laser printer? Not on your life, pal. So let's have another toast. To craziness!"

Miki was the only person I've ever known who wasn't crazy. I lost my insane buddies, but I found her. With the newspaper headlines still floating all around me, Miki grabbed my arm and yanked me free of a gang of boys bursting through the Saigon street crowd. Feeling the strength of her grasp, I was confounded. My biceps stung; it was difficult for me to believe she had performed the rescue all by herself—since she was so small and her hands were thin and tiny like chicken feet. Still in her grip, I tilted backwards and stumbled before finally regaining my balance. Miki leaned me against a restaurant wall, and she laughed quietly behind her hand when she let go. Her laugh seemed holy to me at the time, quiet and distinct, so different from the nagging hum of the restaurant neon and the relentless rumbling in the street.

Miki's eyes were full of clean and simple light. She had eyes like Michael from Oregon; on guard duty once, in a foxhole, Michael told me some of his secrets. Most of all, he wanted to visit monasteries and shrines. He said he didn't care if he never got back to the States again—which I thought was crazy, but I never told him so out loud. Michael from Oregon said he could feel the presence of the monks, despite the fact that we were on the ragged fringe of a battlefield. But for all I knew, those holy men were sending him spiritual thoughtwaves.

When the rest of us in the unit got high and drank beer, Michael lost himself in a dark corner of the hootch and sat with his legs crossed; then, he issued a deep hollow sound from his mouth first and later through his nose, continually, while we smoked and crushed Budweiser cans. He circled his index fingers and thumbs atop his kneecaps, his eyes rolled up into his head, and we laughed and giggled. Billy Reid said he was a trip, a stoned outer-limits trip.

Another night on guard duty, Michael demanded to tell me something important; he claimed he had discovered a precious secret that had changed his entire life dramatically. Instead of watching out beyond the perimeter, he claimed to have been meditating. Michael said he knew the monks were observing him, that they were in close touch with his spirit. In a flash, he realized his involvement in the war was all part of a grand and divine plan—he had been sent to Vietnam because God wanted him to find the monks. It was the only way, the perfect way, he said, tugging on my field jacket when I turned away to peer into the night. Almost in tears, he claimed he had to finish, that he had to tell someone. So I listened, but I kept watch at the same time.

If I missed something moving out there, and if our position was overrun because of Michael's spiritual fantasies, I would be responsible. But he insisted I was the one person who had to hear his story. I listened carefully, staring into his face to show him I cared—even though his eyes were empty then, all the same color gray, enveloped by charged black darkness.

Something called karma was working itself out, he explained. Things were just now unfolding according to plan, in the same way each soldier received orders from above. But karma was a perfect order according to Michael, a law that proved the universe was truly pure and perfect. Only the sounds of his speech made sense to me—the words were familiar, but the ideas lay out of my reach. Even so, the more he spoke, the more faithfully I listened.

Crouching low in the foxhole, Michael said he now understood the truth; his studying and meditation had finally brought forth fruit. He was joyful because he had achieved the goal of his life. I shifted my feet, fighting to stay awake, checking to make sure I had all my grenades and plenty of extra clips.

It was too dark beyond the wire. Anything could have been out there. "I can feel their presence," Michael said. "The monks know I'm finally home." I knew his real home was Pendleton, Oregon, not far from Walla Walla, but I kept my mouth shut.

Counting the points on the concertina wire, I tried to concentrate on standing guard, but Michael tugged on my collar and dragged me down deeper into the foxhole until we both squatted in the bottom, so close our helmets touched. When I stared directly at him, his head disappeared for a second, and I had to blink to make it rematerialize. His eyes returned—two holes in his face that buzzed with the same particles of night that filled in the space around his shoulders and the shiny sandbags. Looking straight up, I could only make out the backs of the sandbags along the top edge of the foxhole, and above that was nothing but a square shaft of darkness. "Now I see my purpose," Michael said.

Michael wanted to be holy—but Miki really was, without trying.

When Miki first smiled at me in front of the restaurant, and as the pain slowly faded from my arm, I felt just the opposite from the way I felt with Michael that night in the *foxhole. She knew something important, also. But her eyes were ten times brighter.*

And if I were honest, I would have to admit that Argo has a little bit of that same special light in his eyes, too, even when he's drunk.

"I need another bottle, Nick. Be a good chap and run down to Esmeralda's for me. I say, here's a few shillings. And a little extra for my favorite procurer. Buy yourself a shiny bauble or something brightly colored. But make mine Wild Turkey. One hundred and one proof. Remember that. Not one hundred, or ninety-nine, but one-oh-one. That extra *one* makes all the difference, my boy. The proof is in the proof. Oh, damnit to hell. Who dropped this perfectly good semiautomatic rifle onto the floor? I'll have to have a word with the housekeeper when she returns from Piccadilly Circus. Now run along, Pipnick. Tallyho, and keep a stiff upper crust."

I wanted to leave Argo and not come back, but I had already stuffed his crinkled dollar bills into the front pocket of my jeans. As I shoved in the money, my hand and prick ached simultaneously from the pressure; the pain flashed up my arm and down my legs, burning and ripping through my nerves. I felt like an overblown bag of skin temporarily encasing a stream of molten steel. Not even LaWanda or the medical officer on board an alien spacecraft could soothe this hurting.

The doorknob to his apartment twisted by itself just before I tried to let myself out. I gave it a hard crank, and someone cursed from out in the hallway. LaWanda was the only person I knew who ever said, "Damn your eyes."

"Oh! I was hoping you were here. How's your hand, honey? I want to apologize. It's just that Harold had to go back on duty. He only gets an hour off, and, well . . . you know. Does it hurt? You want some acupressure or something? Don't look at me like that, Nicholas."

111

"Do you feel stronger now? Do you have a new energy flow?"

"What are you talking about, silly? You sound like Mayananda."

"Is he a monster?"

"No, you crazy thing. He's my Shaktician."

"Nicolitis! Is that your infectious voice I still hear? Get a move on, carrier. Or carrion ye shall be. I need my cure!"

"Is he drunk again?"

"Probably."

"Go fuck yourself, Argo!"

"What? The psychic punchboard deigns to darken my doorway? Out, you sideshow Circe. Exorcise yourself from my pagan premises."

"Sounds like he's got it bad back there. Really bent. Come on, Nicholas."

LaWanda took hold of my sore hand. The feel of her flesh on mine was entirely different from Miki's first touch. I couldn't feel LaWanda's skin because of all the rough white gauze between us. It seemed she was pulling me down the hallway by an invisible rope, and she didn't let go until we reached the stairway. That's when the pain resumed, pulsating through my hand so harshly I thought the gauze wrapping would tear loose.

"Shit, Nicholas. I'm sorry. I'm just not centered today. You want me to put something on that cut? I've got some fresh herbs in the apartment. What do you say, sweetheart?"

"No. I have to go shopping for Argo."

"Do you do *everything* he tells you?"

"Maybe."

"Why, Nicholas?"

"Because he's my friend."

"Friend?"

"What's wrong? Don't you know what a friend is?"

"I do know what a friend *isn't*."

We stood on the middle floor of the apartment building; sets of stairs notched the air in front of us, up and down. I squinted and imagined the stairs extending to infinity in both directions.

"Then will *you* go to the store with me?"

"To buy more liquor, Nicholas? I'm sure I've got something in the apartment we could give him to tide him over. He doesn't sound like he needs any more anyway."

"Only one bottle."

"Maybe he should eat something instead. Positive ions must be eating him alive. I don't think I've ever seen him touch solid food. It's probably alien to his system by now. What's left of it, that is. Which means his damaged brain probably doesn't even remember we exist. So let's just go to my place and relax. Okay?"

"Sometimes you—"

"Yeah. Sure. I'll go, Nicholas. And maybe we can fix his wagon in the process."

"What do you mean?"

"We'll think of something. Come on."

When LaWanda reached for my hand again, I snapped it back and held it over my head so she would get the message. But all she did was roll up her eyes then hop down the stairs two at a time. I followed her and sneaked glances at her ass. The sight of those round curves made me feel nice and warm. But when I lowered my arm, fresh blood pumped back into my wounded hand—this surge scrambled the sexwaves beginning to heat through my belly.

"Hurry up, slowpoke."

"I'm coming."

The sun blazed straight up above the patio, shining down

fierce and hot as if pouring all its heat between the four stucco walls. The girl was still lying out on her towel, and her skin sparkled from all angles as I stepped past. I stared as long as I dared, turning my head away quickly when her boyfriend rustled around and glared back at me. The girl could probably feel my eyes, too—but she didn't look up or even move, because she was no doubt used to being stared at, maybe even tired of it, exhausted.

The girl in the sun and LaWanda had the same sized ass, but LaWanda's didn't swell out as nicely as the girl's did. Plus, LaWanda's hair was too long, down almost to her waist, and she rarely brushed it. The girl on the towel wore her hair short, sweet, and golden brown, gleaming brilliantly in the sun—as if she had dipped her head gently in butterscotch. And the smooth golden flesh around her neck was delicious. LaWanda's neck was white, almost blue, because her hair is too thick and she gets outside only once in a while. As we exited the patio and reached the street, I slowed down, wishing to keep LaWanda exposed to the fresh air she didn't like as long as possible.

"Come on, Nicholas. Let's get this over with."

"Okay."

"You know, sweetheart, I really don't want to do this. But I had to talk with you."

"How are you today, LaWanda?"

"No, no. You don't understand. Nicholas, you certainly acted weird this morning. Is something wrong? Maybe your polarities are scrambled or something. Have you been eating enough fresh vegetables? What is it? You can tell me."

"Sure. Something's wrong. That light across the street keeps flashing 'Don't Walk' even though the other lights are green for the cars."

"That light's always been broken. But Nicholas—answer me! I won't let you cross the street until you do."

I felt no reason to offer a reply; she didn't deserve one. I could always lose myself in another memory, and there was nothing LaWanda could do about that.

Miki's eyes appeared to be much larger than they really were; her eyes glistened soft and brown, and they seemed to belong to something more expansive that spread all the way through her—inside and outside—something that extended deep down into the center of her small body, broadcast through her eyes, with the same force that pumped blood steadily through her veins and propelled her precious breathing—a feeling that lived in and around her that I could not name; a feeling that I could only call her, just Miki. In comparison, LaWanda's eyes were simply eyes that were part of a face that was attached to the front of her head that just so happened to be enclosed by wild hair drooping down in pliable spikes across her thin shoulders. LaWanda's head seemed to be constructed from many different parts, and somehow her hair held everything together. With Miki, I had the feeling that even if her hair were shaved off to the bare skin, she would still survive as one solid person—because she was held together by something much truer than LaWanda possessed.

"I'm just nervous, that's all."

We stood on the corner of Seventh and University, in front of the enormous window of a furniture store; on display were clean new puffed-up couches, and glossy tables surrounded by lamps dangling from silver stalks. LaWanda and I were reflected in the window, and it appeared we were standing in a strange living room, cleaner than any hotel suite. We were inside the store and we were out on the street—and occasionally we could be seen in the cars that cruised past, despite the fact that our curved and tilted reflections in the car windows re-created us as inhabitants of a world tormented by unpredictable gravity and unnamed colors.

"You're nervous? You've been giving *me* the creeps all day. I thought you and Harold were going to kill each other, and I couldn't handle it. I just ran downstairs to the laundry room, and I didn't have to. But the way you acted . . . I didn't want to deal with it. You're usually such a sweetheart, Nicholas. Ever since I first met you, you've been the sweetest person of all. Until today. I just freaked."

I sent her a dark thoughtwave, hoping to make her shiver in the sun.

Across the street, on the Sixth Avenue corner, stood the phone company fortress—satellite dishes of all sizes cluttered the top of an enormous brown concrete cube with no windows. Argo said people actually worked inside that cube, but I didn't believe him. Who could work in the midst of such intense wave bombardment, in and out, day and night?

I wanted that dark thoughtwave to zing into the center of LaWanda's brain—but it would never reach the target. All thoughtwaves would be scrambled beyond recognition by the telephone dishes.

I had never made the connection before; that wave-production station was awfully close to LaWanda's apartment complex. Most likely all thoughtwaves sent from my house to hers would be zapped by Pacific Bell.

If technology grew any stronger, there was no telling how scrambled up the world would become. Soon, we would need special thought-transfer helmets immune to jamming from unwanted and overpowerful sources. Then again, it might be fun to be overloaded and infiltrated by a variety of waves. We could follow our impulses more freely—our next move triggered by an electrical signal, a satellite transmission, a super-intense radio broadcast out of Mexico. Argo said even sunspots could determine the course of our lives and change our moods and influence the stock market. Why not the flick of a light switch or the burst of a car alarm or the whirring of a NASA computer?

Maybe that explained why the traffic signal had been stuck on "Don't Walk." That signal was too close to the phone company wave-generating station.

And what was *my* correct signal? If I had been born in a time before all these technological waves were being produced, would my life-signal be different? Purer? Easier to receive?

"Nicholas? Why are you staring at me like that? Talk to me. Why do you keep disappearing all the time? Are you in there? Nicholas! Earth calling Nicholas!"

I pretended not to hear her, and I concentrated on sending her that dark thought. The simplest way into her brain was through her eyes. But since her eyes seemed divorced from the rest of her personality, I focused just a little higher, directing the thoughtwave straight out in a perfect line into the center of her forehead. A coil of hair slipped down across her face, and LaWanda brushed it away. My thought was still off target, deflected by her skull. In basic training, the drill sergeants taught us how to aim our M16s using Kentucky windage— shifting the barrel slightly to the left or right of the target to compensate for minor problems like an inaccurate gunsight or foul windy weather. So I tried that technique as a last resort, aiming my thought at LaWanda's left eyebrow.

"If you're just going to stand here, I'm going back. My eyes hurt in this sun, anyway."

Still off target, I must have arrowed my thoughts into a sensitive spot in her eyemeat by mistake. The phone company had to be more powerful than I first imagined.

For the moment, I had to give up. That dark thought ricocheted through the front part of my brain, loose like a mad bee, and I felt frustrated not being able to release it.

"Let's go. Now!"

Since the traffic signal was broken and it was too dangerous to cross the street, we continued down the north side of University, past an almost-mall containing the vitamin shop and soup-and-salad restaurant LaWanda visited occasionally. LaWanda went through odd cycles. Sometimes she refused to eat meat, and other times she wouldn't eat anything at all. Once I dragged LaWanda to the soup-and-salad place and attempted to force-feed her. She didn't cooperate and sucked on a brown bottle of imported beer instead while I went back for seconds and thirds. The waitress provided her a large frosted mug, but LaWanda didn't have the strength to lift it.

That incident occurred during the time LaWanda was at war with one of her witch enemies; she was convinced an evil spell of revenge had been cast. Her hair was falling out and her nose bled without warning. The three-legged coffee table in her apartment was littered with crumpled tissues blotched red encircling a black hairbrush so thick with lost hair the bristles were hidden. For most of the day, LaWanda would lie moaning on the couch. I came by to visit, and upon seeing her in such agony my first thought was to get her something to eat. That's when I dragged her to the restaurant. Her body was so fragile, though, I had to restrain myself from squeezing too hard; I was afraid I might poke a brittle bone through her cold skin—skin that felt as papery as one of her bloody white tissues. Her tits were still big, though, and I felt guilty staring at them in between bites of salad dripping with bleu cheese dressing.

After the evil-spell crisis was over, I visited that restaurant again a few months later with LaWanda and Argo—and she gobbled down more food than I thought possible. LaWanda went back for thirds on soup and fourths on salad, and she devoured five cornbread muffins. Before heading home, she took us to the vitamin shop next door and purchased eleven bottles of pills. She rushed us home, and first thing she cracked open the pills and eventually swallowed three handfuls—white pills with lines down the middle and brown ones shaped like little footballs and others long and thick like cut-up pieces of rubber tubing. None of those pills looked like candy, but LaWanda relished them nonetheless. Later, the three of us drank beer and Argo told dumb jokes. When I walked home that night, I spent blocks trying to figure out the one about the pygmy and the explorer's wife. Even after passing sixteen streetlamps, I still didn't get it and gave up—though I had laughed just as hard as Argo and LaWanda did when the joke was first told.

The memory of that confusion brought on sadness, so I shut it off.

By the time LaWanda and I reached the corner, waiting for another light to change, I was tired—tired of her and tired of Argo—even though they were the only friends I had left. Mrs. Raylak was nice, but she was still my landlady and not really my friend. And the rest of my friends had been sold, traded, or killed.

A city bus rumbled up from behind us and cut the corner. I tried to count all the heads inside, but the bus flashed by too fast. The heads all looked like the same one, each in its movie-frame window, evolving quickly from old lady in the front to different women reading to young punk with purple mohawk to school kids laughing to tattooed man sitting in the last seat smoking even though that was against the rules: one head, developing, changing shapes and sizes and colors, but all the same head—The Bus Head, the new monster of the cities sucking up fresh victims on every corner and roaming out of control, stopping only for gas and to unload rivers of silver coins from the money machine churning next to the zombie driver.

Argo told me that people spent so much money and time trying to change themselves that they never had time to do anything that *really* mattered. I didn't understand that, either. And I didn't ask him to explain.

It now seemed important for me to buy Argo his bottle—that mattered. Somehow. But anything more than that . . . well, it was scrambled like all the cars and trucks and motorcycles struggling to turn left or right or continue straight ahead in the center of the intersection.

"Come on, Nicholas! Run!"

A silver grinning grille and bug-eyed headlights swept toward me. I leaped forward . . . could feel fender skinclose . . . radiator heat. Then my left leg jerked up hard. *Sniper fire and the RTO calling for air strike.* The car struck my leg, ripping my jeans and knocking me flat. I dragged ass to the other side of the street. . . . "Nicholas!" I hugged LaWanda's ankles.

"Nicholas, my baby. Here, get out of the street. Are you all right? Get up, sweetheart. You silly matador."

"Okay."

"Hey, lady. He all right?"

"Did you get the license number? It was a silver Oldsmobile, I know that much."

"Silver? Hell, it was green. Light green."

"You don't know what you're talking about, ace. That was an Impala."

"Oh, my, he's bleeding. Young lady, you best get him to a doctor."

"Nicholas? Let's go. Okay? Please? Can you walk. Oh,

God, Nicholas. Come on. Nicholas! Good. That's it. Good. Easy. Can you put pressure on it? God, these people are strange. Please, Nicholas. Why don't they just mind their own business. Please!"

"Jesus, he's a big one. Gonna take more'n a lousy Oldsmobile to put him away."

"If I were you, lady, I'd sue."

"Yeah, hit'n'run. That's a felony, for sure."

"Call the police. They'll get him."

"No, please. We'll be all right."

"Ma'am, I might be able to help you. My brother-in-law is a lawyer. His number's in the book. Bob Robertson, Attorney at Law. That's R as in *robbery*— Hey, you don't have to be so rude. I was just trying to help."

"Leave her be, pal. Can't you see she's in shock?"

"Shock? Looks like she's wigged out to me."

"Wings? She said the car had wings? Brother, I know it's hot out today, but that's too crazy."

I brushed off my pants and shirt. I picked pebbles out of my wrinkled elbow skin. When I stepped forward to test my foot, everything felt fine—except a big sliver of chrome poked through my pant cuff and scraped on the sidewalk behind me. Easily, I slid the chrome strip free, but I felt like a fool standing there holding an imitation El Cid spear. Luckily, there was a public trash can close by, next to a bus stop bench. "Pitch In!" said the little white decal on the side of the can that depicted a stick-figure man with a perfect-circle head and a triangle groin. I pretended I was him. It was no problem bending the metal strip in half, then in half again. Inside the trash can it went, and everything was over. That much I could prove. It was just like Argo said: "There's nothing you can't prove, as long as your perspective is limited enough."

" . . . lucky he didn't get his foot shish-kebabbed."

" . . . pants are all ripped to shit."

" . . . thought for sure he was going to be runned over, 'cept that car looked to bounce off 'n him if they woulda hit."

"What the hell are you talking about?"

"It was a miracle."

Only memories could erase all those heckling voices.

Near Chu Lai we got ambushed. We all hugged the earth. I didn't move, even though dirt crumbs leaped into my nose when I inhaled. Splinters of wood rained out from the trees around us. Bullets pinged overhead, then a machine gun opened up. It seemed like the red-hot top of a monstrous frying pan was floating over our platoon, pressing down slowly, ready to singe my buttpack and melt my trenching tool and poach me alive inside my fatigues.

When the shooting finally stopped, we lay in silence, waiting. Time vanished. I could hear the grass growing and absolutely nothing else, until Lieutenant Wheeler yelled an all-clear that cracked open the air between us. No one was hit, miraculously. The RTO had taken a round through the radio, but it still worked.

And that was it. Back to normal. On the way out, Billy Reid finished explaining the words to "Purple Haze," right where he'd left off before the ambush.

LaWanda shivered and hugged herself. "Nicholas, if you're okay, let's go buy that bottle and get out of here. I sweat too much on days like this."

I pushed her through the crowd, and we moved forward, closer to our destination. But I felt removed from the action somehow. We were just following genetic orders or something, at the mercy of waves concealed and unidentified.

We still had to cross two more streets. Each time we stepped off another curb, I glared at the drivers turning our way and sent out protection waves, forcing myself to look mean and horrifying. I didn't change my expression until we arrived safely at Esmeralda's Liquor Emporium.

LaWanda ran the last few feet. With the strength I had left—which hadn't been exhausted by the aches and the wounds and by dodging runaway sedans and gear-grinding buses—I sent one last angry thoughtwave, designed to trip her and send her crashing face-first into the Black Velvet ad in the window. She kept running, however, and I wished I were out in front so I could study her tits bouncing. Instead, I was forced to imagine how they looked. LaWanda only wore a bra underneath her fluffy, ruffled waitress blouse; today, all she wore on top was a faded black T-shirt.

There are moments when I dream my body can transform itself into soft black cloth sewn into the form of a clean shirt lying next to LaWanda's bed—so she can pick me up first thing when she awakes and slip me over her head. Then I would belong to her tits and protect them—spending my life as a shield against harmful sunlight and the eyes of hungry men.

But I didn't recall that dream this time while LaWanda dashed into the liquor store.

By the time I was inside, LaWanda had already purchased a pack of cigarettes; she hugged the counter and leaned over talking to Stevie Esmeralda, who stood at a safe distance behind the cash register. Stevie is so fat he can't tuck in his shirts. His belly button is always in full view—where brown hairs twirl out across his roll of flab.

"Hey, Nicky. Long time no see. I hear you've taken up a new sport—destruction derby on foot."

"I'm okay."

"Good, good. Glad to hear that. And what'll it be today? Your buddy Argo has a raging thirst in all this heat, I imagine."

"He's okay, too."

Bottles saturated the wall from floor to ceiling behind Stevie; against the opposite wall stood more bottles plus cheap wooden racks for wine and champagne. Boxes slashed on the diagonal were stacked high in the center of the store, full of still more bottles and decorated with a flat paper-advertisement lady who stood on top of the highest box. She wore a shimmering black dress, a pearl necklace, and no shoes. She rotated on a vertical gray pole. When she turned her back, she became nothing more than brown cardboard with a tiny electric motor taped to her nonexistent shoulder blades.

Since there was such an abundance of bottles in the store, I considered buying Argo something exotic for a surprise. He'd already had enough Wild Turkey for one day. Even though I was spending his money, I could still turn the bottle he wanted into a present, if it was something he didn't expect. Eddie Elvesizer always enjoyed brandy, and one time he was entertaining a French lady spy in his Paris apartment when he discovered his special stock had been depleted. He threw a distinguished fit, and she poured them vodka drinks instead— that's how Eddie discovered she was actually working for the Russians. So, even if Argo was upset initially when I brought him a different bottle, something good would result.

In the midst of such a variety of bottles, I had trouble making a decision. Vodka was clear and appeared harmless. The labels were designed to resemble silver-and-white shields. But it didn't seem worth it to pay so much for something almost invisible protected by colored paper and fancy writing. Besides, I knew Argo didn't like things he could see through— he rarely opened his curtains, and all the drinking glasses he owned were alligator green or pimp-jacket blue.

"Hey, Nicky. How's it hangin', eh?"

"Stevie, don't."

"You been gettin' any lately?"

"Argo gave me about twenty bucks."

"Oh, he did, did he? You got a nice tip, eh? And he'll give you the rest of it later, I bet. Ha!"

"Stevie, if you don't quit I'm going to—"

"Going to what? You gonna cut me off, lambchop? Huh?"

"Argo demanded Wild Turkey, but I think I'll surprise him instead."

"Well, ain't that a kick in the butt," Stevie said. "What'd you have in mind, big boy? We're all out of flowers and candy."

"Leave him *alone*."

"Aw, go peddle your pussy."

"The man deserves something decent for a change," I said.

"Oh, I heard that," Stevie said. "You should give him a little taste, sweet thang."

"Shut up, would you?"

"He's been having trouble finishing his book," I said. "And he works harder than any of us. That's the truth. If you can't respect him for anything else, you at least have to give him credit for that."

"Well, Nick, I didn't realize. But I think you should know something. You oughta see the people that come in here and buy his kinda books. I wouldn't want to meet them down some dark alley. You, LaWanda, maybe. But me, no way. Fucking geeks lookin' like they got their wangs all tied in knots, ain't had no pussy since pussy had them. Right, Wanda, sugar? We all know you never have to read no books like that, don't we? Hell, you're the number one knot untier in these parts, ain't you?"

I felt like throwing up watching Stevie grab onto his crotch and squeeze it with both hands. His belly jiggled, and he laughed his greasy round laugh. His long hair shook like fringe across his round shoulders, and his teeth beamed white from the mouth hole in the center of his hairy jaws. Thinner hair fluffed up around the collar of his T-shirt; his chest looked like a heavy peat moss sack stuffed with hair, overflowing out against his neck and arm muscles and blubbery waist. After he let go of himself, he slapped his puffy hands against the glass countertop; his fingers appeared carved from rotten wood, with bundles of hair taped to each knuckle.

"Now what'll it be, young man? Yes, you, the one with the bloody diaper wrapped around your paw. Whatever you want, you'll find it here someplace. Right, Wanda? Eh?"

Stevie winked at her. One side of his face crinkled with creases, like a block of ice cracking and not breaking after getting smacked with a ball peen hammer. A piece of pink tongue floated between his nonexistent lips.

"Fuck you."

"Where and when?"

"Nicholas, how about if you got him some wine? Just grab something cheap and let's get out of here."

"Sure. We got some good stuff, Nicky. Thunderbird. Mad Dog 20-20. Wild Irish Rose. All the big names."

"Don't give me any shit. Not after what I've been through."

"Such a violent tongue, Nick. But you can save it for the next war. I'm on your side, I really am. In the meantime, why don't you just go ahead and look around. Take your time. You don't want to go about this thing half-cocked. Ha!"

Stevie's voice forced out another memory.

On the streets of Saigon, there were tables set up full of liquor bottles and cigarette cartons and toothpaste boxes. It was confusing to see all that familiar stuff for sale there—stuff I usually saw on TV advertisements back home on our black-and-white television. Behind those tables sat tiny women, thin shoulders just barely propping up their black shirts from the inside, white bamboo hats shadowing their flat faces. Every brand of liquor was jammed onto those crowded tables, in the midst of packs of American razor blades and soap bars.

In Esmeralda's, the bottles were lined up so perfectly, I felt if I took out even one I'd upset the pattern beyond repair, denying its beauty. The bottles seemed to be supporting the roof of the store, and if the bottles were moved the whole place might cave in.

Usually, when things that are already perfect are upset and rearranged, the result is monsters.

If I pulled down a bottle, I didn't know if I'd be the monster that would result from the mistake, or if somehow that mistake would give life to some other kind of monster. At the time, the destructive results didn't seem that awful— particularly if LaWanda could have been demolished in the ensuing chaos.

I could feel Stevie staring at me, but I refused to look back at him. Out of the corner of my eye I saw him tap LaWanda on the shoulder, reaching farther out over the counter as she inched away from him. Finally, he grabbed hold of her near the neck with his wooden hands. LaWanda squirmed. Stevie's arm was so thick with fat that his elbow was submerged beneath the white doughy lump hanging from the backside of his upper arm.

"But I was drunk."

"So was I."

"I didn't know what I was doing."

"You coulda fooled me, honey."

"You're hurting me."

"So are you. You don't know how bad it hurts. Come on. I get off in a coupla hours. We can go out for smorgasbord or something."

"You're a pig, Stevie."

"I love it."

"Come on, Nicholas. I've got to get back and iron my blouse."

All the bottles gleamed like jewels. The liquor store was a treasure chest, and the three of us were interfering with the beauty. If our bodies were peeled inside out, and the blood was washed clean, would we shine like jewels, spread out like fresh-cleaned fish? Or would we be too frightening for words? Or both? Did our bodies digest food and circulate blood in total darkness? Inside my head, was it dark like the space between stars at night? Or did light twinkle through my brain, shining in the fluids, highlighting the cauliflower-clumped ridges of my brain while I thought? Did changing thoughts change the colors? If I always entertained certain positive thoughts, would my brain work better? Would the colors shine brighter?

Stevie was still connected to LaWanda. I thought he would emerge from behind the counter and spread toward her like The Blob, attempting to swallow her up the same way his flab had already consumed the point of his elbow. I'd have to become Steve McQueen and rescue her. If it happened fast that would be the best way, because if it went slow there would be too much time for me to think about what to do. I'd empty liquor on The Blob until I found the right brand—the one that would melt The Blob's oozing unshaped body. I'd break open the necks of bottle after bottle, and I'd splash booze all over—forcing that monster to squeal like a piglet.

"Nicky! What the hell you think you're doing? Put that thing down, for Christ's sake."

When I found the right one, I'd take a fresh unopened bottle to Argo and explain how special it was, how it had saved the store from destruction.

"Nicholas! No!"

The Blob attacked me instead, wrapping around my neck tight so I couldn't breathe, knowing just what to do. I still had one bottle left. I tried to break it open and splash it around. I hoped it was the right one, the one that would do the trick—but blue hazy circles flitted across the store. I couldn't suck in air. Then my head got crushed. LaWanda's face filled all spaces. She was a picture on the giant movie screen spread tight and pasted against my eyeballs.

"Jesus, Stevie. You almost killed him."

"What the hell would *you* do if some guy was busting up your inventory? Cheer him on?"

"You didn't have to choke him like that."

"Yes, I did. I'm a businessman."

My pants were wet but cool, and they smelled of paint thinner or liquor, not piss. When I swallowed, spines ripped into the soft skin of my throat.

"You better have enough to cover this, Nicky. Jesus, where did I leave the fucking mop? Look at this place! Like a damn sleaze pit. Smells to high heaven. Is that all you got? You bimbos get out of here. And so much for your joke on Argo, bitch. Now the joke's on you. Don't bother darkening my door again—unless you got somethin' to lay on the table. Know what I'm sayin'? Coupla fruitcakes from way back, that's what you are. Get outta here!"

"Nicholas, what the hell's wrong with you? Come on, get up. How could you do this to me? I can't take you out there and let everyone see what a mess you are. Don't you ever think about anyone but yourself? You're sick, Nicholas. And now you've got me all tangled up in your disease. What am I supposed to *do* with you, anyway? Here, get off the floor and let's go. Now. Oh, you're such a jerk. Look what you did to my hair!"

My crotch was icy. Billy Reid said you felt frozen and

empty with a bullet in the belly. Blood oozed from my hand; the gauze unraveled. Boris Karloff starred in the original *Mummy*.

LaWanda continued thrashing her lips but I put up a barrier to deflect her words. It felt good to stand outside, listening to the cars swish and rattle in the street. I could even hear the traffic signals clicking inside the yellow light poles. The traffic lights changed colors; the cars and people streamed through the streets in multiple directions, creating mixed patterns. If red meant stop, and green meant go, what did yellow mean? What did it *really* mean? The sky was blue—for a reason? My blood was red, the bandage used to be snowflake white. LaWanda's T-shirt was black as telephone-pole pitch, and her skin was almost as white as the gauze bandage fresh from the box. Argo's money was gone, though it was still green. My army uniform was green—officially, olive drab. Green.

"Nicholas, say something!"

"Go."

"God damnit, Nicholas. Look what you did! You're an asshole for this. A big spooky asshole! Now what am I supposed to do?"

Blood fell onto the sidewalk.

"Now my hand is messed up."

"Nicholas, I can't fix that here, in front of all these people. God, I'm going to *freak!*"

"Help me."

"Okay, okay. It'll be all right. All the booze you spilled will kill the germs. You can't get any more infected than you already are. Yes, I know, it stings. Oh, shit. I don't care. Let me have your hand, then. And if it's any consolation, Stevie's hurting more than you right now. Serves him right, the letch."

"You seemed friendly enough with him."

"Things aren't always what they seem, I guess. There, Nicholas. That should do it . . . for now. Oh, shit, I hate all these people *staring* at me!"

The touch of LaWanda's hand was soothing, even though she shook nervously and her white fingers were cold. Something passed between us in the midst of the shivering and the pain. My feet seemed to rest steadier on the sidewalk, my thoughts seemed less like figments.

"What's wrong with being a letch?"

"Nicholas, really. All that fat swine thinks about is sex."

"But why not? If it's good for you."

"Good for *him*. Look, keep your hand in your pocket or something for now. I just want to get home and out of this crowd."

"Maybe Stevie would be nicer after more sex. Maybe he wouldn't have to suffer all that extra weight. He just wants to be stronger, doesn't he? Like anybody else. That's all. It's simple if you really understand. Colors are simple. Sex could be simple."

"Look, Nicholas. The man just tried to switch your lights off. And now you want me to sacrifice my body for him?"

"It wouldn't be a sacrifice."

"Sometimes I don't know who you are. And right now I don't really care."

Down the street from Esmeralda's stood eight different newspaper dispensers. LaWanda could be stuffed very easily into any one of them. Beside the daily papers, there were sex newspapers depicting naked women—black bars slashed across their tits and eyes. I discovered one of those papers in Argo's laboratory; it contained small ads offering more naked women and some men—all with black bars obscuring their nipples and pricks and pussies. Argo circled seven of those ads in thick red felt pen.

"What the hell were you trying to prove back there, Nicholas?"

"I was just trying to figure something out, that's all."

"Please explain it to me someday. If you find the time. Now let's get back home. I'm burning up out here."

"What about Argo?"

"You should have thought about that before you busted three bottles of top-shelf whiskey."

"He's going to be angry if we come back without his bottle."

"When *you* come back."

"Sure."

"And *if* he's still conscious."

"Let's not go back yet. We could just go to the park or something."

"Nice try, Nicholas. But I've got to get ready for work. So you might as well head for your grand opening, or whatever it is tonight."

"The alien watch."

"Whatever. You could deal with Mr. Argo later. He probably won't even remember anyway. Now look, I've got things to do."

"Don't you even care?"

"Sure, sure I do, Nicholas. You know I'd do anything for you. But not right now. Understand?"

"I don't mean about *me*. Don't you even care about the *aliens?*"

"They didn't show up last month, so I doubt they'll make an appearance tonight."

"How did you know about last month?"

"I don't know. You must've told me in one of your disjointed rambles."

"They're coming tonight. I know it."

"Fine, Nicholas. You get going, grab yourself a ringside seat, and tell me all about it tomorrow. It's been real."

"LaWanda, this isn't fair."

"Maybe not."

"Let's walk on the other side of the street."

"No. Hey, not so hard."

"Now. The light's green."

LaWanda was bigger than Miki, and she smelled like a pet animal. I pulled her closer as we joined a crowd crossing the street, holding on tight when she tried to sneak around two men wearing black sunglasses and carrying briefcases. If I were a competent sculptor, I could carve a duplicate of Miki from within LaWanda's body. Since her tits are larger and her ass fuller, the project would require simple modifications: restyle the body, dye the hair, color the eyes, tighten the facial skin, soften the voice.

LaWanda attempted to spin free. I wrapped my arm snug against her back, curling one finger through her belt loop.

She parted her hair down the middle, but the part was crooked in two places, overlapping and revealing too much white scalp. Her hair needed to be fixed, but I didn't have a comb, and my fingers were too big and numb for the job.

I struggled through the crowd, slowing us down, hoping to reach the curb the instant the light changed—even though pedestrians in the rear had to change course and veer around us. The signal changed to a blinking red "Don't Walk." La-Wanda dragged her feet; she forced me to yank her up out of the gutter. She kicked me but missed wide. Carved into one square of sidewalk was the year 1924. The square next to that one was cracked and didn't line up. I wondered if I was strong enough to move it into alignment. Brak would have sufficient strength. But he could never do anything requiring care or patience. Only one leg of the blue mailbox on the corner was bolted into the concrete.

"If you don't let go of me I'll scream."

From the restaurant on the corner, a man stared at me from the window, slurping soup. His eyes widened above the spoon buried between his pinching lips. White soup burbled down his chin. His eyes held me. I tilted my head, rearranging the window glare, and stars of sun sparkled across his face. If I held my head at the proper angle, a bar of reflected light streaked over his eyes, the reverse of the black bars on the girls' faces in the seventy-five-cent newspapers.

Why would anyone throw a bomb into a restaurant?

"Ni-cho-las, you're hurting me. If you don't let me go this instant—"

"Did you go to the pagoda today?"

"Oh, God, Nicholas, you're blowing it, you're blowing it for Christ's sake let me go!"

"Do you want to stop in that store and buy some flowers first?"

"For your grave, damn you."

"There's fruit at the Arab market."

"You're the fucking fruit. Look, watch my lips, Nicholas. Let's be gentle now. Just ease off the pressure. Hey, just a little. It's . . . okay. There. And . . . would you like to hold hands on the way back? How does that sound?"

"Your hair is so shiny. There's a special light in your hair, burning from inside."

"Right, Nicholas. All the guys tell me that. Just give me your hand now. We'll be home soon."

"Will you marry me?"

"Oh, of course. Turn me loose and I'll do anything."

"In the pagoda?"

"On the moon, if you want. I don't give a shit. I mean, just ease up, Nicholas."

The man in the window extracted chopsticks from his mouth, slowly, and wiped some rice off his chin. The slash of light still cut across his eyes; I didn't know if he could still see me or not.

"I have to go back tomorrow."

"Go back? To Esmeralda's? Nicholas, please, do whatever you want. Just let me go before I flip out!"

"Sergeant Ascencion and Billy Reid will be looking for me. I have to go back."

"Nicholas, I don't know. Maybe we should take the long way. Okay? You just keep cool and keep on walking. It'll be nice. Just you and me out for a walk. A nice walk. And maybe we can stop and visit my friend over by the hospital. You remember her. That'd be fun, wouldn't it, Nicholas?"

"My father's in that hospital."

"Your father is . . . yes, Nicholas. Everybody's father is in the hospital. If we hurry, maybe we can make it for visiting hours."

I wanted to suck on LaWanda's tits—but there was too much pressure, too much heat, too much tightness and fear in her voice. I wanted to go home—to my real home. Get out and go back. Freedom in the dark corners of memory. Away.

My father was fifty-eight years old, and we sat together in front of Walter Cronkite on TV. We never spoke, we just watched. He had no favorite shows, but he didn't care for monster movies. The same channel could hold us for an entire evening. Usually, we didn't go to bed until the late news reports were over, denying ourselves Johnny Carson. My father always awoke the next morning before sunup to prepare for work. He used the bathroom first. I would wait in the hall, listening to

him gargle and swish clean his teeth. Then we traded places
smoothly and silently.

But the night we watched Walter Cronkite for the last
time, my father dropped out of his chair flat onto the floor. He
gripped his left arm with his right hand, and his mouth swung
open. He wanted to scream. Nothing came out. Walter
Cronkite announced the votes were finally in, and Richard
Nixon was the new president, winning only 43.16 percent of
the popular vote.

I didn't go to school the next day.

"Now what's wrong?"

I never missed a day of school in my life, until the day after
my father's accident. I spent more time at school than I did at
home, staying after for baseball practice and games. The last
year I played, when I hit .472, my father came out to see me
only once.

"Come on, Nicholas. You can't just stand there. What
are you looking at? Nicholas. This isn't right. These people.
They won't stop *staring* at me. Just a few more blocks. There.
Take my hand. My *hand!* Don't do this to me. God damnit,
you're making me look ridiculous in public. Please, baby.
Here, take my hand. That's nice, isn't it? Easy. One step.
There. Now another. Come on!"

Miki's hands were easily lost inside mine. I always took
care not to squeeze too tight. Once I hurt her. She wouldn't tell
me it hurt, but I could tell by the way she breathed deeply,
forcing a smile. Her hands were so small and stiff, almost all
bone.

I once killed a sparrow with my BB rifle. With my
pocketknife I attempted to slice meat off the bird's ribs, but there
wasn't much to cut. The dead sparrow floated in my hand,
back and forth, it was that light. Its eyes were bright black, and

its beak popped open in rhythm to the poking knife blade. Ribs snapped like brittle matchsticks. Even though the sparrow's chest held the fluffy mess of a hole, the bird still seemed capable of flight.

"Nice day, don't you think, Nicholas?"

"You said it was too hot."

"Yeah, I guess I did. But that was before. I think it got cooler all of a sudden. Don't you think so?"

"No."

"It is."

"Too many things are out of order today. Too many."

"No they're not. Are they?"

"Yes."

"You really think so, Nicholas?"

"We were supposed to buy Argo a bottle. Now we're not. Listen to how the tires sound on the cars. It's hot, and the tires stick to the street. Listen when they go around the corner. Hear it? The rubber's melting. The tread's peeling off. Argo's going to be furious."

"He's not going to remember, Nicholas. There's still beer left over in my refrigerator if he needs a drink that badly."

"That's *your* beer. It was a gift."

"Yes, and thank you, Nicholas. But there's nothing wrong with sharing, is there?"

"But that's different. It was a special gift."

"*You* drank one, Nicholas."

"That's different."

"Okay. Okay."

When he fell from the recliner, my father thumped into the floor solidly. That was the final sound he made. I could feel the quick vibration through my feet. The TV screen provided the only light in the living room. My father's eyes were open, and I could see Walter Cronkite reflected there—as if my father had two tiny screens built into his head. Our TV was black-and-white, but within my father's eyes Walter Cronkite appeared in color. My father's teeth were gray in the TV glare. A shadow passed over his face as the news report shifted to a commercial.

"You know, my friend over at the hospital can lend you some money."

"We should just tell Argo the truth."

"Ow! No. Let's go this way, Nicholas. Your father. Remember? The hospital. Argo can wait."

"He's my friend."

"That's what you think. Hey, we're going the wrong way. You've met *my* friend before. Remember Alma? She likes you."

I lay down on the floor next to my father, careful not to touch him. His body was twisted almost all the way over. Arrows drawn out from his chest would have struck the floor between us, piercing the scruffy carpet. Yet his head faced straight up. More arrows shooting out of his eyes would have dented the ceiling. Walter Cronkite said, "November 6th, 1968." I received my draft notice three weeks later, the day before Thanksgiving.

"She does? Can she give me strength? Through sex?"

"Nicholas. We've got to cross the street now. Slow down. Don't pull me like that. Look out. There's cars coming, turning left."

"I'm stronger than you are, because you can't escape. But I didn't even have sex."

"Oh, my God."

"It would be good for me to have sex, I think."

"Nicholas! That fucking RV almost squashed my toes. Snap out of it, would you?"

" . . . looks like you've got a wild one there . . ."

"You children should get out of the street before you get hurt . . ."

" . . . did you see the rack on that gal?"

"Shit. You'd still have to answer to that gorilla she's got wringing her neck."

A fly flitted across my father's forehead, then stopped. It seemed like nothing more than a black mole above his eyebrow. After grinding its hands together, the fly danced down along my father's nose, poked its head up inside a nostril, backed out, then disappeared. I tried to follow the fly but lost it the instant of takeoff. My head tingled. It felt like the fly was walking across my skull, stepping on hairs with its suction feet.

My father lay next to me, and my neck itched. I scratched all the way around because I imagined more flies were spearing their dirty feet deep into the pores of my skin, plugging them up like they were switchboard holes.

Then the backs of my legs prickled. My father lay still. I pictured thousands of golden fly asses vibrating from my ankles to my neck in a solid sheath, in the same thick golden pattern I saw once shaped tight around fresh dogshit turds in the front lawn on a hot summer day.

I fought not to scratch too hard, afraid of disturbing my resting father. I fought to remain just as still.

"Come on, Nicholas. Walk steady. We're almost home."

"So, where's the booze, Nick Barleycorn? Where's the relish for all that's left of this hotdog day?"

"I didn't . . . couldn't get it."

LaWanda convulsed, winking at Argo. I tightened my fingers into the strip of muscle atop her narrow shoulder. She grew motionless as I squeezed harder. Argo stared at her curiously, as if reading messages tattooed in tiny letters across her eyes.

"Oh, yes, I see, said the blind man. I . . . I suppose I can do without, for the time being. If that's okay with you, Mr. Nick. I wouldn't want to interfere with your . . . plans. Understood?"

"It was my fault, and I'm sorry."

"Yes, if you say so. Why don't you sit down, then, and tell me about it. I mean, if you want to. Only if you want to."

"It just happened."

"As do many things, Big Nick. Which I'm certain you already are aware of. These things. That happen, I mean."

"*Some* things."

"And I daresay you've got quite a grip on things at the moment. Am I correct? Have you these things well in hand, Sir Nicholas? We, your loyal subjects, are prepared to serve you, m'lord."

I concentrated on Argo's moving mouth, sighting between his feet veed on the edge of the clear glass coffee table.

He scrunched low against his purple couch, neck jammed into the slot between two plump cushions. Fat upholstery buttons formed a square pattern on either side of his head—evidence of a marksman's careful target practice; shadows silhouetting the buttons converting them into empty holes.

The living room was as dark as it could be on a sunny day, with the drapes swung closed and the lights shut off. Argo's mouth remained in shadow, too, furry around the edges, his teeth lost behind a bar of shade.

"Why are you staring at LaWanda like that?"

"No need to fling such invective, Nick. Just admiring her teasing smile, the sparkle in her eye. You can't begrudge a man that, can you? No? Well, I'm sorry. Even though this is my home, I suppose, considering the circumstances, it's *your* castle. Until we get this thing cleared up."

"What thing?"

"*The* thing, Nick."

"James Arness starred in *The Thing* in 1951. The original."

"Yes, I'm sure he did, Mr. Channel Changer. But that was a long time ago, O cinematic one."

"I saw it on Channel 5 last month."

"Yes, yes, Nick. The next day you were over here beseeching me to watch the skies, watch the skies. You remember that, don't you, Wanda? Hmmm? Don't be afraid, my dear. Everything's fine. Harmless and . . . excuse me . . . fine."

"No. The Thing was an alien from another planet, and he desired to conquer the earth."

"Quite right. Conquer the earth!"

"And the scientist argued with the soldiers. They were determined to kill The Thing, but the scientist wanted to save it and communicate with it. He said in that movie, 'No pain . . . no emotions . . . no heart. How superior!'"

"Bravo, Nick-Olivier. Bravo. Now. Wanda, why don't you march into the kitchen and fetch us guys something hearty to drink."

"She can't, Argo. You don't *have* anything to drink. That's what I'm trying to tell you. I'm sorry. We went to Esmeralda's and I couldn't do it."

"Yes, that's an honorable confession, lad. But I'd like to hear LaWanda's version, if you don't mind. So just ease your hand away from her mouth and allow her to speak. All in the name of fair play, Nick. You follow me, don't you? Equal rights, and all that?"

"She tried to trick me, Argo. You have to know that, too. She had it in her mind to take me the wrong way, to the hospital."

"Yes, I see."

"That scientist in the movie begged The Thing, and he said he was just trying to help. He was just like the doctors at the VA. But The Thing smacked him in the face and knocked him straight into the permafrost. LaWanda was dragging me to the *doctors* again."

"But you hurt your hand terribly. She just wanted to have someone treat it. That's all, I'm sure."

"She tried to take me to the hospital. But she doesn't know that I don't have to go there anymore, Argo. I was discharged. Officially."

"This we know, son. And LaWanda wasn't trying to trick you. She was just trying to help."

"That's the same thing the scientist said at the Pole."

"In a movie, Nick. In a movie. There's a big difference."

"You don't know what you're talking about."

"Trust me, Nick. I really don't care about the booze. Let's just forget everything and try to have some fun for a change. I'll stumble into the kitchen and whip us up a snack and put on some records. We'll have a party, just the three of us. How does that sound? You could use a little loosening up."

"No."

"Sure, Nick. Whatever you say. Hey. Look at your hand. It's starting to bleed again. Come on, big guy. You know it's not polite to bleed on a lady."

"Movies are just as true as we are."

"Certainly. But movies never hurt anyone, either. And you're hurting Wanda. Let her go, Nick. Be a good guy like in the movies and let her go."

"Don't. Stay on the couch, Argo. I have to figure this out first. Something's not right."

When The Thing's hand was bitten off by a husky, the scientists analyzed the hand and discovered it was constructed from vegetable matter. The army captain, Hendry, was furious, and he wanted to know how they were supposed to kill The Thing if he was nothing more than a walking vegetable. There was only one girl in that movie, and she shouted at Captain Hendry, "Boil it, bake it, fry it." Her name was Nikki, and on long frozen nights she drank Captain Hendry under the table in the Quonset hut.

Argo was too drunk to understand, or even to get up off his couch. One of his sock-covered feet slipped off the edge of the coffee table; his heel slammed into the floor. Argo replaced his foot onto the table by hand, and it took him three tries.

Earlier, on the way down Argo's hallway, LaWanda bit my hand, the same hand I slashed open in her kitchen. She wouldn't bite me again.

Miki never bit me. She did everything she could to please me—touching me, smiling at me, feeding me. Once she pre-

*pared me an elaborate fish dinner. I helped her clean the fish,
and she giggled when I couldn't cut off the fish's head. As hard
as I tried, I couldn't saw through the spine. I pressed down as
hard as I could and drove the knife back and forth. With each
push of my arm, the fish head flopped against the edge of the
cutting board. The head wobbled faster; the knife blade was a
blur. I squeezed the slippery fish body tightly, but it threatened
to squirt free of my hand, as if the fish were coming back to life.
Still giggling, Miki reached up as high as she could and gently
rubbed my shoulders. Her hands were warm and smooth, and I
wanted her to stroke the bare skin underneath the rough fabric
of my fatigues. As I imagined her caressing me, the knife
became still. I breathed in slowly and closed my eyes. The fish
head slapped down onto the cement floor.*

"What motion picture are you viewing now, Walt Dis-
Nick? A sweeping epic of love and adventure? Or just a
throwaway teenage comedy? Or both? Any monsters in this
one, Nickenstein? How about your old pal Godzilla? Is he still
tromping around in your dimbulb wide-screen rumpus room?
How do you fit all this stuff inside that dollhouse closet of a
mind of yours, anyway? I didn't think such a freeze-dried
kernelmind could hold so much. What have you got sprouting
in there *now*, composthead? What scrawny twisted growth is
going to come creeping out your cranial bungholes next? You
think we enjoy suffering through your manic hopscotchisms?
Hell, Old Nick. I used to think you were a genius, a regular
Kaspar Hauser. Why do you think I continued allowing you to
come around here all the time? Material, Nick. You were my
material. The stuff meal tickets are printed on, you big lug.
You think you're pretty clever, sneaking into the lab and
reading my shit, don't you? Well, I could care less. You never
saw the stuff that mattered. The script, Nickuloid. The script.
I've just been feeding off you, writing a screenplay. I was going

to make myself a bundle. At *your* expense. Just sucking your blood all this time. Draining you dry. Using you, Nickknot. Plain and simple. You understand now? Can you figure *this* one out? You're a stupid shit, Nicholas. Do you read me? A stupid fucking shit-for-brains slab of psychosis dreck. Hey! Are you just going to stand there, in all your basket-case glory, or are you ever going to *do* something? Look at you. Pinching a woman's head off because she tried to help you. Well, *I'm* done trying to help you, Schitzolas. And if you don't release Wanda by the time I count three, you'll be pulling five-point-six-five-millimeter hollowpoints out of that hall of broken mirrors you try to pass off as a brain. *Comprendes, compadre?* Three strikes and you're out. Does that ring a cracked bell, Mr. Minorleagues? And how'd you make it through Nam without getting zapped, you hyper-lucky fuckhead? Just let me count three, Private. One-two-three and no more beat the reaper. You'll be a dead man, Nickorpse. You'll finally be able to play the movie role you've been practicing for all these years: *Maggotfodder,* starring Nicholas Ames as The Cadaver. The chilling tale of a professional jerkoff artist lying prone with a head full of lead. The *New York Times* calls it 'literally breathtaking.' Get ready now, Nickwit. One . . . two . . ."

"Stop."

"Two and a half . . ."

"Get out of there!"

"Two and three quarters . . ."

"No, Argo."

"Two and three quarters and four dimes . . ."

"Get away from your guns!"

" . . . and five Nick-Nick-nickles!"

"Argo!"

"All right, Bozo. Let her go!"

I hugged LaWanda close to my chest as a shield. Along

through the part in her hair I sighted on Argo. He held the AR-15 straight out from his right eye; the muzzle vibrated in small unsteady circles. Argo's other eye twitched open and closed.

"You hear that familiar sound? Lock and load, mother-fucker. Turn loose your meathooks and leave that woman be. There's a full clip in here waiting to galvanize the back of your head into next week."

"Okay."

"Damn veterans like you think we owe you something special. Shit. Look at you standing there. Mr. Combat Experience. They got monuments stuck up for you, and movies based on your alleged heroics, and half the country's feeling guilty because you're all supposed to be suffering some time-bomb syndrome effect and will never be able to enjoy the wonderful feeling of being an integral part of American society like the rest of us red-white-and-blue homebodies. Well, take a number, and hurry and wait with the rest of us, Nickson. We're *all* fucked up, whether we know it or not."

"Argo. I can't take any more of this."

"Shut up, bitch. Get out of the line of fire. That's better. And don't you be getting any ideas, Nick. Just back off. One more step back. Until you're up against the wall. Right. Now, hands on head. Do it! Put your fucking hands on that bag-of-cement head of yours."

Argo poked the rifle in and out. I refused to move. Then Argo swooped the rifle up close to my face; the gun oil smelled greasy and evil.

"How does it feel, GI? You poor sorry gastrointestinal war-torn orphan. The world weeps for you daily. You wish. And what do the rest of us get? The ones who fought *here?* That's right, Nicky. Right here, we were fighting to get your ass back home. Out in the streets, that's where I was. On the TV.

On the covers of the magazines. To blame for the venom in the president's speeches. No monuments erected for *us* in Washington, D.C. No mobs of friends and families trekking across the fruited plains to kiss the names of *my* fallen comrades. No. And in the meantime, I've got to sit around while a nation tries to change memories of humiliation and guilt into honorable recollections. You're a hero, Nicky Murphy. Do you realize that? A fucking hero baptized by fire and aged in the Vietnamese sun. Just put on your hero badge and all doors will open for you. Which you'll never be able to figure out. Because you were just as fucked up before you went overseas as you were when you got back. Stop looking at me like a damn walleye beached in the desert. Get with the program. Hear ye, hear ye. You are an American. And it was Americans that started that damn war in Vietnam. Americans that lived and breathed good American air for years before you were granted the privilege of breathing it yourself. And once you slipped out of your mother's hole and took your first breath, you tasted that sickness, too. Rally 'round the umbilical cord, gang. We got another one for the crusades. You didn't see anything in Vietnam that the rest of us didn't live with back here. You just had the good fortune to be sent where the sickness was the worst. The cancer was here all the time. You just brought some of it with you over there in your field pack, spread it around, and watched it grow. For that, you are now being praised. More sickness. The brass bands were late, but they're all playing your tune. That good old thanks-for-fighting-our-war-it's-been-good-to-know-you tune. A catchy little melody, wouldn't you say, Nicktoven? Hey! Answer me! Face the music, buddy boy. Do you like it, or don't you? Spit it out!"

"I don't hear anything."

"Leave him alone, Argo. Leave *us* alone, for God's sake."

"Look who's talking. The Queen of the Black Arts. What

did *you* ever do that made any sense? When did *you* ever put yourself on the line? Even Nick must have thought, in some fetid recess of sensibility, that he was doing the *right* thing as a GI. I wish I could say the same about you."

"What gives you the right—"

"It's my apartment, and it's my gun."

"That doesn't mean shit."

"You're right. It means anything *but* shit. I got the power, babe. Isn't that what it comes down to in the end? Power here and power there, shifting in a fucked-up grid of give-and-take, of promises and lies, of expectations and the glistening knife-edge of betrayal? Dig it, babe. Just like I was reading it out of a book. Which gives it power. Authority. Just the way I say it. Power even in words. And when you got it, sweetheart, you flaunt it. Want to run my gauntlet? Step right up. There's a sucker drooling and supplicating every minute, with lip aquiver, choking on sour candy with cheeks caved in—a great American tradition. You're in good company. Just stand in line and keep taking your medicine four times daily. Doctor's orders. Yours is but to gaze on high, and praise the Lord. Glory be. Right 'round the corner, sweet glory. Sugar and spice and everything redemptive, with a greasy bag of French-fried puppydog tails for every millionth customer, yes sir. Let me hear you say, 'Yeaaahhhh!'"

"Argo, I'm sick and tired of you! And Nicholas, you're just a crazy little punk. You two are bad news and I should call the police, have you arrested for kidnapping and drunkenness, just clear you off the face of the earth, you're ill. Both of you!"

"Look who's talking—the pot calling the kettle black," Argo said.

"You guys are no better than my husband, and I hope you end up the same way. Or worse!"

"Ah, yes, dear demented one. But he was trying to prove something. Perhaps you've forgotten, your dear departed hubby gave his life for what he believed in. Nothing more glorious than that. So you bestow great honors by including us in Vincent's ghostly company."

"Argo, just shut up. Vincent died. Plain and simple, he died. So shut your mouth. He was no hero. It takes more guts to stay *alive* these days, if you ask me. Even if you didn't, faggot."

"Yes, thanks for the ultimate insult. Going for the jugular, the deepest fear of all men, amen. But we can handle it, right, Nick? Did you hear what the little lady just suggested? Sure, we don't have the dynamic staying power or the potency of a behemoth like Stevie Esmeralda. But we do the best we can, apparently content to play with one another's soupy noodle. Yes, Nick, you might be a homo, I suppose—

homogenized and homiletic and ho-ho-ho-phobic. But not heroic."

"Argo, you're not fair. Just shut the fuck *up!*" LaWanda said.

"You're no hero, Nick. But you're still alive. You released the damsel. And now *you're* distressed. Yet never fear. Never. Little did you both know, the gun wasn't loaded. Just loaded for bear, with words. And you couldn't bear it a moment longer. To my delight. How happy—"

"Nicholas, I don't care what your friend says, I don't care what my husband did, I don't care what you saw on television last week—I just care about the truth, and the truth is this: I've had it. I was just trying to help you. It's that simple. And what do I get for it? Do I see any appreciation here? No, just bullshit, and it's making me insane!"

"—how gay."

"Shut up, Argo!"

"You were trying to help him *what?*" Argo said.

"You were the one who said you were using him for an experiment. At least I don't try to use him."

"Use him, schmuse him—"

"But in the liquor store you tried to play a trick on Argo. You and Stevie were planning something—"

"Shut up, Nicholas—" LaWanda said.

"What's this? Revealed deception augurs poorly. How can we maintain our gaiety, our homeostasis, in the face of such treachery?"

"Stop it! I just want to be his friend. He needs *somebody.*"

"How touching. Friends to the end. In the end."

"You're drunk, Argo. Ugly drunk. Maybe I should take *you* in, instead of Nicholas."

"Maybe so . . . maybe so . . ."

"I have to leave. I should just leave," LaWanda said.

"Be my guest."

"Make me."

"I beg your pardon."

"I have to get *out* of here," LaWanda said.

"Nick, be a good sport and show her the door."

"You can't just kick me out. Nicholas, sit down. You scare me standing there in the corner."

"Woman, you're loonier than he'll ever be."

"I've got to get to work."

"Then *go!* For heaven's sake, get on your way. Please."

"Argo, it's really time."

"I don't follow you. If it weren't for the pleading look in your undernourished eyes, I'd boot you out myself. What is it?"

"Time to talk."

"What? Speak up!"

"Talk! We have to talk about this, get it out in the open."

"Listen to the woman, Nick. What is she saying? She sounds so practical all of a sudden. But I don't comprehend this 'it' she continually refers to. Is 'it' my sexual proclivities? Or is 'it' you? What do you think, Nick-rotes?"

"For once, Argo. Please."

"Oh, yes, why not? Let's raise a little consciousness. That's how you ladies do it, is it not?"

"Whatever you say, Argo. But it couldn't hurt. Assuming you've got any fucking consciousness left to raise."

"*Touché*. Now I'll play. Good show. Good job. Blowjob. Blow the man down."

"You're babbling."

"Mommy, do we really have to raise consciousness now? Me and Nicky-Wicky wanna go out and play."

"Playtime's over, Argo."

"Oh, another hit, a palpable hit indeed, Nick-let. Using one of my own favorite lines on this old favorite himself. Two against one, I can't argue with those odds, you odd fellows you."

"Good, that's more like it, Nicholas. Sit back. That makes me feel better. Relax."

"Sometimes Argo relaxes so much he falls out of his recliner."

"Yes, yes, that must be something."

"Jesus."

"But for the time being, let's not worry about who's falling where. Today was too heavy for me, and I don't know what else to do."

"Oh, I'm blitzed, Nicky's neurons are out of whack, and you're transforming into Oprah Winfrey right before my sodden eyes."

"Don't make me lose my patience, Argo."

"Patients? What do you mean, losing patients? Here we are, Doc. Who's on first? Let the games begin."

"You're a real asshole, you know that?"

"Yes, I do know that. Next question."

"What are you afraid of, Argo?"

"Sometimes he's afraid of his editor."

"Yes, how true. And I'm afraid of the dark, too."

"So am I."

"Oh, yeah? Who's your editor, Nickingway? Maxwell Perkins? Maxwell Smart? Maxwell's Silver Hammer? Ummm, good to the last dotted *i* and crossed *t*."

"Argo, this is your last warning. Get serious or we'll never get anywhere."

"Can I write that one down? I can see Eddie Elvesizer now, captured by un-heretofore-contacted African tribesmen about to turn loose their pubescent sons on the occasion of annual rites-of-passage shenanigans. Foreskin lies in heaps near the council fires. With bleeding cockbuds, the terrified boys are driven out into the veldt. Eddie is forced to join them. His shredded multicolored silk parachute drags behind him in the dust. His weapons are useless, having shattered upon impact. As he struggles to join the fleeing boys, prodded by a wall of spearpoints, the chief—the wizened old man astraddle a throne of antelope hides, his face smeared with greasy white paint—cries out: 'Get serious or we'll never get anywhere!' "

"What book was *that* in?"

"That was your last chance, Argo. I'm as serious as a heart attack now."

"Okay, okay, I'll play the game. God, I wish I had a drink. But I'll play. I know when I'm beat."

"I wish you wouldn't look at it like that, Argo. You haven't been beaten. You haven't lost. Don't you see what we're trying to do, in spite of ourselves? It's these secrets. They're killing us. It's time to talk."

"I remember that time your husband died. As clear as a movie I remember it."

"Yes, Nicholas. I know. Why don't we open those curtains? It's too dreary in here."

"Dreary? Look who's talking dreary. You're the one who burns black candles and summons succubi."

"Is that what you think I'm all about? We really *do* need to talk. There's more than one of us here with misfiring neurons, or whatever it was you said."

"Maybe three."

"That's a start, Argo. If we could all appreciate that, we'd be able to get somewhere. Do you know what he means by that, Nicholas? Or at least, what I *hope* he means? You *were* trying to be sincere, weren't you?"

"Yes."

"No."

"Why does everything have to be so crazy?"

"What do you mean, LaWanda?"

"I second that emotion. Why are you all of a sudden so needful of illumination? What's in it for you, anyway? You could have been gone long ago, leaving us two silly boys here to dork our dolphins."

"Because we've gone too far, that's why. I can see that. You can see that. What else can we do, living like this? Who else is going to help us if we don't help ourselves? We've been hurting so badly, fooling ourselves."

"How?"

"Part of it has to do with you, Nicholas. I mean, ever since we've known each other, well, we've known about your problem. And—"

"Argo said I only have one problem, and all I need is . . . some . . . pussy."

"Yes, that doesn't surprise me. But, Nicholas, remember the first day we met? Down at the beach? Remember when Vincent pulled you out of the surf?"

"I can't forget that. He saved my life."

"You had no business being out there. You couldn't even swim."

"I know. But the water was so beautiful. I just wanted to be part of it."

"I never heard *this* one before."

"Quiet."

"Sorry. Go on, Nick."

"There's a story behind it."

"Then tell it, Nick. Tell it."

"Well, the day they cut me from the team in Walla Walla, I went alone straight to the bus depot. Downtown I bought a paper and looked for Ernie Lazaro's name in the box scores. He was a friend of mine who got sent to another team. It said he went one-for-three against the Padres with an RBI and a sacrifice. I was happy for him because the Astros were the best team for Ernie. His personality was like an asteroid."

"Wait a minute, Nick. Let me write that one down, too."

"Argo!"

"Anyway, I slept on the bus most of the way back to San Diego. It was a long, long trip. The only stuff I took with me were my glove and bat and a few clothes. I gave the rest of my stuff away, even my cleats—they were too big for anybody on the team, but they wanted to keep them for a souvenir."

"Touching—"

"Then what happened, Nicholas?"

"At the Greyhound depot in San Diego, I stored everything in a locker. Mine was next to a marine who was trying to cram a duffel bag into his locker. The big green bag wouldn't fit, and I laughed to myself, because that's how I felt. I didn't have a place to stay or anything."

"Oh, I wish I had a violin—"

"Then, from the depot downtown I just started walking. If I couldn't play baseball I really couldn't do anything else. I strolled all the way down Broadway until I reached the wharf, and there I almost bought a ticket on the harbor excursion boat. But when I thought about having to listen to the captain tell me stories and historical jokes over a loudspeaker while I sat on a wooden bench on the foredeck shooing away sea gulls, it reminded me too much of having to sit through Coach Mulhauser's lectures on signs."

" . . . and secret handshakes and such—"

"What's a sign, Nicholas?"

"When the coach shuffled his right foot with his hands in both back pockets, that meant to steal. I think. So I just kept walking, past the tuna fleet with their nets dotted with orange floats spilling out onto the sidewalk, past the airport, the navy training center, and over the Narragansett Street hill until I reached the main lifeguard tower in Ocean Beach. Behind me, everything I owned was crammed into a metal box in the worst part of downtown. And in front of me, the ocean was bluer than the sky."

"But why did you do it, Nicholas?"

"I just wanted to go swimming, that's all."

"Famous last words."

"Hush. But why'd you go in with your clothes on, Nicholas?"

"He *what*?"

"Let him tell it."

"I didn't own any swim trunks."

"Likely story."

"More likely than all your Elvesizer junk."

"Hey, whose soul are we trying to cleanse here? Let the boy speak."

"All right. But you're next."

"What do you mean, next?"

"Then what happened, Nicholas?"

"You know. You were there. Why do I have to tell it again? It doesn't make any sense."

"Yes, it does, Nicholas. Everything makes sense, one way or another. It just depends how you look at it."

"What about us sitting here, jacking our jaws like a bunch of touchy-feely freakniks in a hot tub steaming with epsom salts and spilled cocaine? What kind of sense is this?"

"Does it make sense to be so afraid, Argo? Does it?"

"I wasn't *afraid* to go into that water. I wasn't even afraid before Vincent . . ."

"Before Vincent *what*, Captain Nicko?"

"Easy."

"Easy, schmeezy. If you're going to tell a story, tell it."

"Careful."

"I just wasn't afraid. Everything was all connected together. You know? The people in the waves were playing, and the sun was shredded yellow across the ocean all the way past the pier. There's a pulse in the ocean, too. It was pumping through me, easily. The waves busted shut and swooshed onto the shore. White broken water rushed out again, sucked back into new waves curling green. I was in the middle of all that. And I just had a tinier pulse, that's all. But it was the same pulse. And I wanted to get closer to it, to submerge in it. That's all."

" . . . which reminds me of a song."

"I wish you'd stop that. Right when we're starting to get somewhere, you spit out something dumb."

"What's wrong with that? Here, the boy's getting lyrical, and I say it reminds me of a song. Isn't that somehow appropriate? Isn't it?"

"It's the way you say it."

"Oh? And what's wrong with that? What don't you like about it? Just because things don't go the way you want them to doesn't mean they're fucked up. Be like Nick. Step into the middle of things, and let them wash around you. I think that's pretty good, myself. That's all."

"You really do?"

"I just lost track of things. I heard something and could hardly understand it, so I went where the voice was. I was just reading the signs."

"This is more your terrain, Wanda."

"It's where we *all* are, in case you'd like to know. I don't see why it's so difficult for you to follow that."

"Forgive me, Mother, for I have sinned. For I have failed to see. Fo' Ah be blind as dee day hab dee night."

"Don't push it."

"And why, Nick Spitz, did you have to jump—literally jump—into the fucking ocean?"

"Ar-go . . ."

"Ex-cuse me. Why, perchance, did you find it so compelling, so perfectly perfect, to choose that moment in which to immerse yourself—"

"Ar-go . . ."

"—immerse yourself in the brine, in the amniotic effervescence of the Ocean Beach tidal consonance?"

"Right when I thought we were beginning to make some progress—"

"Why, Nick? Why?"

"He didn't just jump in. It was different than that. I watched him. You couldn't help but notice. I mean—"

"You don't have to perjure yourself."

"He just had this look in his eyes, that's all. I noticed his eyes more than anything else. If that's all right with you."

"Sure."

"I was talking to Mr. Argo over there."

"Oh. Do I detect a note of disdain in your formerly concordant voice?"

"A person can only take so much, Argo. It's just the way you say things sometimes."

"He's just afraid. Like you said before."

"Herr Doktor Nickmann! Such cogent analysis. Will you take me on as a patient? Or is this hysterical woman more than enough for you now? Might we trade places? I'd prefer the recliner if I'm going to be coughing up dreams and such, for your appraisal. The entrails of my mind. Is divination one of

159

your specialties? Or will you refer me to the shaman-woman over there instead? You two should go into practice. I'm certain you could secure a license of some sort, hang out your shingles, your herpes zoster advertisements. They'd flock to you in droves; those in need are legion, are lesions. Seekers abound, another born every minute, craving the minutiae of inexplicability you could cleverly pawn off as the miraculous. No sweat, guys. Be here now, and then—rake in the shekels. Dig?"

"Why do you insist on destroying this?"

"Nick? Where are you going? Was it something I said?"

" . . . something you didn't say."

"Shut up, bitch. Nick. Open your eyes! Don't leave us, old man."

"See what you've done."

"Gag me, witch."

CHAPTER FIFTEEN

A MAN JUST DIED

"Movie time again, Nick?"

LaWanda was working the night her husband killed himself. I was visiting Argo, helping him fix his dinner at home. Out on his patio, Argo instructed me to find the proper place to stand, to block the wind, while he fumbled with matches and lighter fluid and black charcoal briquettes. The wind sneaked in all around me, whistling through my legs from different directions to attack the hibachi grill. Argo tossed a handful of black matchsticks over the balcony; I watched them float down into the patio. Two cops ran past the laundry room and ducked into the stairwell. Argo squatted down close to the coals, and when he spotted the cops he grabbed hold of my pant leg and hoisted himself up. "Maybe Ed and Cindy finally did the deed," he said, dusting black charcoal from his trousers.

The cops ran up to the third floor, holding their hands close against their black leather holsters as they ascended the stairs. Argo pulled on my shirt, and I followed after him. The cops knocked on LaWanda's door. When he was close enough, Argo asked the cops if they needed some help. But since Argo wasn't the manager, the cops didn't talk. Argo turned nasty, and I held him back. I assumed if the cops smelled all that liquor fuming from Argo's mouth, they would lock him up for sure.

The only thing the cops shared with us was this: "There's been an accident." Argo demanded to know if LaWanda was all right. He told the cops he was a relative, even though this was a lie. Reluctantly, the cops told us that Vincent Hernandez had jumped in front of the Amtrak train near Del Mar. They needed someone to identify the body. The cop with blond hair said, softly, "What's left of it." Argo didn't hear that last remark, but I did—loud and clear.

I rode with Argo in his Jeep, and we followed the cops down to the Beaumont Station restaurant. It was refreshing because we drove so fast. Since we were with the police, in a two-car convoy, there was nothing they could do to us. We were safe. I held tight to the handle Argo had welded beneath his glovebox. When he hit a bump or screeched tightly around corners, I pretended we were swashbuckling out in the desert sliding around the sand dunes near El Centro.

Argo drove like a robot. He didn't say one word the entire trip, which dried up some of the excitement. "A man just died," he told me, yanking hard on the emergency brake when we halted in the restaurant parking lot. "Doesn't that mean anything to you?" At that moment, we traded places, and I became the robot until we met LaWanda inside.

Forcing the cops to wait, Argo announced he would give LaWanda the news. He had been drinking all afternoon and I was afraid the alcohol would cripple him, but he managed to talk with force, with purpose. Even so, he had to explain himself to the cops twice. The first time, the police radio crackled loudly and erased his words. A female dispatcher spoke—a crushing sound cut short her voice—and neither of the cops answered. "I'll break it to her," Argo said again. The blond cop nodded while staring at his fingernails. His badge was shinier than his eyes. Next to his shoulder rested a shotgun, mounted in the front seat pointing straight up through the roof.

Inside the restaurant I stood next to a hand-painted sign: "Please Wait for the Hostess to Seat You." When no one was looking, I snatched a silver mint from a bowl beside the cash register. Jerry Lewis's face was printed on cardboard next to the candies. He was blue, and red letters announced, "Give to Jerry's Kids." He hugged a boy who wore metal supports along the sides of his legs. The plastic bowl attached to the Jerry Lewis card held only nine cents—a nickel and four pennies.

The mint filled my mouth with coolness. I didn't chew steadily, just once in a while, so no one would know I was eating something stolen. That way, the coolness lasted longer. I tried to make it last as long as I could, taking smaller and smaller bites. When the mint was chopped down in size too small for me to chew, I sucked on it until it disappeared.

Searching for Argo, I stared over the top of the cash register into one of the dining rooms. He had told me he'd be right back. But he had vanished. I walked from one end of the waiting area to the other five times, in a hurry, stopping only when the squeaking of my shoes on the rug sounded louder than the clatter of hundreds of knives and forks on plates. My heart beat through me and ricocheted off the cash register. The front door creaked open. Out in the parking lot, the police radio crunched into silence. The door slapped shut. No one stepped inside the restaurant. The door just opened and closed on its own.

Inside the Beaumont Station, a black locomotive was painted on the swinging kitchen doors. When a waitress or busboy burst through those doors, the train split in two. Argo slammed through—the train broke in half again—LaWanda nestled under his arm. She hid half her face behind a thick linen napkin. Part of the bun of hair on the back of her head had exploded, and strands of long hair twisted through the ruffles on her white blouse.

They stepped toward me slowly, easing their way through the maze of tables—each time they passed a table, the diners stopped talking and eating to stare. As Argo and LaWanda approached the front door, the restaurant grew quieter. I didn't want to stare, like everyone else. Photographs of old trains cluttered the walls around me. I turned my head, but in the glass of the frames my reflection gazed back at me—in each frame another Nicholas, like a ghost hovering above boxcars, flatcars, tankers, cabooses.

Outside, in front of the restaurant at night, the white roof of the police car seemed too white. As the three of us stepped in front of the still-hot radiator, the police radio sputtered again. The cops inside looked like toy men—like they had been purchased from the mall down the street and plugged into the car battery. Their tan uniforms fit them perfectly, so clean and pressed, creases knifing straight down each side of their chests.

One cop had blond hair, the other brown. That was the only difference between them—trapped inside their car, staring through us, trying to talk. The radio was their incomprehensible voice of crackling and crunching and code words.

I didn't like those cops, and I wished they were gone, instantly invisible. I wanted to jump into the Jeep and bushwhack through the tules down the riverbed behind the restaurant, past the condominium network and the golf course and the gravel plant, to reappear on the other side of the valley— coming home from a perilous safari. We didn't need those cops. But they wouldn't disappear, no matter how many thoughtspears I heaved against the slimy window of their car— windows that reflected LaWanda and me in twisting tangled shapes as we climbed back into Argo's Jeep.

Argo ground the gears shifting into reverse, drowning out LaWanda's sniffling. I hid in the back, hanging on to the cold metal roll bar.

The Beaumont Station boxcar looked like it had crashed gently into the rest of the building built around it—crashed without breaking anything. The syrupy red boxcar had the name of the restaurant standing on top, the letters slanted suggesting speed. Clouds of curly black smoke trailed out from the Ts—cutout clouds gleaming black.

As we rolled through the parking lot, with the cops leading the way, I studied the smoke clouds; they remained solid and flat, turning almost invisible as we rumbled into the street— from the side, sharp cloud edges and nothing more.

Argo missed second gear and slowed down to double-clutch. When the gears meshed, he turned to LaWanda and attempted to say, "I'm sorry," with his eyes. She didn't see him; she looked the other way, wiping her nose with the napkin.

I wanted to drop a hand down and rest it on her shoulder, but I was afraid. They said Vincent, her husband, was dead; but we had only the policemen's words to go on. That's why we had to drive downtown to view the body.

The morgue was illuminated with too many lights; it reeked like a science classroom. Argo stumbled, pushing LaWanda closer to the examining table. A handicapped man in a white coat revealed Vincent's head beneath a green sheet. La-Wanda sucked air hard through her teeth. Red shreds of flesh and black knots of hair surrounded a mess of raw crimson pulp. Fluorescent lights sizzled above us. Vincent had saved my life. I could never forget; pulling me up onto the sand, he said over and over, "Now kiss the earth, kid. Kiss the fucking earth."

"So, Nick. You still there? Let me try and picture this. It's a sunny day. You're at the beach. You decide to go for a swim. You get a strange look in your eyes. You hear voices. You're hypnotized by the play of light on the rippling water. Right so far?"

"What?"

"Answer me, idiot."

"The beach? I was on the team, then I got cut. C-U-T, cut. Is that wrong or something?"

"What are you saying, lad? You were trying out for the swim team? Ouch! You didn't have to do that, strumpet."

"Try to see between the lines, Argo."

"What lines? That's the whole problem. This boy don't *have* no lines. He's a walking comic strip without word balloons—without edges to the pages, even."

"So what does that make you?"

"It makes me smart enough to know you've got to have those lines. Otherwise you've got nothing but madness. Isn't that what we're discussing here? Isn't it?"

"No."

"You don't think he's—"

"No—"

"Come on, Wanda. I mean, look, Nicky. We're friends. Right? We've been through a lot together. Correct? Blink. Nod. *Do* something. There. That's better. Since we're friends—since you agree we're friends—and I agree with you on that—I think we've earned the right to say certain things. We can take a few chances. You follow? No? Well, let me try and explain it this way. If a friend saw another friend in trouble, shouldn't that first friend try to help? If he didn't help, he wouldn't be a friend. Right?"

"But Vincent helped me, and he wasn't my friend until we got out of the ocean."

"Yes. Yes. So you're right. But we're not talking about Vincent here, Nick. We're talking about *you*. About Nicholas Ames—bon vivant, raconteur, boy for all seasons, man with no reasons. None other than. Your carcass is on the table, son. Baby, it's you."

"So."

"So? You're a trip, Nick. An absolute trip. Take me for a ride on your magic swirling ship, Mr. Tambourine-for-Brains."

"If you could just speak your mind, maybe he'd understand. Did you ever think of that?"

"Understand *what*?"

"Don't make fun of him. Stop looking like that. He's sitting right there, Argo. Jesus, you're so immature."

"Hey, that's rich. I haven't heard that one for ages, since my mother slapped me—for making fart noises with my hand in my armpit at the dinner table."

"So that explains those weird noises and the funny way you walk. Take your hand out of there and tell Nicholas what's on your mind. You're the writer in the family. Use your words, Argo."

"Look. We're not getting anywhere with this stuff. It's cutting into my drinking time, anyway. Wanda? You understand what I mean? Does anybody understand what I mean?"

"No."

"Nick the Merman jumped into the slime-dark sea. Vincent, the trusty stud, ran to his rescue, grabbed the hulking lad

167

firmly about the head and shoulders, pulled him free—yea, free—from the anthropomorphic clutches of the thrashing surf. And a myth was born."

"Shut the fuck up, Argo."

"Easy now, Nicholas. Easy. We should be going. I'm getting a massive headache . . . all this crazy stuff. Nicholas?"

"But it was different. Vincent saved my life. A wave broke over his head and he disappeared, but he still held on to me with both arms. I couldn't breathe easily. White water fizzed all around us. But he rescued me—which is more than you ever did for me."

"So what the fuck do you want from me, you primordial pygmy?"

"Argo! Let's just quit it, all right? You didn't want to play, you never wanted to play, so let's just quit it."

"I could smash your face. I could give you a face like Vincent's."

"Yes, certainly. Ah, playtime's over, kiddies. Wouldn't it be loverly if you two could be, yes, running along now? Old Ogre Argo has to get on with living his life. Take pity on an old sot, please."

"You're a dead man, Argo."

"Wanda, come on! Get him *out* of here!"

"Why? This is getting good."

"Please, lady. Do something."

"Forget it. You just run and hide, little man. You anonymous little man, who won't even put his real name on the books he writes. Pick up your toy gun and hide. Ha!"

"It's too late to run now."

"Leave me alone. Is that too much to ask? A little privacy. That's all I want. Not much. Just a little. Respect my desires, and I shall grant you peace and good wishes forever and ever."

"What do you think, Nicholas?"

It was impossible to climb out of the reclining chair. Something was caught on the bars and springs inside. I pressed down with my legs, straining to push through whatever it was, kicking the footrest. The muscles in my legs quivered. My heels dug into the Naugahyde upholstery. Something broke. A spring twanged, vibrating and echoing inside the hollow tomb of the chair. The reverberations trembled up through the seat of my pants, irritating me.

"Damn, boy. You gone and broked mah chair. Why'd y'all have to do that to mah po' chair? Ain't there nothin' subtle 'bout you, boy? Eh?"

"It was already broken. Here, let me help you, Nicholas. Get on your feet and let Mr. Argo take a look at you."

"Take him out of here, bitch. I mean it."

The footrest snapped back into place, crookedly. I arose from the chair and found LaWanda's hand waiting.

"You're a sick man, Argo. There's no hope for you. No bloody hope at all."

"Kiss my ass. The two of you, just kiss my ass."

"You hear that, Nicholas? Nicholas!"

Argo's face froze. I smashed him into the shadows. He tumbled over the couch and skidded onto the kitchen floor, grunting.

"Ooo, Nicholas. You . . . do you think he's all right?"

"I'm leaving."

"Wait. Not yet. Here, let me look at that hand. My God, Nicholas, you ripped it open again."

"I don't care. I've got to get going now. I've got to get ready for tonight."

"No, Nicholas. You can't. Not yet. Please, let me help you. Please."

CHAPTER SEVENTEEN

A HOLE IN THE SHAPE OF MY FATHER'S HAND

My father was thirty-six years old when I was born. I didn't have any brothers or sisters. My father did not keep a picture of my mother around the house. Once when I was sick and had to stay home from school in the fourth grade, I sneaked into his bedroom and searched everywhere for her photograph.

Each drawer in my father's clothes closet was in perfect order—socks in one small top drawer, boxer shorts in the other, all neatly folded and stacked in piles. After I dug through them, the piles were left crooked; I couldn't rearrange them as neatly as I found them, no matter how hard I tried.

As I left his room, I felt I had done something dirty. Slipping back beneath my comforter on the couch, I sneezed worse than I had all day. I used up more than half a box of tissues before my father came home from work. By that time my nose was peeling and raw. Flakes of skin roughed against my fingers when I sneezed into my hands.

My father opened the door down the hall and closed it softly behind him. I listened closely to his steps approaching me, his steps clicking on the linoleum then muffled by throw rugs, then clicking again until he stopped in back of the couch. He said nothing. He lowered his hand and rested it against my forehead. His skin was cool, like the thought of snow.

Taking back his hand, my father stepped quietly down the

hall and into the bathroom. I had a cold, but I didn't feel cold. The spot on my forehead where my father had set his hand felt open and empty; a hole in the shape of my father's hand melted through my skull all the way to the pillow.

My father had a heart attack.

Vincent Hernandez galloped down the railroad tracks at night into an oncoming Amtrak locomotive.

Sergeant Ascencion died from wounds inflicted by splinters of American artillery shells.

Miki was eating a nice lunch when a homemade bomb exploded in a Saigon restaurant.

Billy Reid got shot up.

The pope was shot and wounded.

I don't know if I'll die or not. I feel caught up in a humming wave pattern most of the time. I don't know whether I'll die or if my waves will simply hum at a different frequency. Waves of the ocean, waves of death, waves of pain.

I was beaned once by Doug Zoffel in high school. The curveball he tossed swooped wide. I didn't think it would break so quickly, just at the final second. The moment before the ball slammed into my temple, it appeared to be gigantic. I could see the seams, frozen in flight, the stitches crisscrossing neatly around the white leather sphere. When I was struck, it felt like the entire baseball field had tilted and flipped over, crashing straight down on top of me.

Death will come just the opposite. I'll hear a vacant noise or feel a strange breeze or see a quick shadow slide across the floor and vanish into the corner behind me. I'll turn to look. Then I'll be dead.

I closed Argo's door behind us. I imagined more doors and gates and fences clicking shut behind Argo, one after another, as he rushed through an endless hallway screaming.

"He wasn't moving, Nicholas. Maybe . . . oh, God, you were great."

"He deserved it."

"Yes, I'm glad you could see that. But what about you, Nicholas? You deserve something . . . much better than . . . look at your hand. Here, come with me. Hurry."

LaWanda pulled me along, her hand encircling mine. I still felt a biting sting, left over from the impact with Argo's cheekbone. Blood seeped across her fingers, across her white wrist. A frantic energy vibrated between us, increasing the force of my heartbeats.

In front of apartment 37, LaWanda dug into her pocket for the key, smearing blood on her jeans, on the doorknob, on my tattered bandage.

"Get in here."

Her living room possessed more light than Argo's, but the air was thick with the smell of ripe garbage. The refrigerator was open, the shelves snapped in half; beer cans and a shattered mustard jar lay on the floor, vibrating from the hum of the overworked motor.

"Don't go in there, Nicholas. Ah, when Harold left, he was a little angry, that's all. The jerk."

LaWanda's voice slipped underneath my skin and erupted into my blood with the gnawing nagging force of fleabites and toothache. I shuddered before her, a force without shape, a mangled screen of electrons and molecules and pulsating cells. I, myself, Nicholas, leaked out the hole in my hand; my energies escaped in currents of pain flowing from the stem of my prick; I was vanishing; I was expanding.

With a bundle of black candles in each hand, LaWanda passed before me, beckoning, out of focus, cloaked in cobwebs or mosquito netting or wisps of cloud.

"This way."

That voice—the edge intent on capturing me, entangling me in something secret. I flowed behind her, into the bedroom. LaWanda locked the door.

I wanted to demolish her dresser, shatter the mirror, rip loose the hanging lamps and burst them against the walls, gashing holes that would disgorge chalky sheetrock and two-by-fours and naked electrical wires. I wanted to tear the sheets and blankets off her bed, shred the fabric into particles of dust—hollering, bellowing, shrieking. I saw myself doing all these things—ruining the world around me, fighting to clear it away, hunting for something more authentic underneath the remains. But I could not move. I could only stand there, hovering before LaWanda, immobilized by the sound of her T-shirt slipping off her shoulders. Her breasts were larger than I imagined—full, white, capped with tawny nipples, delicious.

"You don't know what you did up there, do you, Nicholas?"

From the closet LaWanda extracted a box of brass candle holders. She placed them carefully around the bed, whispering an incantation over each one before inserting a fresh black candle.

"Light them for me. One match per candle."

A box of wooden matches ejected from her hand and flew across the room, bouncing off my chest. I caught the box, the box caught me. Kneeling, I began to work, scratching each match into life—inhaling bursts of bitter smoke as the white match heads fizzed orange; then I converted greasy wicks into yellow-and-blue crescents of hollow flame. Blood on the carpets, blood on the splintery ends of matches, blood spread against brass. I left a trail of dead black sticks behind me as I floated from candle to candle.

"Very good, Nicholas. Now watch me."

LaWanda stood at the foot of the bed swaying in the fluttering candlelight. Shadows swam across her face, her breasts, as she removed her jeans, revealing more luscious whiteness, nakedness, simplicity.

"Now you do the same, Nicholas."

"But—"

"Now!"

Kneeling by the bedroom door, I fought with the clasp of my belt; I couldn't flex the fingers on my sore hand. Struggling left streaks of red across my pocket and zipper.

"Such a brute. Upstairs. Now what's wrong with you?"

"This isn't—"

"Nicholas, you showed me something. That power. God, that's what Vincent wanted. That's what he craved. And you have so much. But you don't even know it's *there!*"

"Help me."

"No, Nicholas. You help *me*. You get rid of those clothes, and you help me."

I wrestled with my shirt, tearing it off over my head, briefly immersed in thick darkness.

"Now the rest, Nicholas. Stop playing these games."

My hands wouldn't cooperate. The candles sucked up oxygen, glowing brighter.

"Do it!"

LaWanda slid a hand across her belly, smoothing it in circles, smoothing it down between her legs, smoothly digging her fingernails into her skin, crackling her fingernails through those thick hairs.

"I want to see you, Nicholas."

My pants constricted my waist and legs, heavy as El Cid's bronze trousers, tighter than fire ravaging a frayed candlewick.

"I want to really see you."

With her other hand, LaWanda stroked her nipples, pinching them, tweaking the ends between her fingernails, stabbing her fingernails into her breasts. Her mouth opened wide, another shadow. Her eyes closed. Her hands seized her body, stroking, scraping.

Instantly, she appeared at my side, delivered across the room on tides of flame.

"Stand up."

I felt myself rising. LaWanda worked quickly at my belt and tore my pants free, lifting each leg and flinging the pants against the wall. Her skin was not warm, though, and as she gripped the elastic of my underwear I shivered.

When she took me into her mouth, I was drawn into emptiness, into a dimension of absent horizons and disembodied voices. She sucked, she rolled her head against my belly, she shoved me back against the wall. With my eyes closed, I drifted softly, thoroughly soft, while she swallowed me, while she scuffled between my legs. I squirmed as she dug her fingernails into my backside; I trembled as she bit me, as she attached herself to the center of my body and slurped and groaned and stabbed me with her chin.

Spitting me out, LaWanda leaned back on her haunches. Her face was waxy and wet, varnished with yellow red candlelight. She wiped off her mouth with the back of her hand.

"Damn you, Nicholas. Twice in one day."

"I—"

"First Harold, and now you. I'd be better off with Argo at this rate."

"Just . . . let me lie down."

"There is a last resort, though. It's dangerous. But you're strong enough, Nicholas."

"Let me—"

"See that green box in the closet? Get it. Go over there and get it! Not that one, the other one. Good. Now bring it here. Hurry up! That's my boy. Now you can lie down. But keep your legs spread wide and your arms straight out. Like that! Wider!"

Her bed was nothing more than a mattress cluttered with knots of blankets and sheets and flattened pillows. I carved out a place for myself, feeling as if I had sunk below floor level. The candles burned like torches; the bed was ringed with snapping flames; LaWanda scurried back and forth rattling the box over her head.

"Crystals, Nicholas. Sources of power."

Miki was the most powerful person I ever touched, even though she was afraid of the dark and couldn't lift heavy bags of rice. She could speak without talking. She could reach inside me with her eyes. She could erase memories of Billy Reid's blood-drenched legs or Sergeant Ascencion's shattered bones with one simple smile.

"There! Now it's working. Oh, Nicholas. Can you feel the power now? More. Here, take this in your hand. Squeeze it while I chant. Squeeze it tighter. Here's another one. Concentrate on the crystals, on those hard crystals, Nicholas. Visualize their power, their perfection. Absorb them into your mind's eye. Take them inside you, Nicholas! Take them *deep* inside, plunge them into your heart, force them to release energy, energy, energy!"

My hands knotted around the crystals so tightly I envisioned my own fingerbones exploding into powder. LaWanda crept onto the bed and scattered more crystals on my chest, inside my navel, in a cluster around the sudden stiffness between my legs.

"Now, now, now, Nicholas."

Like a creature, LaWanda knelt at my feet, hissing, sighing, slithering her tongue across her lips.

"Do it, baby. Get off your back and do it."

I released the crystals and squatted behind her—drawn by the surging warmth of her thighs, her hips, her pussy—lured by the radiance mirrored in her eyes and teeth. The aching in my prick—a taunting rhythm. Inside her, inside her. Blood oozed from my hand and fused us together as I grabbed onto her ribs and pulled myself closer, deeper.

"No, baby, no."

The fever, the shuddering, the blind cadence, the need.

"Higher, Nicholas. Put it . . . there. Up . . . there!"

LaWanda—so small in my hands, so delicate, her flesh so white, almost blue, writhing beneath me, against me.

"Yes, baby . . . yes. Deep. Don't . . . be afraid."

I surrendered.

"Hurt me, Nicholas. Please!"

I heard the war snapping inside her neck.

While LaWanda slept, I tiptoed outside the ring of melted candles and gathered my clothes. Not wishing to create unnecessary noise, I dressed quietly in the living room. Even though LaWanda was late for work, I wanted her to sleep.

Tucking in my shirt, I knew these small considerations were the genesis of love.

She wouldn't have to work much longer, anyway—once I found a job. For a change, the future seemed like the future, clear and possible, instead of a crudely edited conglomeration of memories and illusions.

Rummaging through LaWanda's old rolltop desk, I uncovered a pink notepad. I left a message for her explaining that I would return for dinner—with good news about employment, I promised; the House of Hospitality was hiring, no problem—especially since I was a veteran. Also, I suggested she take the night off, so she could accompany me to the alien watch with Mrs. Raylak.

Now I knew something else—if anyone had an alpha body, it was LaWanda.

Resting the note next to the bedroom door, I discovered my hand had stopped bleeding. Perhaps those crystals were potent after all. Nonetheless, I replaced the old bandage Argo made for me and tightened it down with Scotch tape.

After cleaning up the kitchen and discarding the broken

refrigerator shelves, I lined up the cans of beer in a neat row on top of the crisper. LaWanda would see them first thing.

The green plastic garbage sack was overstuffed, and I pinched my fingers fastening the twisty-tie. The sack rattled as I picked it up, but not loud enough to disturb LaWanda. I was happy she slept so soundly, happy to be part of her life.

Running downstairs, I slapped my feet against the concrete steps to drown out my thoughts. I skipped the last three steps and jumped out into the patio, holding the garbage bag against my chest as if it were a sleeping child. In the laundry room across the courtyard, the dryer tumbled a full load of clothes—broadcasting repeating sound patterns that expanded and rolled out, bouncing against the four inner walls of the apartment complex. The music spread louder and deeper as I raced over to the dumpster; hefting the garbage bag over my head, I urged myself to run as fast as I could; the dryer thumped more brutally, a symphonic bass-line soundtrack driving me forward, begging me, propelling me, inspiring me to heave the garbage sack into the empty dumpster as ferociously as I could—a crescendo, a final crashing note, a celebration.

The sun had slipped down from the center of the sky. Looking straight up, I saw nothing but a square film of blue stretched tightly at the corners where it clung to the top edges of the apartments—the azure canvas roof of an enormous suffocating tent. The dryer crunched to a stop; the sides of the dumpster vibrated faintly. In that sudden silence my thoughts returned. Reappeared. Resumed. In a flurry. My father took me to the circus only once. Only once. I had to get out of there.

The day I returned to school after recovering from my cold, I didn't spend my lunch money. Instead, I saved it for the walk home. *Stopping at a liquor store, I bought a Big Deal cola and a Hostess fruit pie. I never bought Coca-Cola or Pepsi. The Big Deals were just as good, they cost less, and they had better flavors, like cream soda and strawberry. The fruit pies were sweet, and berry was my favorite; I liked to crunch the tiny seeds between my teeth. Those little pies were actually turn-overs, smothered with a white sugar coating almost as thick as plastic around a rough crust.*

That liquor store was in the center of our neighborhood shopping center. A low green hedge encircled the parking lot, separating black asphalt from the sidewalk. Inside this hedge were caves kids had hollowed out, a series of winding honeycombs. With my pie and soda, I enjoyed sitting inside one of the natural tree-caverns, surrounded by leathery curling branches and crisp brown leaves.

Soda cans and pie wrappers were piled in a corner of the cave. Portholes opened out on each side of me. I sipped my soda and studied cars rolling into the lot, parking under the light standards propped up by concrete pedestals—some of those concrete foundations were chipped, like the statue I saw in an art book at school of a woman with no arms.

The light poles, silver and tall with dangling globes, jutted up between rows of cars like dying streamlined trees. Women wheeled metal carts to their cars and fought with crinkling paper sacks and babies, shoving them all into back seats, then driving away so someone else could take their vacant parking slot.

Attached to the trunk of the light pole closest to me was a small poster. I squinted and was unable to read all the words— but at the top I could see clearly "CIRCUS!" and the orange-and-blue face of a clown with Bozo-style hair.

Clowns threw pies into victims' faces. I saw that all the time in cartoons and on the Ed Sullivan Show. *But I never witnessed it live and in person. I held my pie at arm's length, stiffening my muscles all of a sudden. Part of me wanted to smash that pie into my own face.*

By the time I arrived at the House of Hospitality, the sun had evolved into a radiant orange disk generating an extravagant sunset. I felt calmer in the park. The trees seemed to know me, I had walked this path so often.

LaWanda was probably still asleep, dreaming secret dreams, unaware of my motives. It felt good to have a surprise in store for her. And my poor friend Argo had no doubt recovered sufficiently to make the trip to Esmeralda's himself; as the light faded, he probably stumbled up the stairs to his apartment slowly, his fingers wrapped around a fresh bottle, his cheek still throbbing.

The House of Hospitality would be a good place to work, guarded vigilantly by El Cid. He still reared back on his horse in the parking lot. My shadow dissolved into his as I crossed the street, then it reappeared, born out the other side—my headshadow flat and spread out on the lawn like a Bozohead, my hairshadow dispersed among the thin black shadows of the grass blades.

Watching all those shadows combine and disintegrate disturbed me; I wished I hadn't noticed, I wished I could erase the memory. All I could do was turn in different directions, trying to hide my shadows in uncommon places—between the cracks in the sidewalk where ants streamed in parallel rows, across the leafy roughness of shrubs, among the muddy wheel wells of parked cars and tourist buses.

Between the parking lot, where El Cid stood, and the sidewalk next to the fortress of the House of Hospitality, a black wrought-iron fence restrained an uneven hedge. In the plush light of the setting sun, the black metal seemed as temporary and one-dimensional as shadows. Before the building's old-fashioned wooden castle doors, I looked behind me quickly to see my shadow sliced by the metal bars of the fence—my shadow vaporized into the bushes in pieces of weightless devil's food; crumbs from my Bozohead sprinkled harmlessly across the scalloped leaves—food for the invisible boys hiding inside the honeycomb caves.

The last swallow of my Big Deal cola was warm. My hands were sticky with sugary pie crumbs. I scooted through the fallen leaves and dirt, crouching like a duck, carving furrows similar to the ruts in Invisible Invaders—*a movie I wouldn't see for ten more years.*

I interrupted my snack to read the circus poster. Slipping free of the hedge, released into direct sunlight, I dusted myself off. Dirt from my pants coated my gluey hands. A station wagon slid into the empty parking slot in front of the light pole. A girl in the back seat stared at me. Framed in the window, she looked like she was on TV. Her little fingers tendriled around the top of the door, so tiny, without fingernails.

"Look, Mommy," she said, turning to address the back of her mother's head. "That boy was borned from the trees." The mother's head rotated. She wore black sunglasses. Her eyes were open, round Os of darkness.

A convertible sports car was parked between me and the departing station wagon. Its hood appeared silver, full of the burning sun—yet I knew it was blue, the same color blue as the outline of the clown's face and the long, thin letters in the word "CIRCUS!"

Beneath the poster, I stood reading as the station wagon pulled out. The little girl screamed and leaped up and down on the back seat. The mother swatted her, blindly slashing her arm in and out, her eyes forward, her other hand gripping the steering wheel. The girl dodged her mother's arm like Sinbad evading enemy swords. CIRCUS! *The Greatest Show on Earth. Three Nights Only.*

At the House of Hospitality, the castle doors were held back by rubber-tipped metal stoppers—cats' hind legs screwed into the thick brown wood. I wanted to kick them, flip them up, permit the doors to swing free. If they were supposed to close, they would close. If they were going to remain open, they would remain open. What would decide the outcome, I didn't know. The wind. The heat. A woman rolling a baby stroller not looking where she was going. Powerful thought-waves from a man who had not lived among men for very many years—like the one who sat on one of the wrought-iron benches just inside the patio, beneath the green dragony fronds of a gangly bird-of-paradise plant.

I saw this man in the park many times. Usually, he could be found searching through sand-filled urns for cigarette butts. He gathered them carefully, brushing off gritty sand before dropping the butts into the side pockets of his coat, the same coat he always wore no matter the weather—a gray coat, with greasy lapels and brown stains edging the front and side pockets. In winter, he wore a sky blue windbreaker underneath the coat, but still the same brown creaseless slacks and black high-top tennis sneakers.

This man enjoyed sitting with his legs crossed at the knee, leaning back against the bench. He rested his hands flat at his sides, fingers together and parallel to his thin thighs. For the longest time he would sit this way, staring, his face as solid as the face of the statue lady pouring water from her jug inside the wishing well. Her jug was carved from rock. The man just stared, occasionally smoking one of his stubby used cigarettes.

I saw this man so often, I was certain he lived in one of the nearby canyons. Once I caught him washing his hair in the sink in the House of Hospitality men's room. Still wearing his gray coat, he bent over and dipped in his head. The drain was jammed with paper towels. He pulled up his head and let the water stream off. His hair was so dirty, the water didn't change its shape—combed straight back, a small black plastic helmet.

The bird-of-paradise plant behind him was part of his costume. When I walked out farther into the courtyard, I glanced at him sharply from the side. In that quick take, he appeared as one of the Mayan priest manikins on display at the Museum of Man. Orange flowers in green pods the size of praying hands circled his head. I felt he could see something no one else could see; he was staring at an importance right there in the middle of the tourists, in the middle of the customers exiting the restaurant, in the middle of us all—all wandering around the wishing well staying out of one another's way.

I surveyed the courtyard attempting to see what that man saw, squinting, peeking behind the shrubs, behind the statue of the Indian woman pouring water, even up around the balcony on the second floor.

The man with the greasy hair continued gazing among all of us captured in the patio, and his eyes frightened me. I was terrified by the thought of succumbing to their power, to his exclusive, sweeping line of sight. Sometimes he appeared to be laughing at all of us, holding his black eyes steady and unblinking. But he was trying to tell us something else. That was what I wanted to know, that was the secret he possessed. But that was also the scary part.

His secret would provide me with something new. But something new always erased part of the regular old Nicholas—and that process was like dying in slow motion.

Argo's answers to my questions initiated that slow death. New answers killed off old ideas—ideas I considered true and accurate for years. But if lies were burned out with truth, and later that truth was shown to be a lie, burned out by a newer, stronger truth, and that cycle continued, wouldn't everything—everything—be a lie? The man with the greasy hair would know the answer.

I leaned against the wishing well, absorbed by the pennies on the bottom—copper scabs embraced by algae and gum wrappers. Movies could be just as believable as real life, I thought, but only for a short time. Life continually changed; therefore, new movies were steadily created.

The monsters in movies were derived from life, if only because a real person had to create them to begin with. But once created, a monster was a monster. More movies needed to be produced, because people required new monsters. Old monsters became silly. Not so silly that they became unappreciated or unsympathetic, but silly because they were no longer more threatening than modern realities.

The Thing was a perfect monster, because in 1951, Americans were afraid of things they didn't understand. There was a Cold War, a war no one could fight. Communists frightened America; The Thing terrified scientists and soldiers. The audiences in theaters enjoyed the cycle of fear, turned inside out by Hollywood and the evening news.

But today The Thing won't work. People demand new terror.

The man with the greasy hair realized what scared us the most. And he never looked afraid. Even Brak would fail to scare him. But sometimes people can't reveal their knowledge even though they know things, inside. That's why I think I love people, all people, and why I think all these thoughts to begin with—because we eternally battle with fear, together, mute and alone.

I approached the light pole. The concrete pedestal was as high as my waist. Reaching around the hot metal pole, I hoisted myself up. Even though the silver gray metal burned my arms and hands, I held on and stretched. I gripped the bottom edge of the CIRCUS *poster and struggled to tear it loose. The poster ripped. Just the bottom corner flaked off in my hand. A gray triangle. I jammed it into my back pocket, hugging the scalding pole with one arm, pressing my cheek flush against the pole to maintain my balance. Slowly, I tilted my head and gazed all the way to the top. The poster was attached directly above me. The pole went on forever, supporting the sky, guaranteeing the sky remained secure and taut and did not collapse like a broken tent.*

Above me, the lamp was cut into thousands of rough squares. I tugged at the bottom edge of the poster and imagined that lamp shining in the middle of the day, showering me with light from hundreds of beautiful angles—light that flowed in slow motion, in golden syrupy columns, columns that encased my body gently, suspending me inside a pillar of buttery radiation.

The light pole was too hot. I forced myself to hang on a few moments longer, pulling down on the poster just so, ripping it a little on one side when I finally tore it free.

I lost my grip. The poster floated down like a runaway kite, twisting. It slapped onto the asphalt parking lot facedown. I sprang from the pedestal. My entire face and the insides of my arms burned intensely. I glowed red.

I had no coins to toss into the House of Hospitality wishing well. I wanted to wish for happiness—happiness for LaWanda, happiness for myself, always and eternally happiness upon happiness.

The man with the greasy hair sat behind me, his eyes beaming solidly into my back. Tunnels attached directly to his brain extended from his face as cones. Inside those cones, atoms changed colors. The shaft from a flashlight beam at night catches bits of dust and charges them—the dust is always there, but unseen without the light. Those cones had the same effect on invisible particles.

To check on that man, I turned around suddenly. He remained beneath the bird-of-paradise. He had not moved. His fingers still pointed straight out toward me, and he never blinked.

What he saw was astonishing. Whether he considered it beautiful or frightening—or both—was another story. He never smiled. But his expression was deep. He didn't show the ridiculous look of a child that Argo wore when passed out on his couch. And he didn't exhibit the new grimace of pleasure LaWanda had revealed to me for the first time that afternoon. Instead, he reminded me of my father that last night in front of the TV. Even though his face was dirty, and even though his face was fixed into one expression as hard as the Indian statue, the man with the greasy hair exhibited a unique redness through his skin, a color wavering between visible and invisible—fresh as the peelings of red orange fruit remembered in the mind's eye.

I wanted to go sit with him and talk, but I didn't know what to say. It was safer standing next to the statue. The water splashed gently, soothing to watch, distracting me from the clackering of forks and knives and dishes inside the restaurant—the flapping of the double doors to the men's room—the busy hum of conversation about plants, the architecture, the nice weather, things to eat, things to do next.

When I returned home from the shopping center, I taped the CIRCUS *sign back together. I lined up the torn corner and carefully stuck tape on the back. When I finished, the rip was almost unnoticeable. Using the rest of the tape, I placed the* CIRCUS *sign over the television screen.*

It would be simple to toss a coin into the wishing well and concentrate on making LaWanda happy, on making love grow, on getting a job—while I shut my eyes and listened to the coin plop into the water and flutter to the bottom. But I had no coins—more wishes than coins. Beyond all my thoughts lurked The Large Wish, the wish for something I couldn't even imagine yet, something that would spread out wide and full inside of me. I wanted to see the things the man with the greasy hair could see. But for now, LaWanda was enough. She was all I deserved. If I could just make her life easier, that would be enough.

The man with the greasy hair had arrived at the point where he no longer needed to wish. That's where I wanted to be. After my work was done. Argo wrote books. He worked hard. Now it was my turn, to do something that mattered, to find the right work. When I was a soldier, I had a job, I was working—but I don't think it mattered. To someone else, perhaps. No more than that.

While in the middle of it, I spent hours wondering why that war had been created. I asked Sergeant Ascencion for an explanation—our appetite for monsters?—and he said, "Ours is not to reason why, boy. Have another beer and cool your socks." No one understood any better than I, but that didn't stop us from running patrols or setting out mines or calling in air support.

Playing baseball wasn't much of a job, either. I never had a real job, a reality that bothered me, that froze my voice when someone asked me what I did for a living. But the man with the greasy hair no longer held a job; he was too small to play baseball; yet he had discovered truly how to see. When I stood rooted in the batter's box, analyzing the pitcher challenging me from the middle of the baseball diamond, I could see clearly his expression—disgust when he shook his head no to the catcher's signs; snarling satisfaction when he got the sign he wanted. The fans were too far away to see that closely into the details of the game; the fans were too far away, watching a different long-distance version of the real game we played on the field. When Coach Mulhauser squeezed his belly in the dugout, he reacted to a genuine agony—his twitching ulcer; and instead the fans thought he was sending out signs.

If the man with the greasy hair were an umpire, he would ignore all those details, gazing directly into the heart of the game. He would overlook facial expressions and burning stomachs and terrified young batters ripping at deadly unpredictable baseballs. He would see the true game, an entirely different game from the one viewed by the fans, the players, the coaches, the sportswriters, the pilots of small aircraft overhead, the patients in hospitals listening to the game on radio, the fathers of the players reading their sons' letters.

"You must be making one hell of a wish."

"What?"

"You've been standing there for half a lifetime."

The gray man with the keys, who I had seen in the courtyard earlier in the day, glided in beside me. He enveloped the blue and yellow tiles that edged the wishing well with his large hands. His skin was thick and wrinkled. His fingernails were chewed on and dirty and dull; they didn't shine like normal fingernails. Gently, he swung his bundle of keys back and forth; the keys drifted down in a wide arc until almost skimming the water.

Our reflections gazed out from the surface of the wishing well—eight eyes connected by a mirror of water. The keys curved over the gray man's face, concealing his reflection, then curved back over my forehead, slicing me in half. Coins lying on the bottom of the well gnawed holes into our images. The keys floated and floated, never connecting, never knocking anything over. The earth continued to revolve on its axis and the keys continued to swing. No pegs to topple. Pegs carved from the stuff gnawed out of our faces. Pegs set in a row all around the wishing well, a nice even row. Pegs in a circle. The gray man and I standing straight within that circle. The man with the greasy hair staring intently at one peg, the peg closest to his wrought-iron bench. He concentrated powerfully enough to topple the peg. The peg teetered then collapsed. A slow-motion fall. The gray man and I watched in silence, taking three deep breaths in the time it took that first peg to tilt, in the time it took that first peg to click against the neighboring peg, toppling the imaginary circle.

"We should get a good sunset today. Too bad you can't see it from in here."

"Do you work here?"

"No. Of course not. I just wear this outfit and jangle these keys for the hell of it."

"Oh."

"Who wants to know? You writing a book or something?"

"I just asked."

"Yeah, sure. I work here. Night watchman. I seen you around here before, ain't I?"

"Sometimes."

"Sometimes? What kinda answer is that?"

"I don't know."

"You're telling me. And I thought you were a smart kid. Yes, sir. I been watching you. Right. I been watching you standing here a long time. I woulda thought you were figuring out some kinda trouble or something if I didn't recognize you. Yep, I seen you before. Hard to forget a nice-looking boy like you. You been makin' wishes? What you been wishing for all this time? Jeez, you been standing here half the afternoon. You been wishing for me to come around, haven't you? You been wishing for Big Mel to come by and talk with you. Don't be shy. I can tell. You can't hide nothing from Mel. That's what I always say, all the time. You can't hide nothing from Mel."

"Almost."

"Almost only counts in horseshoes and hand grenades, son. Ain't no almost the way I look at it."

"It's almost five o'clock."

"No way. It's exactly four forty-seven p.m. Now, you tell Mel exactly what you been wishing for. Okay? Don't be bashful. Don't be standing there fixing to talk to me about the weather or no nonsense like that. Life's too short. We can't be wasting time, no sir. Men where I come from like to cut through all that nonsense and get right to the point. Makes sense, don't it? Sure it does. Lots of sense. Trust the things what make sense, son. Trust 'em. Trust 'em good. You hear me? I ain't scaring you, am I, son? Old Mel ain't putting no fear in you, is he? Speak up, son. Speak!"

"A job."

"That's all?"

"I need a job. I want to work right *here*."

"Well, well. That's mighty fine. Mighty fucking fine. Excuse my French, son. But us guys can talk like that. Mel's your friend, son. And Mel's the man to talk to about a job. Yes, sir. Today's your lucky day. Your wish done come true. A job. Now, I can't *guarantee* anything. But there is something opening up. And I think you're just the man we've been looking for. What's your name, son? What do they call you?"

"Nicholas."

"Nicholas? A fine name. Ni-cho-las. Not too many of them around these days, are there? Eh? Not the most popular name in the world. But a good name. Yes, sir. A good name. Pleased to meet you, Nicholas. Put 'er there. Hey, that's quite a grip you got. You can tell a lot about a man from his grip. Easy there, boy. Lighten up. Lighten up! Hey. Now, you don't mind if I call you Nick, do you? Of course not. Nick. I like that name. I like that name a lot. Or do people call you Nicholas?"

"LaWanda does."

"LaWanda? That your girlfriend? Eh?"

"Well, she's sort of, but . . ."

"A big boy like you, and no girlfriend? That's hard to believe. Yes, sir. A big one like you. Jeez, you're a big one. And no girlfriend."

"Today was the first day—"

"Well, well. No girlfriend."

"What is it that's opening up, anyway?"

"Eh? Opening up? Sun's going down and the flowers're shutting up tight. Restaurant's been open all day, but they'll be closing down directly. I gotta lock the gates after that. Things closing in and closing down all over. What're you talking about, opening up?"

"The job. You said there was a job."

"Just kidding, son. What's the matter? You don't like to laugh? There, that's better. Smile. Here. Turn up your mouth. Like this. Boy, you got soft skin. Nice soft skin. Anybody ever tell you that before? Hey, don't lose that smile. I put that smile there myself, with my own two hands. That's a Mel special.

Keep that smile, Nick. Right-o. You wanna work for Mel, you gotta learn how to smile."

"What kind of work?"

"Well, I'll tell you. Usually, Mrs. Devens over there in the office handles these things. But she's not there on Saturdays. So, when she's not here, I take over. I've got my own office, you might say. Upstairs. Part of the bargain. Part of the night watchman's deal. My own little apartment way up high in the House of Hospitality. Got the place all to myself most of the time. So, we can go up there and have you fill out the application form. For starters. But I can't guarantee anything. Remember that. Then on Monday, when Mrs. Devens gets in, I'll give her your paperwork. And my recommendation, of course. Yes, Nick, I think you're the man we've been looking for. Mrs. Devens has the final word, though. But I know how to handle her. She's no problem. I got her all figured out."

"That's good. Maybe my wish *will* come true."

"Maybe so, son."

"I come here all the time. But I'm not like that guy over there on the bench. He comes here all the time, too, but we're completely different."

"You mean Kevin? Oh, Lord, yes you're different. Kevin's nothing but a bum. Nothing but a down-and-out homeless bum. He's seen better days, believe me."

"I don't know about that. I think the days are all the same to him."

"You might be right about that. You just might be right, Nick. He used to be in the circus or something. Fell off a ladder and hit his head. We look out for him, don't you worry. He stays around here someplace, but we look out for him."

"I think he might be looking out for you."

"Hey, Nick. Now wait just a minute. What do you mean

193

by that, anyway? I'm trying to do you a favor here, Nick. This is Mel talking. Kevin ain't got nothing to look out for and neither do you. You try and do folks a favor these days and where does it get you? I'm talking to you, Nick. Watch my lips. Mel says, you can trust me. Ain't nothing to look out for. What gives you these ideas, anyway? Kevin ain't been telling you no stories about me, has he? Don't let that crazy man bend your ear. Kevin ain't nobody to listen to nohow. Do you see *him* wearing a uniform? Toting keys? Living in his own apartment? No way, son. You got to learn who you can trust. Mel. You can trust Mel. You don't have to look out for Mel. Unless you're afraid of somebody doing you a favor. You understand me, Nick? There's nothing to look out for here. Nothing to be afraid of."

"It's in his eyes. The way he looks."

"Yeah. He does look funny. But you would, too, if you fell off a ladder and split your head open."

"I've never even *been* to the circus."

"What? Never in your life? That's too bad, Nick. Everybody should go at least once. Like those Moslems. You know? Once in their life they've got to go to Mecca. Pilgrims, Nick. So, once in your life you gotta go see a circus. Simple as that. Makes you remember what being a kid was for. Too bad about Kevin. Hell, he probably had the best job of any of us, working for the circus."

"Sounds good to me."

"Good? Damn, boy. Good ain't the word for it. He had it as good as he's got it bad now. Look at him. Just turn around slow and take a quick look. You see that? You see what the walking wounded of this world look like? Yep, that's one right there. Missing in action."

"I was in Vietnam."

"We all were, son. It was on television. Remember?"

194

"I was *there*. We even saw a camera crew once, when we were on patrol. Guys were screaming for medics down this road. When we reached the wounded, these French guys with cameras filmed it and didn't help us or anything. They just watched."

"So, you're a big star, are you? Maybe that's where I've seen you before. On the boob tube. Mr. Nick, GI at large. Yep, that had to be you. The one with the helmet. Right?"

"I never saw anyone like Kevin in the war. He sees different things than we do. I believe that."

"Boy, he don't see nothing."

"That's what I mean."

"What *do* you mean, Nick?"

"I mean, he's wiser than we are. He can see through everything. He doesn't have to worry about the same things we do, because he's learned something—with his eyes—that we haven't learned."

"And just how do you know all this, Nick?"

"I can feel it, I guess. Nobody told me, or anything like that. I just figured it out, through my feelings."

"That's mighty interesting. Mighty interesting. Through your feelings. I've got feelings too, you know."

"We all do."

"Right, Nick. But I think my feelings are different from what you think they are."

"You can't really think your feelings."

"You can't? It feels pretty strong to me, Nick, that Kevin—our little friend over there—is out of whack. That's what I think. And I also think that *you* think he's *in* whack. If you catch my drift."

"The only problem is, what he knows he can't tell me."

"Yeah. I see. Well, you still thinking about this job we got here? You still gotta fill out the application. Yes, sir. I got the forms upstairs. You could fill them out today, just to be on the safe side, and I'd hand-carry them to Mrs. Devens first thing Monday morning. You're just about in, the way I look at it. All you got to do is fill in the blanks. You following me?"

"Maybe I should ask Kevin about this place first. Maybe he could tell me if things were right or not. I need a job, you're right about that. And this place would be perfect. But I want to make sure my feelings are all lined up first. That's not too much to ask, is it?"

"I don't know."

"I've got other . . . people to think about, too."

"Sure, but I ain't got the slightest idea what you're talking about. You ain't trying to tell me you don't trust Mel, are you? Hell, boy, I'm giving you every break in the book. I wouldn't do this for just *anybody*. But I happen to like you, okay? I seen you around and I got this hunch you can be trusted. Besides, you're a fucking veteran. That means plenty when it comes to job applications. Don't you know that, son? You done served your country. You kept us free to breathe sweet democratic air for another few days. So you get a payback. You get what you earned. What goes around comes around, Nick. Simple as that. Even Kevin could tell you that much."

"Yeah?"

"Come on. Let's go upstairs. I'll give you that form, maybe even cook you up a little something. It's gettin' to be dinnertime anyway. What do you say, Nick?"

"All right, Mel."

Mel and I stepped off the wishing-well pedestal simultaneously and walked through the courtyard into a rectangle of
shadow. My shoes changed color. Darker. Scalloped arches led
to an inner walkway. Mel passed through first. It was cooler
there, next to the beige stucco wall and the row of doors to the
hospitality rooms.

The information office was closed. Through the locked
screen door, I saw a large-scale tourist map on the wall; in the
center, a black X marked the spot, "You Are Here." The
administration office next door was locked and dark, also—
opposite a cluster of shrubs and palms like those enclosing
Kevin, diagonally across the patio.

We continued walking. Just before turning the corner, I
took a last look over my shoulder. Kevin was gone. Uneasily, I
took hold of the edge of the building, pausing, wanting to ask
him a final question, wanting his advice. Mel jingled his
keys—"Come on, boy." I needed a job more than advice—
Argo would agree. It would be better to brag to Argo that I had
found a job, to announce to LaWanda that she could quit
hers, than it would be to seek approval from Kevin.

I would have keys and a uniform. I would evolve.

"Up this way."

Between Mel and me, across the hall from the ballroom
and a reception room, stood an empty phone booth; the
receiver dangled, swaying by a thick silver cord. I reached

inside to hang up the phone, but Mel waved me on, stomping up a narrow tiled staircase. I ran after him, ascending the smooth steps until I met him on the second floor.

"You ever been up here before, Nick?"

"No."

"Real nice up here. You can stand quiet and watch all the people, watch guys like you hover around the wishing well, watch those rich fools nibbling away in the restaurant. Real nice. Especially when these honeysuckles are in bloom and everything smells sweet and sticky. Here, take a whiff. Nice, eh?"

I couldn't move up close enough to tell.

"I always wanted to be a gardener. You know? Make things grow, and all that. But this job ain't half bad. Working here is good, matter of fact. You're gonna like it, Nick. A little hard work's good for a man. Yes, sir, you're gonna like it."

Mel smiled and buried his nose in the orange flowers. He inhaled deeply; bits of pollen dotted his nostrils.

He was a night watchman, but he wanted to be a gardener. Argo wanted to write for the movies, but he wrote Eddie Elvesizer novels instead. When I was younger, I wanted to go to the circus. The government told me to go to Vietnam. My father wanted me to play baseball, but he never attended the games. Now I just wanted to be something, for LaWanda. She wanted to move to a better apartment. She wanted a better life. Like anybody else. Like Mrs. Raylak. She wanted to see the aliens more than anything in this world. I could help, somehow. Somehow I could help them all.

"You like this place so far, Nick? Things look a lot better from up here. A different perspective. You can really get away from it all, if you know what I mean."

"What *do* you mean?"

"Hey. Not to get testy, pal. I didn't mean nothing. Just an

expression. Okay? I ain't trying nothin', Nick. Jeez, what're you so paranoid about? Look who's throwing stones now."

"Get away from *what*? I don't think you can ever get away from anything, no matter how hard you try."

"Is that so? Well, maybe I underestimated you just a little bit, son. Yep, you are the man for the job, no doubt about that. Mrs. Devens is gonna be mighty proud of me for snatching you outta the crowd. We've got it made now, son. Made in the shade."

The sun was almost down; shadows seeped into the court-yard, concealing more and more of the benches and tiles and plants and tourists. Past the knifing leaves of the honeysuckle, through the windows of the second-story room directly across the patio, I could see the tip of the spear-flag on the El Cid statue. Straight through, past a piano and rows of folding chairs and a wooden podium, in front of drawn curtains and windowpanes fitted into the shape of a peaked church window, the tip of El Cid's bronze spear-flag pierced the sky. That bronze flag would never flutter no matter how strong the wind, and it would rust slowly and grow blacker like the shadow that it was—that entire statue the antireflection of El Cid, no more than a hollow metallic model mounted on government con-crete.

The empty room grew darker, as if the spear-flag had punctured the side of the House of Hospitality, letting all the light seep out. Air out of a balloon. Billy Reid's blood. The bloom withering from the flowers that Miki placed before the Buddha shrine. Argo's empty bottles lying sideways on the filthy linoleum in his kitchen, one last taste of brown booze filming the glass. The two home runs remaining in the base-ball bat stored in my closet, the power draining away like juice from a corroded car battery. My father. He told me I'd make it one day. He said *he* always tried, he said it was the American

Way. To make it. But I never learned what it was he wanted to make.

My father tore the CIRCUS *sign off the TV screen and flapped it above his head, dancing, declaring me to be the greatest son on earth. "Ladies and gentlemen," he said, "presenting now for your continuing entertainment, the Young and Wild Nicholas Ames, who will, right before your very eyes, jump through these hoops at the crack of my gentle whip and land face first in the red-white-and-blue glory of Hog Heaven."*

He teased me with the CIRCUS *sign, tapping my behind, wiggling that cardboard through my hair, trying to tickle me and make me laugh the same way he sang his pretend-giggle kootchie-kootchie-koos. I tried to run away down the hall to my bedroom, but he chased me in circles around the TV and blocked me off when I changed directions, slapping me with the cardboard sign. His pretend-giggles grew into hard laughter. He stung my ears with the poster.*

On the curved gray glass of the TV screen, another father chased another son. Created from shadows. Reflections. Monster movie without title. Black-and-white reruns. The hogface of glory.

"Ain't nothin' going on tonight in any of these rooms. No weddings, no revival meetings, none of the usual stuff. Gotta lock up pretty soon, after we get something to eat. If you got time, maybe you'd like to make the rounds with me later. We'll chase these folks out and I'll show you what this place is made of. Maybe later. Nice place. You like tacos? I got some stuff for tacos back in my kitchen. Good stuff. Puts meat on your bones. Yes, sir. Looks like *you* eat right, anyway. Nice and strong guy like you. You know what's good for you, eh? You read me, Nick? Listen up here, now. You know what you like, don't you? Hell, we all know what we like. If you don't even know *that*, you ain't worth a damn. Nobody gets my respect more'n a guy who knows what he wants and goes out to get it. Nice way to live, that. You get hungry, you cook up somethin' good. Easy. You just gotta be good to yourself, Nick. You know what I'm sayin'? If you ain't good to yourself, most likely no one else'll do it for you. Rules to live by, boy. I got plenty of 'em. They got me this far. No sense in tradin' them in. They been workin' fine for Mel. Just fine."

"Where did you get them?"

"Where? I made 'em up, son."

"Like people make up movie scripts or write books?"

"Maybe. But if you think I just made 'em up for entertainment, you got another think coming. Just the opposite, Nick. Ain't nothin' entertaining about survival."

"If I had a job or something, things would be easier."

"Yes, sir. That's a start. And we're fixing to do something about that, aren't we? A little basic survival. You and me, Nick. Carving out a little breathing space here. Got this whole place to ourselves, just as soon as the tourists clear out. You'll be good at that, Nick. Clearing out the tourists. You got that kind voice, but something in your face says, 'I mean business.' I admire a guy like that, Nick. I really do. Really. Not too many of them around anymore. Getting thinned out or something. Hard to find the good ones anymore. Hard to come across what you want sometimes, even if you know exactly what it is you're looking for."

"There's still a lot of people wandering around down there. If any of them were lost, they'd have to wait until the information office opened up tomorrow morning."

"That's a good one, Nick. And we'd have to shove the poor souls out onto the streets where they'd wander around in circles. Not like us, eh? We got it made. Just the two of us, locked in here. Hell, there ain't nothin' we can't do, really. Get us a nice meal, stroll around the grounds for a while, get to know this place. I got some wine, too, Nick. You like wine?"

"A little bit. But I want to fill out those forms. It would be nice to stick around, but I have to get going soon. There's something important I have to do tonight. Something really important."

"Hey, Nick, it's all relative. Ain't that what they say?"

"I don't know. I have some friends waiting for me, and we're supposed to go out past Jamul."

"Jamul? Ain't nothin' out there but mesquite and Mexicans."

"Maybe for now."

"Hell, son. What are you talking about?"

"Aliens."

"That's what I said, boy. Mexicans. Ain't you listening?"

"It's what *I* want to do."

"Oh. I see. And I suppose you think you've just earned more of my respect. Is that it? You *want* to go all the way out to Jamul. You *want* to fill out the application forms. You *want* this and you *want* that. Aren't you being a little selfish, Nick? I mean, there comes a time when you have to draw the line. You can quote me on that, too. Another one of Mel Freeman's Rules of Order. You have to know where to draw the line. I've got *more* respect for people who know what they want but who know when they're asking for too much. You gotta think about other folks, too, you know."

"But I am."

"Yeah. But think a second on *this*, Nick. You want an awful lot, the way it sounds to me. It takes a *real* man to know when he's getting carried away, when he's doing nothing but stepping on other people's toes. You follow me? You can just continue trampling your way through life, fooling yourself into thinking you're the cat's fucking pajamas. Only one day you'll have to wise up and slow down. Otherwise, you'll end up like your pal Kevin down there. He didn't know when to stop, Nick. Got himself burned in the end. Ruined his fucking life."

"Ruined? He knows more than we do."

"What makes you say a thing like that, Nick? You ever talk to him? Or are you just jacking your jaws because you enjoy the sound? Think on it, son. Think hard."

"You can tell by his eyes. He *knows*. I bet he doesn't care about jobs or aliens or wine. My friend Argo wants to make a million dollars in Hollywood, but that's never going to work."

"Yes, but there's nothin' wrong with dreaming, Nick."

"You don't understand. What would people do if they got everything they wanted? What if Argo sold his book to the movies and got rich? *Then* what would he do? What would he want next? He wouldn't want what Kevin wants, because Kevin doesn't want anything. He doesn't *need* anything. And that's why he's so beautiful."

"Oh, sure, he's a pretty boy. Is that what you're saying? You go for the pretty ones, is that it? I'm not your type, eh? You trying to tell me something, Nick? You trying to tell me something on the sly? Just come out and say it, son. Or can't you do that? Is it too hard for you to deal with a man face-to-face? Spit it out, son. I can take it. You don't want to have anything to do with me, right? You're just playing games with me, trying to get yourself a job at my expense. That's pretty low, son. About as low as you can get. I didn't think you were made that way. I really didn't. I must have read you all wrong, Nick."

"Wait a minute. I didn't want you to think *that*."

"What *do* you want me to think? You still playing games? You just fucking with my head?"

"No."

"You promise?"

"Sure. I promise. I like you, Mel. I really do."

"Yeah?"

"Sure. But why do you think Kevin is so . . . so . . ."

"Flaky?"

"Okay. But people are just people. You can be scared of them. But you have to love them, too. You *have* to."

"Really?"

"I'm serious."

"Hey, I believe you. I believe you. You're something else, Nick. You really are."

"I guess you mean that in a good way."

"Sure. Sure I do. Hey, you're a good kid, Nick. Real good. Man, you got some shoulders, eh? Muscles, too. Hell, Old Mel's bear hug won't take. Almost can't reach that high."

"Sorry."

"Don't be, pal. I love it. Just like you said. Right?"

"Sort of."

"Naw. We understand each other. Sure we do. More'n you think. This I believe. Right from the start I believed this, Nick. I could tell just by looking at you, even from way up here, that we would get along. Sure, I did."

"That's what I said about Kevin."

"Yeah, I guess you did, too. As a matter of fact, I some-times think the same way. Really. I just never met anybody who I thought would understand what I meant. You follow me?"

"A little bit."

"Yeah, you do, Nick. You do more'n you think you do. Because great minds think alike. We think alike. We *do*. Now, let's get on. It gets kinda cool when the sun goes down."

"It's still nice out."

"Yeah, but the temperature really drops in here at night. You'd be surprised. Yeah, you would."

My father never got what he wanted, as far as I could tell. What it was he wanted, he should have described to me. But he was as afraid to reveal that knowledge, perhaps, as I was afraid to ask.

Mel made me a little afraid, too. But some things about Argo scared me. And even LaWanda. Mrs. Raylak could even make me shiver—especially when she pinched her fingers into my legs and spilled soda in her lap, explaining how beautiful the aliens were and how thrilling it would be to witness those dizzy colors streaming from the mammoth bodies, the blinding glow of their spaceships, the faithful members of the Nebulae Society attired in seamless white welcoming them with open arms. "White, white," she chanted. "Do you realize how marvelous white is? The presence of all colors, Nicholas. Such beauty. And it shows us how blind we all are. So many colors intensely blended, and all we poor human beings can see is white. It's the thought that provides the beauty. Imagine all those colors vibrating at the same time. There's the beauty, Nicholas. The wonder and the beauty. But only in our imagination can we appreciate it—for now. When the aliens arrive, however, they will teach us to see. It will be wonderful, Nicholas, to be able to see—to feel with our eyes—all those colors resounding as one."

The stucco walls of the House of Hospitality were practically white, fading just a shade into brown. If Mrs. Raylak was correct, the colors were resounding across these walls, too—but I didn't want to share that information with Mel. Kevin would understand, but I didn't know if he would be able to explain much to me—to help me understand more about allcolor. Kevin probably suffered the opposite from the blind—for the blind could hear and smell and taste much more deeply than the rest of us; since Kevin could *see* so intensely, he no doubt lacked the ability to capture his visions with words. Nothing was free. Argo threatened me with that idea enough times—yet since he was so good with words, I wondered how sharp *his* eyes were.

"This way, Nick. Don't be afraid, eh? Down this hall-way."

Mel jangled his keys, searching for the right one. After unlocking a white metal door set into the wall, he flicked a row of switches. Lights fired on, first along the upstairs balconies, then one by one downstairs, until the courtyard was released from shadow. The lights were so bright, the leaves of the trees appeared fake, as thick and waxy as plastic.

Someone in the courtyard below applauded and howled, "All right!" after Mel snapped on the final light—a spotlight that streamed out across the statue lady. Her granite body was transformed into something strange and fragile looking, like spice cake.

"Yes, sir. You gotta remember to turn on these lights every night. You keep it dark in here and God only knows who'll sneak in and hide in the bushes. I don't have to remind you how many poor slobs are out there looking for a place to sleep at night. It's a tragedy, but you gotta face facts. Shady characters, them we don't need. I been robbed once, you know. We caught the guy, and I never woulda guessed he could turn out to be the thief. Shocked the piss outta me, if you want the truth. Same guy used to work in the opera office over there behind you. I even invited the creep over a coupla times. To talk, you know? I like music just as much as the next guy. And the fucker turns around and robs me blind—because he knew when I was in and out. Can you believe that? Tore my bedroom all to hell, too. Trashed it, is what he did. I seen bitches do that to their boyfriends, and outta the blue this guy does it to me. Can you figure that? Crazy, eh?"

My father said a person would have to be out of their mind to pay all that money for circus tickets. The day after I placed the CIRCUS poster across the TV screen, I sketched nutty people lining up next to a tent like the one colored in on the advertisement. I drew lunatics like the ones I saw in cartoons, with Napoleon hats and their hands lost inside their shirts, or with straitjackets on and their tongues poking out crookedly.

When I returned from school, I thought I was the first one there. But when I went to turn on Leave It to Beaver, I found two circus tickets taped to the control panel of the TV set. It was a Friday, and the tickets announced FRIDAY in bold blue letters. I peeled them off and carried them carefully to the couch. Those tickets seemed so valuable, like the ornately printed savings bonds my aunt sent me one Christmas. She sent me a sport jacket, too, for my birthday, but I had never worn it—the original box was still jammed into the back of my clothes closet. I decided it would be best to wear that jacket to the circus.

The sleeves were a little short—I had grown since my birthday. But if I hunched in my arms, no one would notice, I thought. I didn't know what sort of pants to wear, so I tried on most of the ones I owned. I did the same with my shirts, until finally I found the perfect combination. I even shined my shoes a fresh black, spreading out newspapers in the kitchen and working carefully so I didn't leave any polish on the floor.

After I was all dressed up, the last thing I did was wet my hair and comb it just right, standing up as close to the bathroom mirror as I could to make sure the part was straight.

Waiting for my father to arrive home, I paced up and

down the hallway holding the tickets. When I discovered the inside jacket pocket, I slid the tickets inside, tucking them away beneath the silky white lining.

My father still hadn't come home by the time it was dark. I turned on the porch light. Each time I heard a car drive past, I pulled back the living room drapes and checked to see if it was my father. Our driveway was always empty. The tickets said 7:30 p.m. I avoided my thin reflection in the window glass, afraid to check the clock on the wall behind me.

"Oh, ex-cuse me. But when my belly grumbles like that, it can mean only one thing: dinnertime. You hungry, Nick? Sure, you could use a bite. Big guy like you. How the hell you get so big, anyway? You work out? You belong to one'a them health clubs, maybe, pumping iron and sweatin' rivers with the rest of the guys? Must be nice. Yes, sir. Real nice. Big guy like you can handle stuff like that. Right? You can handle just about anything, I imagine. Am I right, Nick? You one'a them guys who take charge, who get off on the unexpected? Hey, just playing with you. Nothing wrong with a little kidding between friends, is there? Don't give me those weird eyes, Nick. I was just kidding. Be for real, kid. Lighten up, for Christ's sake."

"I've been trying to do that all my life."

"Hey, this sounds serious all of a sudden. You wanna tell me about it, Nick? Here, this is the place. Come on in. Make yourself to home, as they say. Kinda nice, eh? The king's lair, or somethin' like that."

A fire door sealed off the end of the hallway. We turned right and entered Mel's dark apartment. I couldn't see very well—just furry shapes in the inky air—so I couldn't answer Mel's question until he clicked on the lamp.

"It's quiet."

"You're telling me. At night sometimes you hear creepy

stuff out in the canyons, down there where your buddy Kevin bunks. But most of the time it's stone cold quiet. Ideal, if you ask me. I lead a charmed life, son. What do they call that, you young guys? Karma? How does that work, Nick? You into that stuff? Some kind of Hindu shit, ain't it? Me, a charmer. A snake charmer. Mel the Fakir. I shoulda been the one in the circus. What do you think? Have a seat, son. The couch ain't gonna swallow you or nothin'. Sit!"

In order to get to the couch, I had to push aside the brittle leaves of a potted palm. Hanging in all corners of the room were plants, overgrowing their pots and dripping, tangled, and curling. I took the far end of the couch, closest to the outside window. To keep from hitting the coffee table—which was overloaded with more pots stuffed with more green and brown plants—I had to scrunch up my knees.

"Smells good in here, don't it? Take a deep breath, Nick. Nice fresh oxygen. Can't get it any better than this. Pure!"

"Pure what?"

"The air, Nick. It's the real thing. No additives or stuff like that. Straight from the source."

"But nothing is *that* pure. Anymore. Everything's changing, every second."

"I'm not sure I follow you, son."

"I didn't know who you were before today. Now that I know, we've both changed. That's how I see it."

"What do you mean by changed?"

"Something new to go on. Something different than before. If things stayed the same all the time, we'd go crazy."

"Right. Now let me see if I read you right."

"No, no. That's okay. I was just thinking out loud. It's nothing. Really."

"Hey, don't sell yourself short, Nick. I don't like to see people put themselves on the back burner like that."

"Do you like movies?"

"Huh? You wanna watch TV or somethin'? Me, I'm hungry. Won't take me but a second to get those tacos off the ground. Mexican food, son. God's gift to the human palate. You like Mexican food? Or didn't you say you were going out to a Mexican restaurant later? But it's rude to eat and run, Nick. Remember that. I command you to respect my hospitality. Get it? Hospitality? Comes with the job, I guess. What's the matter? You ain't got no sense of humor? I think you got problems, boy. It's gonna take more than a job and a hot meal to straighten you out. Don't get upset, now. I'm just trying to help. Ain't no harm in that, is there? Mel's a helping kind of guy. You don't think these plants grow big and strong on their own, do you? It's the Touch of Mel that makes the difference. Green thumb, hell. My whole body is green, inside and out. I oughta patent the damn thing, because I'm so good at making things grow it scares me."

"You can't be afraid of yourself."

"That isn't what I meant, Nick. Damn."

"There're two things—love and fear. The two most basic things."

"You readin' this off a card or something? Hey, are we on camera?"

"See? You're scared of what I'm trying to say. But you can't be. That's where the love comes in."

"Love? What do *you* know about love?"

"It's the only word I can think of. I know what it feels like, sometimes. Like today. Before I got here. But I don't know if I can explain it. That's what scares *me*."

"Well . . . well, maybe if you talked about it some more. That's the ticket. Go ahead, Nick. You can trust me. Really. It'll be all right. Just talk it out. That's what we're here for. I ain't hungry. You don't really want a job. We were just talking about that stuff, weren't we? Just because we needed somethin' to talk about. That's how it usually works when you're tryin' to get around to important things. Like, ah, like fear and love. Right? Hey, don't be afraid, Nick. I mean, it seems pretty obvious to me that there's something on your mind, something you want to share with me. I'm just here for support. I just touched your shoulder, that's all. Perfectly innocent. I don't know what you're afraid of. You can be scared or whatever you want, Nick, but you don't have to fear Old Mel. Nothing to fear here, Nick. Now, just relax. Feel that, son? That's nothing but my hand. Just one simple hand squeezing . . . resting on your shoulder. You can talk with your body, too, Nick. Hand on shoulder equals, 'Go ahead and relax. You're safe here.' You follow, Nick? Sometimes things can be simple. They aren't always complicated and full of mystery and like that. Sometimes things can be so simple they just go past guys like you. You got to learn how to tell when to read the simple signs. Hand on shoulder, Nick. Simple. You know what that word means? Think about it for a minute. Hey, now. You're gonna fall right off the couch if you keep that up. What are you so damn afraid of, son? Don't tell me you're afraid of love."

"Argo said his marriage didn't work out because he confused sex with love. But it's different with me. Today. I know. I know. Argo said that, but when he did he didn't have to touch me."

"I don't know who this guy is, but he can't be all bad, even if he is too frightened to touch people. Just a little touching now and then, and your friend Argo would see the light. He'd be able to get over this sex problem he's got, believe me. It's hard to live right when you got sex things crossing up your mind."

Mel sat down next to me. He smelled different from his

plants, not half as pure. I avoided his eyes when he talked; but when I did glance up at him, those eyes seemed too big for his head. Mel didn't have the same type of stare as Kevin's—a stare that sliced into new territory. Instead, Mel pushed sluggish energy out through his eyes. When Kevin stared, he also absorbed what he saw. Mel shoved things out of the way with his eyes, making room for something else.

"I think . . . I need to find some white clothes."

"Say what?"

"For tonight. For my alpha body."

"Hey, I'm willing to try just about anything. But what's an alpha body?"

"I'm not sure, but it's critical. Mrs. Raylak says *I* have one."

"Sure, son. That's one way to describe it. I could think of others, but we'll go with this Mrs. Ray-O-Vac or whatever for the time being, if you want."

"I want to get over there pretty soon. So, can we . . ."

"Oh?"

" . . . fill out that application?"

"What the hell are you talking about, son? Can't you just relax for once in your life? Aren't you listening to me? What's wrong with you? I've never seen anybody so tensed up, so confounded afraid."

"But that's what I'm trying to tell you. There's something about me I don't like. Do you know what it means to be scared of yourself?"

"I'm listening."

"I hope so. Because . . . sometimes I get so scared, because I don't know *what* I want. Just today, with LaWanda . . . well, things were clear for a little while. But then it all started again. And again. There's something empty inside of me, empty like a monster, without a name or a body, or even without a voice or a growl or anything. It's a vacant place. I know *something's* supposed to be there, something like a strong feeling. And I know it sounds funny to be scared of nothing. But I can't help it. I want to fill up that space so badly. But I don't know what to do. I try. I talk to Argo. And I . . . I talk to LaWanda. But I still don't know what else to do."

"Yes, keep going, Nick. Now I think I understand. Keep going."

"This is the most frightening feeling of all. There was never a monster movie created that could scare people this deeply. How would you like to be afraid all the time, spending your life pretending you really weren't? And when it feels like that vacant space is growing, that it's dissolving your mind from inside out slowly but surely, that's the terror of all time. Don't you ever feel that way? Don't you ever wish you could start something growing inside you that would stretch from one side of that empty space to the other? Like a skin graft, or water bubbling up from the bottom of a well? Don't you ever feel that?"

"Sure, Nick. All the time. Why do you think I brought you up here, anyway?"

Mel's eye. He stared at me with desperation, so densely, studying me inside out—his eyes materialized within the dome of my skull, grazing the edges of my thoughts, slithering through murk and synapse, scavenging light.

Two naked bulbs burned intensely on the ceiling—so bright that when I glanced up I saw two fireballs, like flashbulbs that burst but didn't die, holding steady for one blazing instant.

In that strong light, the leaves on the plants seemed too smooth, too oily, all tilting toward the window opposite the front door. It was dark out, and from the canyons an occasional yelp or whistle reached into the living room. The room felt slanted, because the hanging plants and the coffee-table plants and the baby palms and the green creepers and the fluttery shrubs in the corners and along the walls—they all inclined their leaves in the direction of that window.

I caught myself gripping the arm of the couch more tightly—a shadow of embarrassment streamed through me then disappeared, like a flimsy bit of newspaper ash drifting out of sight up a chimney.

Paralyzed. Mel and I and the plants stuck within a photograph, fixed—we were the spirits of real people trapped on film, silent, unmovable.

Mel's eyes continued to search me out, threatening to uncover stacks of photographs in memory, to rifle through all the moments of my life. Each moment, another snapshot, piled high, thousands of Nicholases framed and captured and frozen.

His eyes crawled through my life—snails on dew-slippery stepping stones; cold eyeslime gleaming in snotty trails across confined Nicholases, sliding slow into the past, gluing memories into a solid heap that grew out from the base of my spine into the white curves at the back of my eyeballs, pressing firmly—the final brain-photo of Mel and me on the couch jammed onto the rest of the heap, until pressure vibrated up through my guts, forcing me to lean toward Mel and away from the window, against the common angle of the plants.

"You want it, Nick. Don't you?"

"I . . ."

"Those lights too bright?"

"No. You can still see me."

"Yeah, sure, Nick. Whatever you say. You need it bad, don't you? You're just crying for it. Oh, sweet fucking Christ, I knew this would happen. I knew it the minute I saw you. This is just too good to be true."

"Like El Cid. Empty. Solid on the outside, but . . ."

"I hear you loud and clear, baby."

"A statue. Sometimes I feel like . . . a . . . El Cid."

"Right. You're into that Spanish stuff, ain't you? Spicy fucking Spanish stuff. I love it, Nick. Love it."

"But there's got to be more. We all . . . want more."

"Now you're singing Mel's song, son. Sweet, sweet music to this guy's ears. The sweetest."

"There's still something missing . . . something . . ."

"Here, Nick. No use us sittin' here wasting all these words. No use a-tall. Oh, man. I tell you what."

"What? I . . . everybody I know, they all want to be doing something else."

"Just cool it now, Nick. I don't wanna hear no more about it. Let's just do it now, all right? You follow me? That's what you want, right? Give it to me, son. I want it all. All you got. Then give it to me again. Damn you, Nick. Give it up! I got to have it, boy. Now! Stop fucking with my head and turn it loose, son. Turn it fucking loose!"

"But . . . I don't have it."

"Shut your mouth, Nick. Shut—your—mouth. I'm begging for it, now. Is that how you like it? You want me to fucking beg? I'm on my knees now, Nick. Look at Mel. On his fucking knees. Please! Nick! Damn, what else do you want me to do?"

Mel tugged on the collar of his shirt. Fabric ripped and a button flipped into the grove of plants on the coffee table. He clutched shreds of his gray shirt, revealing a hairy chest. On his knees, he crawled toward me, in the trough between the coffee table and the couch. There was a taste of Brak inside Mel, too; I could see it in his eyes, the way they trembled like loose, red things ready to shoot out of his head from the pressure.

"I'm through playin' games, Nick. This here's the real thing. And you ain't gettin' out of here till it's finished. Now, Nick. Give it to me. Or I'm gonna take it."

"But . . . I don't have *anything*."

"Cut the shit. You know what I'm talking about."

Mel was a big man, but I could still out-muscle him. When he dove into my lap, I snapped to attention, hooking my arms underneath his, yanking Mel to his feet. He kicked wildly, beating his fists on my back, thumping my thighs steadily with his knees, rushing against me.

"Please. Baby, please."

Brak lived inside Mel, with other monsters and their attendants. I squeezed harder in against his armpits, tying river rapids into knots; he slowed down his squirming. Mel opened his mouth and his tongue slid against his teeth as he attempted to speak. But he used his eyes instead, avoiding words.

Gently, I set him down. When his feet touched the carpet, I let him fall back onto the couch. Our eyes connected. For a few seconds, I felt as if I were staring into a three-dimensional mirror. There I was, starring in a movie, acting, dancing for the monsters.

I walked right through Mel. He didn't turn around, I could feel that much.

The door opened easily, and I stepped out into the hallway. Shivering, I felt like a dog shaking off water. Nothing more needed to be said to Mel. I pushed the door shut behind me. The lock clicked into place neatly.

It was cool in the hallway, but the coolness felt good. Walking was more like floating. I glided out to the balcony and gazed out into the courtyard.

I felt I was in the right place. Right there. For the moment. The job no longer mattered. And LaWanda seemed terribly far away.

I moved to the other end of the balcony, sliding my hand along the smooth wrought-iron railing, and when I stopped it was the right place to stop.

The patio was empty. The tourists had cleared out and the restaurant was closed. Water bubbled out from the statue lady's pot and splashed across her lap, spilling over into the wishing well.

The water went where it went.

I wanted to be like the water, traveling true.

Just as long as I avoided pooling at the bottom of a stagnant well, thick with green muck and penny scabs.

How to learn—I needed someone to teach me, someone who could speak as well as Argo, but who could see as well as

Kevin; someone as gentle as Miki, but with energy as strong as Mel's; someone as curious as LaWanda, but as scientific as Mrs. Raylak.

Waiting, for the river of my self to encounter this teacher who could answer the questions I was too afraid to ask Argo— questions that lived with me like dreams, just beneath the surface, always.

Water never asks and water never knows, but it never stops flowing, either. It continues. Even still water evaporates, invisibly rising into the sky, into clouds, descending as rain, continually.

I had to learn to continue.

Monsters and crystals and galactic maps and empty liquor bottles—more coins staining the underside of the wishing well.

Too much interference—Brak could appear from no-where, nibbling on the inside of my brain like a suckerfish on a shark, gnawing me off course; Miki was dead and I hurt myself with her absence—the river of my self had to rush across her grave and dissolve Brak and spin babbling circles around Argo's feet, around LaWanda's black candles, around Mel's eyes.

Millions of rivers flowing around the globe, crossing in thin ribbons of life, mixing together in a solid pulsating layer—my personal river stretching from California to Louisiana to Vietnam and back again, winding around and around San Diego, running in and out of stores and banks and theaters and doctors' offices and apartments, sometimes no more than a trickle, with a dry spot here and there, but always containing particles from all the places I'd been, particles mixed up and churning right behind me, tumbling off one another in a microscopic water dance, changing, absorbing new particles, exchanging with other rivers, always running and flowing whether I could see it or not, whether or not I could feel its movement, its direction, its dimensions, always running even though for a moment it might pool before an obstruction and gather enough power to change direction or pass through or turn back upon itself, seeking another course, another angle, another detour, always running *somewhere*.

If Argo asked me, what made these rivers run? or, why did they run? or, where did they come from in the first place?—which were the type of ceaseless questions *he* asked *me* about *my* life, about LaWanda's visions, about Mrs. Raylak's investigations—to answer Argo I could only smile, because an explanation would only interfere; explanations could not *be* the rivers, could not take the place of the rivers; explanations were no more useful than the torn bandage on my hand, no more true than calling rivers *rivers* in the first place.

Trusting the movement of my life was all I could really do.

CHAPTER TWENTY-FIVE

SINGING AND SHOUTING

I released the railing, the railing released me.

The quiet splash of water from the wishing-well fountain: amplified by the empty courtyard; sound waves ricocheted up out of the well, bouncing back off the statue lady's solid body—deflected by the leaves and branches of the birds-of-paradise, the palms, the cigarette urns, the iron benches, the pillars—echoing mildly through the arches, spiraling up from the patio, teasing my eardrums—finally absorbed by the purple night sky.

I walked to the stairwell, following cracks in the stucco walls, which at first I imagined to be arrows pointing the way. As I traced the cracks with my fingers, I realized those thin jagged spikes pointed in all directions.

Over the edge, down in the courtyard, a shadow passed— a shifting movement, a figure that could have been Kevin scrounging through the birds-of-paradise, or a bad memory come to life.

A dark shiver twitched my shoulders, but this time I wasn't on Mel's couch and I wasn't embarrassed. I was afraid.

On night patrol, our RTO disappeared. We didn't hear a thing. Without a radio, we waited until sunup before trying to find our way to the firebase. All that night, I leaned close to a tree, gripping the low smooth branches until my hands ached, believing I wouldn't vanish if I kept hanging on. Sergeant Ascencion reported the RTO missing in action, and for the next few days whenever I grew afraid, I said to myself, "RTO MIA; RTO MIA," because in those days I believed if you imagined something was going to happen, it never would.

On guard duty, Billy Reid told me he kept awake thinking about all the different ways he could die—punji pits, Bouncing Bettys, sniper shots, even a heart attack—because he said it was impossible for you to imagine the real way you'd go out— so, the more ways you imagined your own death, the fewer chances there would be for you to get killed.

That tactic didn't work for Billy Reid, and I wanted to know why.

Billy Reid stepped on a mine. A lot of guys stepped on mines, and Billy must have imagined he would, too.

It got so bad, I didn't know what to think.

I stopped at the top of the stairwell and looked down. The steps dropped off to a turnaround hallway on the first floor. I imagined there were ten more steps behind the banister wall to match the ones I could see. Then I stood above myself, afraid, unable to descend the stairs.

Ten steps, MIA.

The House of Hospitality shook violently and began to collapse.

The cracks in the walls widened and sprouted teeth and chomped wildly.

A swirling blast of water rushed up from the stairwell. It smashed into the roof and swept down, knocking me off my feet, rolling me along the balcony. I grabbed on to the iron bars of the railing to keep from being dragged then pounded into the wall where the swirling wave broke back upon itself, twisting and roaring.

Water stormed over my face and I had to hold on to the

bars with all my strength. Through crashing torrents, I could see down into the courtyard filling rapidly with water rising higher than the statue lady.

A steady thumping boomed through the big wooden doors on the other side of the patio. As the thumping intensified, the wooden doors splintered—and El Cid busted through sideways, tumbling into view. His spear-flag was broken off above his hand; a stub poked out from his glove. Half his helmet was crunched in, but he still straddled the metal horse. All the horse's legs had been snapped clean off.

More water streamed in through the shattered front doors and threw El Cid farther out into the patio. He went under, and a hollow ringing smack emitted from a burst bubble signaled his cracking into the statue lady.

El Cid bobbed to the surface momentarily, then he was sucked back under.

The water rose higher, splashing down from the roof, filling the patio up to the balcony edges. I inhaled water, my nose stung, my clothes were soaked and sopping.

My arms ached awfully, and my hands were torn loose—I was tossed into the wild motion of waves and rivers punching me, thrashing me.

Even though half-submerged, I could still hear the screeching cries of Godzilla and the hammering whoosh of chopper blades.

The water climbed higher and I fought to swim to the surface, as high as the roof, and through the scalloped churning of the water I could see out into the parking lot where Godzilla batted at helicopters, even though he was shoulder-deep in the lake rising fast all over the park.

Lightning creased the sky. Thunder busted loose. It began raining so hard, the choppers were knocked out of the sky. They plopped into the turbulent lake and sank immediately.

I swam toward a ribbed palm log that spun close by. The water had risen higher than the roof; the House of Hospitality was submerged.

I managed to reach the log just before a sudden cascade drenched me. Swinging one leg over the top of the log, I hugged the slimy wood with both arms, locking my fingers together.

Floating raggedly.

I couldn't afford to be afraid, there wasn't time. But it did feel exciting to know I was the last one afloat, tossed around above El Cid and Godzilla; the choppers and Mel; Kevin and LaWanda—all of them swirling in silent blue beneath me, underwater, trails of white bubbles fluttering from their mouths and windows and helmets.

I would keep floating until the storm eased, until I found myself drifting east, brushing the tops of freeway signs announcing all the exits out of town—past Golden Hill and Paradise Hills and Lemon Grove, beyond Spring Valley and La Mesa and Mount Helix and El Cajon—all those names like music, and I'd be singing, paddling the log, steering it easily, thrilled by the fact that I was floating uphill, but not disputing it, simply enjoying it.

At the edge of the monstrous lake that had submerged the city, I'd push off from the palm log and wade ashore, somewhere in the valleys outside Jamul. Still singing, I'd hike out to the Nebulae Society X-site. From the top of a hill, standing between branches of dry red mesquite, I'd look down on their watch-circle.

They would all be dressed in white, gazing up at the stars.

I'd look for Mrs. Raylak and Neeta and Mr. Rainey and wave to them all.

Heads would turn one by one until the entire group was staring up at me.

I would keep singing and shouting. When I finished, I would rest my hands on my hips and laugh.

None of us would understand, but that wouldn't matter. Trying to understand only got in the way.

I pried open my eyes. The smell of tree bark snapped in my nostrils. Kevin stood below me, within whispering distance; he gripped the balcony railing, concluding the sad reality: the two of us were there alone amidst the House of Hospitality, which remained cool and dark and sturdy. Yes, another movie, Argo. I'm fighting another movie. Kevin offered me a handful of crumpled cigarettes—stained paper and cinders and shards of tobacco aglow in moonlight, stark and gritty as anything I had ever seen, powerful enough to knock me loose from my own worst enemies, the monsters of memory and desire. Kevin could help me home . . . pus pushing loose slivers and shrapnel . . . "Take one" . . . the first words spoken, the gesture pure, the ritual too stark yet genuine, undisguised, scored and defined by the coolness in the air, the luster in his eyes, the severe beating of my thick heart.

"Nick-olepsy!"

Argo couldn't be here. He'd ruin everything. At the sound of his brutish voice, Kevin withdrew the cigarettes and darted into the stairwell. The soles of his mangled shoes flopped noisily, restoring the fear, the edges of vision, the tides of threatening memory.

"Don't jump, kid. You'll kill yourself!"

His voice infected the patio; the waters had certainly subsided; I was restored to the House of Hospitality, dangling above the courtyard beneath scratchy, knife-edged palm fronds.

"Hey, come . . . on . . . down! You heard me, Nick, you bumbling contestant. No time to waste. Got to get you out of here. Now!"

When I released the trunk of the palm tree, I wobbled then slid down smoothly onto the balcony railing. Pushing free, I stood with ankles locked. With my arms straight out, I lifted one foot.

"Whoa, there, wing-walker. Just take it easy. You got me in a big enough mess already. No need to compound the interest, son. No need to splatter the patio. Good, that's more like it. Now, on the double, Nick. Hit the deck. Front and center."

I followed his orders. But I didn't want to. I wanted to run out of that place as hard as I could, breaking speed and distance records, racing until I became the race, slashing across the whole country in a blur of wonder, of magic, until I had healed everyone—bad credit okay, sixty days the same as cash, in a gentler and kinder America. Televisions, on! Network newscasts, on! Monsters parading at halftime in the greatest Super Bowl of all time, on! And I would be there among everyone, touching everyone as I sped past, exchanging bits of my spirit with theirs, united, in a serious dedicated prayer, one nation, under God, understood, under investigation by an independent counsel—on! On and on!

"Damn you, boy. If you only knew. We've got to get the hell out of here."

"Let go of me."

"No time for this, Nick. Let's move out. I mean it."

"I don't think that's such a good idea."

"Fine, but we're leaving anyway. Look, Nick, the Jeep is double-parked. Okay? Is that a good enough reason?"

"Then what?"

"Listen, this is no time for questions. Either do as I say or stay here and fry. It's that simple."

"What are you talking about?"

"Trust me, Nick."

"Is LaWanda out in the Jeep too?"

"Hardly. LaWanda is . . . not feeling too well right now."

"You're drunk again, Argo."

"'Tis true, jailbait. 'Tis true. And a perfect night to hide . . . to journey . . . down to Old Mexico. I could use your help, Nick. How's that?"

"Now?"

"Sure. I've been planning this trip for some time, amigo."

"But your book. The deadline."

"Yeah, right, Nick. You don't miss a trick. But I'll explain

227

it on the way down. I'm just taking a leave of absence, all right? And I need a valet, a boy Friday, a trustee. Now shake it, Nick. Miles to go before we sleep."

The statue lady's head exploded and her body crumbled into small granite chunks. Bird-of-paradise flowers withered brown and mutated into tumors. Wrought-iron benches melted into gray pools of steaming elements. Kevin's white stone eyes spurted out from behind a cigarette urn, rattling across the tiled patio, disappearing into the rubble and dust of the wishing well. No. No. The movies were over.

"The keys, Nick. Wake up! I can't find the damn keys."

"I'm up, I'm up."

"We don't find those keys, you're a dead man."

Argo drilled his fingers into my shoulders and shook me. His breath was hot and gummy with alcohol. All I could see was his face—his tiny blue eyes, his beaked nose, his snarling, crooked teeth—yet just as sharply and intensely as Kevin's handful of secondhand cigarettes.

"I should just leave you for the buzzards, but now you've got *me* tangled up in this mess. I found the note, Nicholas. And I found LaWanda. Now we've got to get the hell out of here. Out of the country. Is this sinking in, *niño?*"

"But I love her."

"You *loved* her. *Somebody* loved her. Too much. We can talk about this later. Eight hundred miles later. *Vamos!*"

Argo grabbed my hand and led me into the parking lot. His Jeep sat blocking traffic next to the El Cid statue. The lights were still on; a can of beer leaned on the running board.

"They must be in the ignition. So hop in, *gringo.* It's time to leave truth, justice, and the American Way behind us."

Boxes, sleeping bags, a stove, an ice chest, and a pile of clothes were heaped in the back of the Jeep. The canvas top was buttoned securely. I hauled myself inside, sat down, and kicked something hard underneath the seat—Argo's AR-15.

"Hang on, junior. We're off to the land of the midnight *mordida*, where freedom is just another word for nothing left to eat. *Anda, pendejo. Rápido, rápido!*"

"A great man, that El Cid, I'm certain. Even if he did switch allegiances in the middle of his career, killing Spaniards one day and Moors the next. Like I'm doing now, Nick. I pledge allegiance to you, for which you stand, one nation, under God, with liberty and justice for all former literary mercenaries like myself. Temporarily I'm ceasing and desisting as father of Eddie Elvesizer. I have the inalienable right to remain silent. I have the duty to drag your ass south to safety. Now, watch me send currents of life zinging through this rough-and-ready vehicle. One twist of the key, and . . . shit . . . one little twist. Let me finish this unfinished beer. There. I christen you the SS *Promised Land* . . . manchilds be exiled . . . and we're off!"

Argo's beer can sailed out the window, clanking against El Cid's concrete pedestal, swallowed by the wet grass. The Jeep engine revved and the dashboard lights flickered. A white-and-black police car slid around the corner, rolling toward the Organ Pavilion behind us. Grinding the gears, Argo struggled with the stick shift; he rammed it back and forth, pounding his fist into the side of my leg.

"We gotta move, Nick."

"He's turning around."

"Not a good sign, son."

The Jeep lurched forward. Argo stomped on the gas and squirted through the parking lot. Weaving through an empty space, Argo wrestled the Jeep steady and spun out onto the boulevard. I gripped the edge of the dashboard, fighting the changing forces, as my white face flitted through the windows of parked cars.

"By the time he gets through that maze, we'll be long gone, Nick. Home free."

"What difference does it make?"

"You and your questions, Nick-ulosis. Consumption through interrogation. Hand me another beer, would you? Yes. Freeway, that way. See them, Nick? The lights of Tijuana. And to the east? Nothing but nothing. Seductive, no? And just for us. We should hit Mexicali before midnight, easy. That cop still back there?"

"No."

"That's a good boy. Just answer my questions, and all will be well. Well, well, well. You ever been to Baja before, way down there, consumed by those deserts and dead volcanoes and godforsaken reaches of sour land?"

"LaWanda said you needed a tourist card."

"Ah, LaWanda *said*. Clever choice of tense, lad. Past. Alas, I knew her pretty well. No time for tourist cards, Nick-utensil. Don't need one. Never did, never will. Don't need nothing. Drink this. Drink me. For this is my blood."

I shared the beer with Argo, even though it was warm and tasted like spit. As we turned onto the freeway ramp, Argo gunned the engine. He shifted roughly through the gears and swerved into the fast lane. Wind sliced through the cockpit of the Jeep, flapping the canvas roof. Argo moved his lips but his words were lost in the rushing of air and the rhythmic whining of the engine. I merely nodded my head, growing colder.

"One last thing."

"Say what, boy?"

"Is there any way to get outside your own mind?"

"What?"

"Take me to the X-site."

Argo laughed. His eyes filled with purple as he finished off the beer. He motioned for another. I yanked a fresh can from the cooler and handed it over, shouting.

"Mrs. Raylak! They're all waiting for me."

"Not tonight, spaceman."

He drove without speaking for another half hour, until the exit ramp for Alpine, out in the hills east of El Cajon. It was a comfort when the Jeep engine fell quiet as we pulled into a gas station fiery with yellow pumps and harsh droning lamps.

"I got to drain the main vein, kiddo, so you just stay put. Slump down or something, while you're at it."

Argo left me alone in the Jeep. With ease, I could have walked away. I knew how to get back. Mr. Rainey and Neeta had driven me enough times on day trips to the X-site, which wasn't far from the gas station—past the honey ranch toward the lake, on the other side of a hidden plateau. I could wait for them in the little shack next to the white chalk landing circle.

But the color of Argo's voice held me suspended. He was drunk, more drunk than usual; yet something inflexible burned through when he spoke. Mexico. All of a sudden, we were headed for another country, to relax, to forget, to pass some time. I didn't know. His words confined me inside a sticky trap. His invading wet eyes and knifing laughter were hypnotic. Yet beneath the hypnotism, it was clear Argo needed me—his yearning held kidnapped, a glistening gem entangled within the muck that forced him to drink.

Argo fought with the door handle then flung open the door, tottering, lifting one leg uncertainly before crawling back into the Jeep.

"Fucking punks. That's what's wrong with this damn

country. No one trusts anymore. No one. You don't buy gas, you can't piss. You don't make a purchase, you can't perform a natural bodily function. So I let it rip across the side of the building. Organic graffiti. What other choice does a man have? Us, we're leaving. Saddle up, Nick-osabe. It can't be any better where we're headed, but at least it'll be different."

I didn't wait for Argo to ask. As his oversized tires squealed across smooth concrete, I handed him another beer. He accepted it, shifted gears with his free hand, and took us to the on-ramp. But before he could make the turn, I grabbed his arm.

"We can't leave yet."

"No need for terrorism, Nick. Unhand me and speak your piece."

"They'll be waiting for us. We've got to visit the X-site before we go on this excursion you've got planned."

"There's a lot of folks waiting for us. We got to put some miles between us and them, now, boy. Do you read me? Those lunatics don't have a clue, trusting something they can't see, wasting all their hope. The only thing I trust is this Jeep. And this Jeep is aimed at Mexicali and points south, forever."

"To say good-bye, Argo."

"If you trust me, son, you'll release my driving arm and allow us to proceed. I don't know how else to convince you."

"I don't either."

Argo jammed his beer down between his legs. A black highway patrol cruiser appeared behind us, waiting at the sign atop the off-ramp. Studying his rearview mirror, Argo sighed.

"You just got your wish, Nick."

We made a smooth right turn and headed onto the frontage road through Alpine. At night, the town was different than I remembered. I searched for the honey ranch signs while Argo tapped furiously on his steering wheel, pausing only to sip more beer. When it seemed we had gone far enough east, I told him to turn down a two-lane road that cut through a pair of low-lying hills. Argo checked the mirror for the hundredth time, slowing down to make the turn. Then he raced the engine, kicking us forward, plunging us into the two tunnels of light carved out by his headlamps.

"Damn, I feel better already. Something about exile that gets the glands pumping. Oh, this is fine. On the road, out of sight, with bridges burning. Enthusiasm. Or something. You feel it too, Nick?"

"I'm scared, Argo."

"Ho! Get a grip, son. That's not fear you feel. That's *The Way It Is*. Starring Nicholas Ames, All-American Boy."

"I'm scared of myself."

"Here, sample some of these suds. It'll ease the pain."

We chiseled our way through a valley, and in the distance I recognized the hidden plateau—a flat shelf of land behind scrub hills framed by power lines and steel towers. With my mouth full of bitter foam, I pointed the way. Argo glided onto a dirt road fringed by real estate signs and gnarled bushes, bouncing us over ruts and gullies.

"Just say a few words, shake a few hands, then we're gone. All right? And tell them we're going up to Canada, to a writers' conference in Saskatchewan or something."

The beer can was almost empty. I handed the last swallow to Argo. He drained it hungrily and tossed the can outside. I watched it disappear into the darkness and dust. That was a signal for me to scrounge another one out of the cooler. As I turned around and reached into the back seat of the Jeep, Argo yelled—so loud he suffocated the droning of the engine.

"Fucking sheriff!"

A green sedan snapped on its headlights. Argo down-shifted, slowing to a crawl, then stomped on the gas. Our rear tires scattered gravel and sand across the hood of the sheriff's car. In a flash, red and blue light cut through the haze. Argo shifted furiously until we hit top speed, bouncing and roaring through the underbrush. The sheriff tried to follow but hit a deep rut and stopped, the car's headlights gleaming at a cock-eyed angle, the siren fading as our Jeep plunged headlong across the flats then over a hill and out of sight.

We picked up the dirt road at the bottom of the hill. Argo lost control as we broke out into the smoothness, the steering wheel spinning in a blur throwing loose his hands. I grabbed the wheel and held it still, the vibrations throbbing through my arm, rattling my neck. The back end of the Jeep careened in a wide arc. Argo knocked my hand away and took over; the tires ripped and crunched through the bushes until we re-gained the road.

"Now what the fuck do we do?"

"The aliens."

"What? Speak up!"

"They could take us back."

The road curved up the side of another hill just below the plateau. Argo cut the lights and shifted into four-wheel drive. As we ascended, I could see the sheriff's car still stuck, but two more cars streamed down the road, their red-and-blue lights swirling and spinning.

"Okay, George Armstrong. Where's the fucking freeway?"

"Just on the other side."

The Jeep barely cleared the steep rise, chugging the last ten yards. When we hit the flats, Argo sped full-throttle, guided by starlight and the gleam from a sliver of moon.

As we approached the opposite side of the plateau, I detected a curious glow, a canopy of speckled light that ema-nated from the vicinity of the X-site. I pointed through the dusty windshield, urging Argo forward.

Before rolling down into the valley, Argo halted at the top of the hill, slamming us both into the dashboard. In full view below was the chalk landing circle, ringed with border patrol trucks. A crowd stood in a knot behind the shack. Officers fed a line of dark-haired men into the trucks. The Raineys' Buick sat in dull shadows. An old woman, as small as Mrs. Raylak, sat in the back of a sheriff's car.

"Any more bright ideas, Mr. America?"

The unmistakable thrash of a helicopter erupted behind us. Searchlight beams flitted across the hood of the Jeep. Naturally, I leaned over and fished out Argo's AR-15 from beneath the seat.

"You took the words right out of my mouth, son."

Pistol shots cracked behind us. All the movies were over. Dirt kicked up beside me, spraying the front tire. More rounds tore through the Jeep's canvas top. Argo groaned. I checked the bolt action on the rifle and hammered the ammo clip home with the heel of my hand. Blood splashed onto my forearm. The Jeep rolled free, descending. Argo slumped forward, sagging into a rush of gas.

ABOUT THE AUTHOR

David Zielinski served in the United States Army for two years. He now lives in San Diego, where he is a writer and an English teacher.

A NOTE ON THE TYPE

This book was set in Electra, a typeface designed by W. A. Diggins for the Linotype. First available in 1935, Electra was designed to be a modern "fast-moving" face and is characterized by tall capitals, heavy top-serifs on the short letters, and a close relationship between roman and italic.